On a Mission

On a Mission

Ms. Michel Moore, T.C. Littles,
Blacc Top

www.urbanbooks.net

Urban Books, LLC
300 Farmingdale Road, N.Y.-Route 109
Farmingdale, NY 11735

ISBN 13: 978-1-64556-541-3
EBOOK ISBN: 978-1-64556-542-0

First Trade Paperback Printing July 2023
Printed in the United States of America

10 9 8 7 6 5 4 3 2 1

Distributed by Kensington Publishing Corp.
Submit Orders to:
Customer Service
400 Hahn Road
Westminster, MD 21157-4627
Phone: 1-800-733-3000
Fax: 1-800-659-2436

On a Mission

Ms. Michel Moore, T.C. Littles, Blacc Top

Loving a Detroit Savage

by

Ms. Michel Moore

Chapter One

Marley

I put my feelings on safety
So I don't go shootin' where your heart be

I danced around to Ella Mai's hit "Trip" song as it played through the overhead speakers of my boutique. My vibe was right. My energy felt on point. And there had been a steady flow of customers through the door since I'd opened, which meant I was making money and having an A1 type of day.

My boo Maceo gifted me this storefront close to a year ago. Although it was also intended to be a prop operation that would clean the drug money he was raking in, I'd been starting to go straight legit with my books for the last couple of months, or at least trying to. It felt good having solid credit and not having to get check stubs and bank statements made to get whatever I wanted. I'd run my credit into the hole quick, fast, and in a hurry as soon as I got approved for my first credit card—getting rental cars and running check scams through the ATM on fast hustles his mama had me doing—but that's a whole different episode to the drama of our love series.

"Ummm, Marley, can you turn that ol' whiny-ass song off and get some City Girls 'Act Up' bumping through the speakers? That soft-ass R&B gonna have me stalking my ex-nigga instead of making room in my heart for my next nigga." My homegirl Kristina was always ready to turn up.

"Yeah, sis. I got you. All y'all hot-girl summer hoes are going to have the pharmacy jumping by the fall." I scrolled through my music app until I found my ratchet music playlist. Don't get me wrong, I loved a good twerking song like the next chick, but I wasn't obsessing over them. I was more into hip-hop icons like Lil' Kim and Foxy Brown.

"Aht-aht, don't be no hater! Just 'cause you've been caked up with the same nigga for three years straight doesn't mean we all like taking the same dick daily. I'm a ho, and I'm admitting it. I'm not taking it back because I'm still doing it." She remixed the *Love & Hip Hop* star's single that had become damn near every thot's national anthem.

"Ugh, girl, you better hope yo' coochie don't fall the fuck off." I laughed at her silly ass. Kristina was a fluid lover. She didn't prefer men or women, but either and even both whenever the opportunity presented itself. She stayed getting hers, and I wasn't hating. She was one of my best friends, not to mention hustling partners.

Krissy had her own section in my boutique because she was one of the coldest designers and seamstresses in the city, and I'm not just saying that because we were technically on the same team gettin' money. She came through the door with a herd of clientele, which mainly consisted of a gang of dancers since she worked at a slew of strip clubs around the city before we linked up. She and I actually met in one of those clubs when I used to frequent them with Mace.

He was there slanging dope, I was mainly there monitoring, and Krissy was there making dancer costumes. Homegirl never left the club without her trusty needle and thread. She and I ended up getting cool just by being in the same vicinity damn near every night. A lot of the dancers who copped percs, pills, and coke from Mace didn't like doing so out on the floor. So I stayed in the locker room as the candy lady.

Once Caresha's and JT's voices replaced Ella Mai's, almost every chick shopping got to rocking their hips and singing along to the track. And to keep it real, I had a li'l more pep in my step as I danced to the register. It felt good as hell being on top and succeeding even though I'd been counted out.

"You've got some cute clothes in here. A lot of these boutiques popping up around the city be having the same tired two-piece sets and joggers, but you've got a dope-ass collection of fly and unique shit." The customer handed me her credit card.

"Aww, thanks, diva! I appreciate the feedback and love. Tag me on your social media, and I'll give you fifteen percent off today for looking out." I adjusted her total and swiped her card.

"Oh, for real? Thanks for the hookup, girl! I got you, and I'll most definitely be back."

She looked surprised I was willing to take a few dollars off her tab, but my dude taught me well on the first day he dropped the keys to the shop in my hands. "Throw out a few testers. Get a few loyal custos. And keep it consistent. Don't dry up. Once you flatline, you lose a fiend." Maceo knew the streets and taught me the game, and now I was applying it to our business. I stayed branding and using my customers as models with mouthpieces.

Everything in Unique Pieces was tailored for advertise-ment. I had decals on the wall, custom hangers and tags for all the merchandise, key chains, and T-shirts with my logo and website on them that I gave out randomly. I had access to dope money, so it was easy for me to break the bank to make my shop beautiful. I spared no expense when it came to the contractors who designed my layout idea, or when it came to ordering top-of-the-line items from wholesalers. I was able to order from some of the most exclusive labels and designers because I didn't have to budget my money and order small amounts. I went big because I could. My name was on the deed, but the money Mace made off the streets kept the storefront stocked.

"Hey, Jos, I'm about to dip early off the back and take care of some school stuff. You good?"

Joslyn was my other homegirl. We'd met through Kristina, but it was like I'd known her for a lifetime. Jos was cool as hell, loyal, and trustworthy, which was rare to find in females nowadays. She was my one and only employee and never came up short or tried to hustle me out of a few dollars by making side deals with customers when I wasn't around.

"Of course." She was taking pictures of herself in some pieces from our new shipment. Jos had beautiful chocolate brown skin, a sexy, slim-thick body, and a face that was beautiful without pounds of makeup. She was the face of my boutique all over social media. "By the way, sis, what do you and my brother have planned for y'all anniversary this weekend? I'm just asking just in case you want me to work."

"That's why I love you. You're always on top of shit. I actually do need you to close up. I made reservations for us at the London Chophouse, booked a presidential suite down at the casino, and even got a couple's massage." I couldn't wait for me and Mace to dip off for a night of relaxation. Between the boutique, school, and Mace's hustling, we hadn't been spending as much time together as we normally had. It used to be me and him and him and me on the Bonnie and Clyde tip until Unique Pieces opened.

"Oh, okayyy! I know you got some 'come fuck me' boots and booty shorts packed already. It's about time y'all gave me a niece!"

"You sound just like him. But I'm not about to be running around raising him and his kid at the same time. Mace ain't ready." My pussy was cuddled up with an IUD, so it would block any and every nut Maceo shot up in me.

"Girl, bye. If he's asking for kids, you'd better get knocked up and lock him up. Don't let one of them dancers drooling over him down at the club swoop in and make you a stepmama."

"Awwwwww, shit, Jos! Don't stir that crazy bitch up. You know she'll blow the world up over Mace's big-headed ass," Krissy piped into the conversation from out of nowhere.

"Fuck blowing the world up. I'll send a home-wrecker to heaven in style, then raise the bitch's baby as my own." I tapped my hip where my heater was nestled, just in case one of these hot boxes up in here was secretly crushing on him.

Maceo was well-known in the city for being a dough boy and having long money, especially on the west side of Detroit. We couldn't go to Kentucky Fried Chicken for a $5 Fill Up box without a greasy-fingered broad trying to holler. And we most definitely couldn't go to the strip club without a flock of hoes trying to throw themselves in his lap. I was praying I wouldn't have to body a bitch tonight behind my bae, but I would. Mace was more than my man. He was my heart. And one day I was going to rock his last name. I wished a bitch would call herself fuckin' with my future.

Closing the door to my office, I was glad I'd chosen to add a few suites to the space during the renovation. It was originally one large, open canvas when Mace purchased it. I had my office set up with all the essentials since I spent tons of time online sifting through merchandise, communicating with vendors, working some magic on the books, and now doing my homework. I was taking classes toward an associate's degree in business, and the marketing course this semester was kicking my ass.

I'd been struggling since the third week but fighting through it because the professor dropped tons of knowledge. Withdrawing from her class would've done a disservice to myself and the business I was trying to build. My sales had been pumping since I'd been taking her class, even though it was hard for me to retain all the boring-ass statistics the books delivered. Mace taught me how to hustle, and my professor was teaching me how to brand, market, and expand that hustle.

I was trying my best to come out on top so I could finally show my face to my parents. I'd been disowned by them because they hated Mace, what he stood for as a thug, and what they thought he'd drag me down to. I guess I shouldn't have given a fuck, but I wanted them to see how wrong they'd been.

Ding! My iMessage notification popped up.

Lance: Hey, lady. How's it going?

Me: Need to ask? Lol! I'll be lucky to pull off a 70.

Lance: Who needs luck with good friends?

His last notification came with an attachment labeled Miss Marley's Study Guide, which was a PDF of all the notes I needed to pull my assignment out of the gutter. I'd been working on the questions for close to an hour but didn't have enough in-class notes to answer the questions thoroughly.

Me: OMG! You are the best! I owe you big time.

Lance: It's all good, beautiful. I'll see you tmrw. That's a treat within itself.

I giggled at his cornball attempt at flirting, then looked up to Mace walking through the door carrying a bag of food that smelled like heaven. *Oh, shit*. I locked my messages, then started fumbling with some receipts on my desk. Mace would knock my head smooth off my neck if he knew I was entertaining another man, even if it was within the friend zone. Thankfully, he was so engulfed in his phone conversation that he hadn't peeped me looking all suspect.

Maceo was rocking a fresh 'fit, a fitted cap with a snakeskin brim, and the Figaro chain with an iced-out M pendant I'd gotten him for his birthday. The M stood for both money, because he was making it, and Maceo for his name. I always be playing with him and saying he could be Mekhi Phifer's brother because they looked alike except for Mace's bigger lips and the inches of height he had on the actor.

I'd had to throw my fist into a bunch of crushin'-ass women who had their eyes set on what was mine. Just because I shared him with a jump off every now and then during a threesome, wasn't no bitch getting ready to slide into my position and live off the fat of the land I'd brought to harvest. Vernelle might've birthed a hoodlum and trained him to be a hustler, but I was the one struggling with him in the mud day in and out. I was protective as hell over my man and hoping he wasn't about to give me a reason to come up out of retirement.

"Yo, tighten ya shit up, li'l homie. Ain't shit else to be said. You keep coming at me with too many excuses, and that shit ain't sitting right with my spirit. I'm not giving you no more passes to come up short on a package." He ended the call. Mace had the worst explosive temper I'd ever seen, which was why I didn't understand why his workers ever tested his gangster. He stayed strapped with a clip to cause problems.

"Uh-oh, sounds like trouble in paradise. Who's fucking up now?" His crew stayed giving him headaches.

"Who else but Blue?" He rubbed at that throbbing vein in his forehead. "Dex said he dropped short today when he came for his re-up, then got to talking big bullshit when he told him to push on and holla at me. I swear I'm 'bout ready to body that nigga and just be done with him."

"It's nothing for me to send his girl a black dress." I shrugged, caring even less about Blue's life than Mace did.

I never liked him no how, plus he knew too much about Mace's hustle to be given a pass. In our lanes of life, loose ends could either lead to lengthy prison bids or body bags, and Blue wasn't worth either. I wasn't even involved in the day-to-day transactions with Mace anymore and knew of three flips Blue didn't have all his money behind. He was either getting high or flat-out saying fuck the team, and neither of those plays gained you longevity in the game anyway.

"Damn, I really miss yo' sexy, savage ass riding shotgun with me handling business." He pulled me out of my chair for a bear hug and a passionate kiss.

"I know you miss me. And I'm only like this 'cause you got me this way." I met him with puckered lips, then slipped my tongue into his mouth. He must've just been blowing on some good-good 'cause the Kushmints taste was still fresh on his tongue.

"Why don't you get nasty with ya man real quick, baby? You owe me anyway since you were up and gone this morning when I woke up. Ya know I like to start my day juicing." He started sucking on my neck and trying to slide his hand down the back of my hip-huggers, but they were too tight. I was wearing a size too small so my booty would look fatter.

"I'm not trying to get busted wide open while the boutique is full of customers." I pointed at the camera's monitor while trying to fight off the temptation at the same time.

"Girl, stop muthafuckin' playin' with me and take these too-tight-ass jeans off. You know I don't give a fuck about none of them hoes." Mace's response was rough and unapologetic as always. Part of his roughneck personality was what attracted me to him in the first place.

As soon as I did what I was told, Mace had me bent me over my desk with his dick so far up in me that it felt like my guts were about to explode. There wasn't no lovin' in this sex session, just straight buckin' and fuckin'. I was trying my best to throw it back and keep up with his stamina, but he was stroking my coochie with a rhythm I couldn't compete with.

"Ooohhh, shiiit." I squirmed as the pressure started building up. The feeling was familiar. I was about to melt on his manhood like butter.

"Yeah, I feel that pussy talking to me. Let 'er rip for me," he whispered into my ear, then began sucking on it. He was tapping all the right spots.

"I love you." I was stuttering, damn near speaking in tongues.

"I love you more." He licked my face and started tickling my booty hole on some freaky shit that pushed me over the edge.

I always ended up with a sore coochie, hickeys, and sometimes even bruises whenever Mace got into his animalistic zone, but I wasn't complaining and never did. He was knocking my shit out of the frame, and I was loving every second of it. Like he said, fuck them hoes if they heard us. I was all about my man.

Chapter Two

Maceo

"Go grab me a warm rag out the bathroom, with yo' messy ass!" Marley frowned at her cum-covered stomach. "And you better have not shot no nut on my new merchandise either."

"Girl, shut up before I drop this dick back off in yo' guts and leave my nut there. The only time you know how to talk to your man nowadays is when I'm stroking you down." I strategically played with her clit while I wiped her clean. I needed her in the best mood possible for what I was about to ask her to do.

On cue, she started moaning and arching her back, eager for another session. I swear I loved her freaky ass, and my manhood was twitching to climb back in her warmth. But I had business on the floor to handle, and they were hitting me up in the background on silent. Despite the temptation, I finished wiping Marley clean, then stood her up so she could get dressed.

"Don't put them tiny-ass pants back on. You got another size that fits right, I'm sure." I eyed her as I adjusted my jeans. I ain't give a fuck that mainly females shopped at the boutique. She didn't need no pants on that looked like paint. I didn't like for what was mine to be on display.

"Shut up about my pants, Mace. Dang! I see your plan was to come in here bullying me." She rolled her eyes, but she moved toward the stock of pants and pulled out a brand-new pair. "Happy now?"

"Yup, very." I slapped her booty cheeks right before she finished getting the new pair around her waist.

Me and Marley had hella history. We were three years deep into our relationship, which I didn't think was going to last past the few months she held out on a nigga. I thought that three-month rule was some made-for-TV shit, so it really blew my mind when shorty had me waiting, licking coochie like a sucka. I ain't never licked a clit so much in my damn life trying to get that girl to fuck. But I stuck around and fell for her in the meantime.

She knew her worth, and that shit spoke volumes over all the other females yelping in my ear, throwing their goods to me with no strings attached or bills paid. I was a young nigga getting bread, so the older women thought they could control me, and the young ones were too dumb to keep up with the fast life and talking I did. I'd been in the streets since I was 12, so a bitch with some A1 head didn't faze me.

Marley made herself something special out of the gate and even dropped some knowledge on my lap when it came to how I was hustling. Truth be told, she smartened me up. She was the brains, and I was the beast. So once she did drop her panties for me to finally fuck, she pussy whipped me, and I ain't been right since. I was mad territorial over her and our relationship regardless of the li'l creepin' I did in the streets from time to time. A nigga was just a knucklehead. No chick in the world could hold a candle to Marley.

"I'll meet you at the crib in a couple of hours. I've gotta shoot a few moves." I brushed my waves down and threw my fitted cap back on.

"Yeah, okayyy." She eyed me suspiciously. "You better make sure you're at the crib at a decent time or I'm tossing your shit to the curb. Don't think just because

I've been in my bag I haven't still been checking for you."
She crossed her arms and tried cutting her eyes through
my soul. Marley swore she was a fuckin' spiritual mind
reader when it came to my black ass.

"There ain't a day on the calendar safe for you to toss
my shit out," I chuckled. "But you can be easy. I didn't
forget about us hitting Krissy's gig tonight. Are you
talking 'bout getting off with a li'l girl-on-girl action, too?"
Marley wasn't bisexual but was a freak for me. We'd
only had maybe three threesomes but stayed hitting titty
clubs before she went back to school.

"Not the fuck tonight," she snapped, catching me off
guard. "And speaking of that, fun is fun, and I know we
play around, but don't mess around and lose your head
tonight being friendly with them throwaways. Jos told
me how you've been at the bar looking like a puppy dog
who ain't got no pussy at home whenever I'm at school."
She mushed me in the forehead.

"Yo, tell your friends to quit trying to start drama
between you and yo' man and get a man to watch. You
know I don't like that 'he said, she said' feminine shit.
And get yo' hand up outta my face. You know I don't like
that shit either." I knocked her hand away, then quickly
threw mine up to block her from swinging on me. Marley
was feisty when she wanted to be, plus I knew how her
girls could get in her head.

"Don't put the doggish-ass shit you do on my friend,
Mace. I'm not stupid or a fool. Soooo, like I said, don't
make me put my finger back in yo' ugly-ass face." She
shoved past me and started picking up the merchandise
we'd knocked over.

"Are you pregnant or something? You've been acting
hella bipolar with a nigga." I was side-eying her.

"Naw, I'm not pregnant, and don't jinx me!" She caught
even more of an attitude. "The last thing I need is a clone
of your crazy ass running around."

"You think having my seed is a jinx, Marley? Straight up? That's some fucked-up shit to say. A li'l homie I could run around and hoop with would be cool, ma." I was offended, especially since the same throwaways she spoke about were begging me to put babies in them.

"Yeah, whatever. That's what yo' ass is saying now. You're too busy babying the streets to even think about becoming a father. Let's be real. I wish I would jump to get a bump and be left trying to run a business with a baby on my hip. I'm good." Marley always dismissed the topic of us having a kid together. After all the years of us being a couple, I thought she'd be begging me to start a family and make it official.

Although she might've been right about me loving the trap life, I was starting to take it real personal that she wasn't trying to go half on a li'l one with me. It kinda had me wondering if she'd gotten an abortion behind my back before, especially since I'd always gone raw dog and reckless up in her guts.

"A'ight, boo, I'm about to bounce, but I need you to deposit this with your drop tonight." I dropped a bag of cash on her desk.

She rolled her eyes and snickered. "Oh, is that why you called yourself dickin' me down? Well, it didn't knock my senses loose, and I didn't forget what I said. When I told you that I wasn't running trap cash through my business accounts anymore, I meant it."

"C'mon now, Marley baby. Don't start tripping and flipping the script. You already know what it is, what it was, and what it's gon' be for us to stay up." I pinched the bridge of my nose to calm down. She'd been applying hella pressure on my neck to let her run the boutique straight legit, but we'd been up and down the same ropes until I was burnt out. "This shit should run like clockwork by now."

I was trying to hold my temper, but I wasn't vibing with Marley's newfound badge of honor. Up until three months ago, she was doing deposits without any hesitations. She was even hitting me up off schedule to see if there was money to be cleaned. It was all good when she needed the money to get the store up and running.

Although I'd given Marley the boutique to run, it was only supposed to be a basic operating drug front, a way for me to push cash across the country to my business partner and a way to keep Marley out of my hair while I handled the few business ventures I had going on behind her back. Marley's dream to go legit didn't have nothing to do with my get-rich hustle. I was irritated as hell that she was going against our original plans.

"Look, I'm not trying to beef with you, but I don't have time for you to be flopping like a fish out of water. You know what it is! This money has to be deposited into your account, and it must be done before the bank closes. You know what's on the floor and the deals I'm trying to lock in." I was running out of patience because she knew in full detail how smoothly shit needed to run.

Marley pursed her lips, nodded, then growled, "Yup, you've made yourself crystal muthafuckin' clear, Maceo Bryant. Now get the hell out of my office before I stab your disrespectful ass in the throat!" She pulled out her top desk drawer, which was where she kept her Mace, butcher knife, and handgun if some shit popped off.

"A'ight. I'm out." I threw my hands up and started backing out of her office just in case she really decided to go psycho on a nigga. "I love you, and I'll see you at the crib later."

"I don't know. I just might hop on a flight to Vegas and gamble these bands away." She flipped through the cash, then tossed it in her purse. "Now hurry up and get out. I wasn't playing about stabbing yo' ass. If you keep pushing me into a corner, I'ma come out swinging."

"You love a nigga too much to do me dirty, baby boo." I winked, then slammed the door right before the stapler she threw hit me upside my head.

Marley was pissed at me fa'sho, but I already knew she'd forgive me and we'd bounce back from the li'l bullshit-ass disagreement by the end of the night. She hated going to sleep with animosity built up between us, which was something I'd grown to appreciate. I'd always been able to count on my shorty through whatever, and I do mean whatever.

When I fucked up, she forgave me. When I was struggling in the streets hustling backward with Baggies, she held me down and leveled me up mentally. She was the type of woman every hustler needed in their corner. She was down-to-earth, loyal, and sexy as hell. She was my Lauren London, my Teyana Taylor, and my killa Cardi all wrapped up in one. If a nigga were living on the up-and-up, she'd be my Michelle Obama. I've never had to question Marley's allegiance, even on my worst day when I didn't deserve her respect. She deserved to get wifed up, but I was still fuckin' around like a bachelor from time to time.

Ring, ring, ring!

My cell rang through my car's speakers because the Bluetooth was paired. I hated when that happened and normally didn't use the feature, but I was trying out a new music app on my phone earlier. I started scrambling to unpair them. "Damn, fuck this muthafuckin' technology bullshit!"

"You have a call from 313-213—" it was snitching.

"Fuck!" I was ready to break my phone because it was slow and crashing. I was going back to my iPhone ASAP 'cause this Android was fuckin' with my flow with its instability.

I answered before it finished announcing ol' girl's number. "Yo! Didn't I tell yo' hardheaded ass not to call me with your number showing? If you do that shit again, I'm gonna block yo' shit," I went off on Gia, my ex I'd been mixing business and pleasure with as of late.

She smacked her lips and started popping off at the mouth. "Block me? Boy, stop it! You need me more than I need you. I can call about five different niggas in my phone right now who would love to get what I break you off with."

I chuckled at shorty because she was feeling herself way too hard. "Oh, for real? You got it like that, huh? Five different dudes? In your phone right now, huh?"

"Yup, you heard what I said. So you might want to humble yourself before I clip the cord." She was speaking to me like I was some type of sucka-ass nigga.

I snickered again, but this time it was to keep myself from telling Gia I'd fuck her dick-handling ass up in the worst way. I'd never been the type of nigga to play pussy or get fucked, and Vernelle didn't raise me thinking it was wrong to put my hands on a broad if she wanted to get tough. Hell, real talk, growing up I'd seen my ol' bird lay hands on swoll-ass muthafuckin' men. My OG ain't give a fuck about knuckling up with whoever whenever or fighting dirty. You give what you receive, from whoever the fuck you receive it from, and that's law. I was a product of my environment.

"You really love playing me like I'm some chump-ass nigga, G. I know we ain't kicked it like that in a minute, but you ain't forgot how gutta shit can get. Quit barking, li'l bite. I'm about to pull down on you in a minute."

"Don't come up here on no stupid shit. I got bills to pay, and you don't answer the phone consistently enough to make me lose my job." She smacked her lips, still provoking me, so I turned the heat up.

"For a bitch who don't want her head cracked at work, you sure as hell keep planting seeds and putting it into the universe." I hung up and jumped down on the e-way.

I was tired of talking. I wasn't a talking type of mutha-fucka anyway, and Gia knew that better than most people.

Marley

I was sour as hell staring at Mace on the surveillance camera until he sped out of the parking lot. His ego, his cockiness, and his boldness had me wanting to slice and dice him up for real, and then hop that flight to Vegas for a getaway while he healed.

At first, I was 1,000 percent on board with using the business account to clean our drug money, but now I wanted to stop. We needed something legit to fall back on, especially if he wanted to have the kids he kept bringing up to me. We couldn't keep hustling and hoping we came out on top. Only urban fiction stories ended like that.

I didn't want to admit it, but I now understood what my family was trying to teach me when I gave up my scholarship to Tennessee Tech to stay in Detroit playing house with Mace. Playing a dangerous game on a daily was cool or whatever when we were kids, but now we needed to level up and do some real boss shit, like own businesses and properties. Going to school had my eyes wide open. The more I learned, the more I wanted to grow. I was tired of doctoring up paperwork and spread-sheets to make the bank deposits make sense.

There were a few taps on my door, and then Kristina poked her head in. "Hey, sis, are you all right in here? From the sounds of it, you should be good, but your face screams otherwise. What's tea?"

"I'm straight. It's no big deal. You know how your brother gets and then gets me at times." No one knew I was washing our drug money, or at least I hadn't explicitly said it. Kris and Jos might've been my best friends, but I didn't tell them everything.

"Well, don't let him ruin your mood for my party tonight. I hate to be selfish, but I need all my girls rallying around me and rooting me on. I'm nervous as hell. I want the brand to take off sooooo super bad." Kris took my mind off of Mace and our issues to support her, and it was 100 percent cool. I was down for my friends and wanted them to win.

"Awww, sis! You're going to rock it out tonight. You don't have anything to worry about, I swear. And I'm not just saying that 'cause you're my homegirl. Your custom designs fly out of here faster than my wholesale items, plus you keep a waiting list of customers. Hell, I should be the one worried about tonight. You won't need a spot in my boutique anymore. You'll be opening your own." I truly meant the motivation.

"Aww, thanks, sissy. I love you for that." She wiped a tear from her eye. "And instead of opening my own shop, we can open one together and go bigger. Have that black-girl magic thang going on!"

"Sounds like a plan." We did the old-fashioned pinky swear, and then she stood to leave.

"I'm about to clean up then head home so I can get ready. I know I said stay out your mood for me, but for a minute, do you need to vent?" She raised her brow, sympathetically looking at me for an honest answer.

"G'on and get out of here, sis. I'm fine, I swear. I'll see you tonight." I waved her on so she could stay in the zone and I could get to fixing today's earning statements so I could make it to the bank before they closed.

Chapter Three

Maceo

Marley knew I pushed pills. That wasn't a secret of course. Once upon a time, she was a nigga's lookout, bag girl, and ride partner on my hustles until I sat her down to clean the cash. But what she didn't know was that I'd gotten a new pill supplier. That was the one good thing about Marley going to school—her focus wasn't on a nigga like how it used to be when she was in a role like G.I. Jane. I was grateful for the rope 'cause a nigga had been hanging.

Gia worked at this raggedy-ass nursing home that had a large population of people with little to no medical insurance. It was in one of the worst neighborhoods on the east side of Detroit, and most of the workers resided in that same neighborhood and worked for wages under the table. It was unsanitary as hell, and I was shocked the State hadn't stepped in and shut the facility down.

Anyway, the doctor who was on call and did rounds at the nursing home was giving Gia a gang of pills to pass along to me, for a very nice price, as well as the plug to a couple of his pharmacies. I was getting triple the amount of product for 30 percent less than I'd been getting with the original plug. And the blessing just kinda fell into my lap a few months ago. Per Gia, ol' boy was hitting licks on the insurance companies by putting in claims and then having the pharmacies that were owned by his friends and families fill the scripts.

I didn't necessarily like cool-kid-ass white boys or Chaldeans because they were some disrespectful muthafuckas to folks in the hood, but I had to respect their hustles and how loyal they were to their own people. He and his friends owned all the liquor stores, gas stations, urgent cares, and pharmacies in all the predominately poor black areas and were eating good off our paychecks, scams, hustles, and jobs that paid under the table that the citizens of our communities nested. What the Chaldeans were making off insurance fraud was far more than the thousands me and my crew were raking in a month. A debonair savage like myself could live like a king if I could get away with white-collar crime like fraud and embezzlement.

As soon as I got near the nursing home, I set my shooter on my lap just in case I had to blast a young, dumb nigga. Luck wasn't shit but staying ready, and that I did.

"Yo, let see what that mouth work be like now, shorty. I'm in the parking lot. Come outside." I dodged a few man-sized potholes, then whipped up into one of the many empty parking spaces.

"I can't. There's no other CNA on the floor, and there has to be one at all times."

"Naw, G! I ain't trying to hear that shit after you were just on my line running reckless. You better bring your ass out here with my work, or I'm coming up in that dungeon of death to drag you out." I was done playing cool and ready to shake shit up a bit.

"I swear I'm not playing," she yelled in a panic. "I can't leave the floor without coverage or I could lose my job for real. I was on lunch when I was calling you, but now my supervisor is taking hers. She'll be back in about an hour."

"You ain't got an hour." I tucked my heater into my waistband and hopped out. Nursing home or not, I wasn't about to get caught slipping. "What floor are you on?" I started making my way to the entrance. I wasn't but a few paces from the door since I'd parked in a handicap spot.

"Oh, my God! Whoa! Quit tripping and chill out. Please don't come up in here clowning, Mace. You and I both need for me to keep my job." Her words were falling on deaf ears. The only words drumming through them were her previous threats.

"Whatever, G. Kill that noise. What should I tell this lady at the front desk so she can stop looking at me like she's crazy?" The receptionist's face went flush.

"You are out of your rabbit-ass mind," Gia mumbled. "Don't start no shit with her. Just tell her you're here for Gia Sanders, then hurry up here to the third floor. The elevator is to your right." She sounded more worried about the chick behind the desk than of me getting off into her ass for talking slick.

After I gave ol' girl Gia's government, she slid the sign in sheet over to me, and I penned in a fake name and kept it moving up the stairwell to the third floor. I didn't do elevators unless I absolutely had to. I had a fear of getting stuck in one, plus a nigga was claustrophobic. I was about 4 and hiding in the closet from the boogeyman and ended up locking myself in one night. Vernelle was passed out on the couch in a sleep coma and didn't hear my crying and banging on the door in panic mode to be let out. I was in that stuffy, too-small space for at least five hours. I remembered going in when *Married . . . with Children* came on at midnight and getting dragged out and my ass beaten when the news was on. I'd fallen asleep by then, but Vernelle had woken up throwing up all over herself and needing my help, but I was nowhere to be found. I didn't even go to school that day because of all the welts her nutzo ass left on my toddler body.

Gia was standing in front of the elevators when I bent the corner. As mad as she'd just made me, I got stuck on how fat her booty was looking in the hot pink scrubs she was wearing. I fucked around and had to adjust my manhood 'cause it was starting to wake up to the thought of breaking her back out real quick. The thin material was barely containing the natural meat she was blessed with.

Even with the money she was touching with our hustle, it was still hard to believe she wasn't clapping them cheeks for a check anymore. G used to have all the homies lined up around the stage during her sets as well as waving her down for a lap dance. Me included. But she'd been staying out of the club since having a baby.

Gia got knocked up by this nigga who had long bread but not a lot of time left on this earth. He was murdered because niggas saw his potential in the rap game he was about to blow up in and were jealous of his shine. Period. The hate in Detroit was strong, too muthafuckin' strong. That was why I stayed strapped and ready to lay niggas down.

"What was all that stupid shit you was talking on the phone?" I walked up behind Gia without her ever picking up on my presence. She really needed to get a better sense of her surroundings.

She gasped, jumped back, and grabbed her chest. "Damn it, Mace! You scared me!"

"Are you okay, sweetheart?" One of the residents looked up over her red-framed glasses held together by Scotch tape to question Gia. She was only one of many pee-soiled residents lined up in wheelchairs against the wall. Most of them were staring off into thin air or at the television playing a game show, but she happened to be knitting.

"Yes, I'm fine, Ms. Bridgette. I'll be right back to get you changed and to the dining room for dinner. Go ahead back to knitting your blanket." Gia rubbed the lady's back.

"Are you sure?" The lady looked at me and then back to Gia, holding her knitting needle like she was gonna do something.

"Yeah, she's sure, OG. You ain't gotta stroke out trying to worry about some shit that ain't got nothing to do with you. I'll have ya little diaper changer back to you in a few." I was amused at granny's cockiness but not pleasant with her.

"You can't be this fucking crazy," Gia mumbled, pulling me up the hallway and into an empty room by my arm. "I begged you not to come up here acting all uncivilized. The last thing I need is for somebody to be all up in my business. You know half these hoes don't like me anyway."

"Fuck all that. Where's my work at? And who are these niggas you wanted to throw up in my face like you'd sell them my shit?" I backed her into the corner.

"Nobody, damn! I just said that shit so you'd hurry up. You know I hate holding." She slid the stash of pills out of her waist trainer and into my hands.

Shawn stayed in a two-bedroom duplex that was decked up like a true bachelor pad. He had a sixty-five-inch plasma TV mounted on the wall, both the Xbox and PlayStation video game systems, and surround sound installed all throughout the living and dining room area since the floor plan was open. You'd think we were in the middle of a real live shoot-out during a game of *Call of Duty*.

I dropped down on his leather couch and scooped up one of the 360 remotes and opened his music app. Shawn had some killer playlists, but I was in the mood to hear my Detroit faves: RockyBadd, SkillaBaby, and of course Sada. Detroit needed their own Hustle & Grind music label since the industry refused to turn thoroughbreds on. Niggas from the D were cut different.

"Damn, fool! What I tell you about making yo'self comfortable in my crib and shit?" Shawn came out the bathroom from taking a dump. The funky aroma followed him and was lingering in the air.

"Fuck all that, nigga! What dead cat you get some Chinese food from? You stank like death." I fanned around me, then pulled my shirt over my mouth and nose.

"The one by my house. You catching a clue yet?" He plopped down on the couch next to me, pulled the already-stuffed cone out of the ashtray, then set blaze to it. "But naw, on the real, you got some Tums or something? My shit is knockin' like a muthafucka. I think Nakeesha's crazy ass put something in my food or something."

"Naw, her nutty ass probably put a hex on you. That girl got a goddamn tattoo of a witch, but you swear she managing a full deck. And what the fuck I look like, walking around with a pocket of antacids? I flip percs, not Pepto Bismol." I was cackling as Shawn grunted in pain. It wasn't no thang. We always clowned on one another. That was what fam did.

Me and Shawn were blood cousins and had been close as hell since we were kids. Our mothers were sisters, and although they mixed like oil and water, they made us play together and get along. They wanted us to be able to have someone solid we could rely on whenever there was a schoolyard scrap or some dope-boy shit once we became of age to hustle. It didn't matter if Vernelle and Vickie called each other every version of a sack-chasing ho they could think of, I'd never seen one of them struggling if the other one wasn't. Me and this nigga grew up muddy as hell.

Remy joined our two-man crew through Shawn. One day, me and Shawn got caught boosting some fresh sneakers out of a shoe store they'd just opened in a mini-mall a few miles from our house. We'd walked down there smoking a blunt, cracking jokes on all the li'l weak niggas who couldn't come off their porch, and messing with fast-tail girls who stayed giving us play because we were young niggas with game. We were catching the bus back so we wouldn't scuff up our freshly stolen kicks. The cops stopped the bus and arrested us as we were trying to run out the back door, then rode us out separately to the detention center. Rem-Dog was assigned to the unit Shawn was in.

Rem-Dog was thrown into the juvenile system by his mother. He was a knucklehead, the type of kid who did wrong for attention and regardless of circumstance. He was so irrational and out of control at times that muthafuckas really thought he was sick in the head. His mom got tired of taking him to psychiatric appointments, trying different medications that only brought out even crazier side effects, and parenting him all alone. When social services started fucking with her, talking about making her liable for his behavior, she signed Remy over without hesitation and dropped him off to become a ward of the State. Manish-ass Rem-Dog became a menace to society instead of a nutcase though. When he crossed paths with me and Shawn, we three became the wrecking crew.

While Shawn finished getting himself together, I dumped out the product I'd gotten courtesy of Gia.

"Damn, that li'l thot you fuckin' with been coming through like a champ." Shawn started breaking down the bottles of pills and doing his thang. "I hope cuz don't find out about her. We been flipping this boys ten times quicker than that stepped-on shit ol' boy was pushing." Shawn spoke on the quality of Gia's pills because they weren't generics.

"I hope not either. She's plugged straight into the source." Between the doctor and the pharmacies he was linked to, we were hustling grade A narcotics, opposed to all the stepped-on product that was getting pushed through the D. Suffering from a drought was the furthest thing from my mind.

"One of y'all big-headed-ass niggas come open the door." Rem-Dog was looking through the screen window. I got up and let him in, and as I did, he came in talking shit. "Why y'all got the work on display like we're above the law?" He came in, closing the blinds.

"My vitamin D is low, muthafucka." Shawn shrugged, laughing. "But good looking out."

"What up doe, boss?" I dapped it up with Shawn.

"Slow motion. I been in the crib tired as fuck all day."

"Aww, damn. You hitting Krissy's party tonight though, right?"

"Hell yeah, I'm sliding through. I already got my 'fit ready. Hopefully Marley's homegirl Jos will finally throw a nigga some attention tonight." He was crushing hard on Joslyn, but she'd yet to give him any play. Jos got mad attention in the club plus called herself a social media model, so it was hard to get that girl out of her head.

"Maybe she will, maybe she won't. Good luck on that, playa." I wasn't hating, just not feeling how she dry snitched on me to Marley. It wasn't Jos's business what I was at the club for.

The thought reminded me to touch base with Marley before she started hitting my line on tip. I also wanted to make sure she followed through with that wash because my connect out in Cali was scheduled to hit the account by morning. Her plans might've been to go legit, but I was trying to go global with my grind.

"A'ight, fellas, Gia got all ninety-day scripts this time. Plus, the dosages are higher. We should be able to flip

these boys for at least five dollars more a pill, maybe ten."
I was multiplying money in my mind as I broke down the
new recipe.

"Yeah, yeah, yeah, nigga. We got it. Stretch it, don't
stomp on it." Shawn got to work, and unlike earlier when
we clowned back and forth, I followed his lead. Playtime
was over. It was time to get our product ready for the
streets.

We never sold the pills in the same form they came
in from the pharmaceutical company. For one, that shit
could be tracked because there were only ten mainstream
pharmaceutical industries in America, and two, I'd be
hustling for a hobby. We took their pills, ground them
down into piles of powder, then made our own brand
to distribute in the streets. We even added shit like
methamphetamine and fentanyl to stretch batches out.

Once we had Detroit feenin', we pushed our pills to
Pennsylvania, plus large quantities of coke and heroin.
Shawn or Remy ran the product there at least twice a
month to this nigga named Kurtis we all knew from juvie.
Kurt ended up doing a bid right out of juvie instead of
hitting the pavement like me, Rem, and Shawn did, and
he ended up in the country-bumpkin-ass town that had
stepped on everything. I swear to God them fools were
rolling up oregano and dried-up grass, the weed was so
garbage. Kurtis sent word to the D, and we were on the
road with some testers in less than twenty-four hours.
It'd been smooth money ever since. The money we got off
a delivered package in Pennsylvania was what we made
here in a month's time. Fiends in P-Town ate our product
up like candy.

"Yo, which one of y'all are making the trip this week?"

Shawn spoke up first. "I'm down for the double back.
I gotta check on this shorty. I gave her some abortion
money two weeks ago and wanna make sure that's
handled."

"Damn, fool! You'll trick with everything. I ain't seen not one female worth buying an Extra Value Meal for, but you running up in 'em raw. Ya dick is gonna fall off." Rem-Dog wasn't lying. Shawn had been like that since we were kids. He stayed sliding off with females who looked dusty, claiming they were easier to control and didn't come with ego, expectations, or "pretty-girl issues" he wasn't trying to entertain.

"Nakeesha is gonna put a hex on your ass and my heroin if she finds out you're using those runs to run up in another woman, cuzzo. Do me a favor and quit mixing business and pleasure. Make sure whoever ol' girl is really deaded that situation, and then you dead that situation." All the joking and laughing had come to an end. I was serious as hell. Shawn fucking with a local could put us all at risk, and right now, I wanted us moving like ghosts in and out of their city. We didn't know enough about Pennsylvania's laws, layouts, or who was loyal to whom to give locals access to us. The easiest setup came from a woman getting a man to engage in pillow talk. I wasn't trying to lose no sleep over a potential setup queen in another city.

"Damn, a nigga might just be thinking wayyy too much with his diznick." Shawn sat back in his chair, looking like he'd been hit with an epiphany. "I'm most definitely about to make sure that situation is handled. The last thing I'm trying to do is catch a case or get caught slipping out there."

"Nowww you're thinking with your right head. I swear to God I think Auntie dropped you on your fuckin' dome sometimes." We got back to cracking a few jokes on one another, then homed back in on business. We each had moves to make, re-ups to fill, and spots to stack.

After about an hour longer, we'd finished whipping up the work and separating it for distribution. The three of us evenly split the profits from all the Pennsylvania runs, but we each had our own customers as well. There were enough drugs and money to go around as long as the laws of loyalty were enforced at all times.

Chapter Four

Marley

I was at home, pre-turning up with my homemade drink of Tito's and cranberry juice while waiting for Mace to make good on his word. He'd texted me that he was en route home, but that was twenty minutes ago. He had ten more before I slipped on my clothes and hit the streets solo-dolo. I wasn't about to miss my bestie's fashion show or a chance to promote the boutique.

I laid my outfit on the bed, then picked out an outfit for Mace that matched my fly. I was rocking a royal blue bodycon dress with matching thigh boots that tied all the way up my legs with the peekaboo toe, and he was going to rock a royal blue Balenciaga jogger set and some fresh kicks. Mace's wardrobe was hella cold and low-key had me thinking about carrying some men's pieces at my boutique. I could see my ladies shopping for their men, especially since most of them were using a sponsor's cash to shop anyway. I'd really been on my A game lately when it came to thinking like a boss-ass entrepreneur.

Ding! My text notification went off.

Jos: This MF is slapping! Where are you? She threw in the "pair of eyes" emoji.

Me: I'm getting dressed. OMW in a few. Is Krissy on one already?

Jos: U know she on 10, boo. Hurry yo' ass up! This time she put a whole bunch of yelling emojis after her message. I swear Jos could have a whole conversation with nothing but emojis and GIFs if she wanted to.

Me: I am. I am. See u in a minute.

I closed our chat and got ready to text Mace for his exact whereabouts, but another message came through. It was Lance checking back in to see if I'd submitted the assignment for our business class yet. The deadline was almost an hour away, so I thought it was sweet he was looking out to make sure I didn't miss it. I used to be an overachiever like Lance until I fell in love with a roughneck. Now I was trying to balance two very different lives. I sat down at my vanity to reply. Lance had been looking out for me all semester, and I really appreciated it since I'd been struggling trying to juggle school, the boutique, and the relationship he didn't even know about.

It wasn't that I was keeping Mace a secret, but I was keeping all the chunks of my life that involved criminal activity a secret. I even went to the extreme to drive forty-five minutes to and from school so the likelihood of someone knowing me would be slim to none.

Me: Hey, yeah, I actually buckled down & submitted it earlier. Imagine that. Thx for looking out, as always.

Lance: Wow! Look at you, taking care of business. I'm proud of you. And it's all good. No thx needed. U know I got u.

I sent back a smiley emoji, then opened the Pandora app to my hip-hop station, paired it to my Bluetooth speaker, then started putting my makeup on. Thankfully, my wand curls were finally falling right, so I could start on the rest of my look. I'd gotten my eyebrows arched and some mink lashes installed at the beauty bar with Krissy and Jos the other day, so all I had to do was apply a little foundation, some eyeshadow, and of course my gloss. I didn't have a face that required a bunch of makeup, so I never overdid it. I had a cute, chic, sexy look going on. A lot of people said I put them in the mind of socialite Jordyn Woods but a shorter version since I was barely five foot two.

"Did you handle that for me, bae?" I felt Mace's breath on my neck and then his lips.

"Awww, shit! You scared me." I jumped and started turning the volume down on my phone.

"That's 'cause yo' ass think you're at a concert in here."

"You know I like to catch a good vibe before I go out."

"I dig it. Just let me know if you handled that wash for me and you can get back to your set."

"Yes, Maceo. You know I did," I huffed and went to push him back, but he grabbed me up by my arm instead.

"Thank you, babbyyyyy." He then started playfully kissing me all over my face.

"Oh, my God, you can be so damn goofy." As much as I loved Mace's rough edges, I equally loved how he'd let down his guard with me.

"Look, Marley, you know a nigga ain't the best with his words, but I just wanted you to know I appreciate you for holding me down and just being solid with a nigga all the way around. I know it ain't easy thuggin' it out with me sometimes."

"You're welcome, and you know I'm always going to have your back, but I really want you to consider all the preaching I've been doing about switching up how we hustle and operate. At the end of the day, all I want is longevity with you and for us to start moving differently. This street shit been getting reallll grimy, and I don't want to lose you to the game or getting caught up. We can hustle on the books and still bank hella bread, bae."

"Whoa, chill. I wasn't trying to kick it with you so you could convert me to your beliefs. I'm standing on this street shit until they put me in the ground. That's who I am and who you met." Mace kissed my forehead, then picked up a bag from the floor beside us that had been there the entire time but that I hadn't noticed. It was a bag from my favorite jeweler. "I copped you something. Open it up."

"I don't know if I should be happy you shut me up." I loved getting gifts, especially jewelry, but I hated that Mace wouldn't give himself a chance to see something different.

"C'mon with the energy," he huffed. "Don't mess up the li'l special shit I tried planning." I could tell he was starting to get annoyed. "Open what I copped for you."

"Okay." I took the bag, not wanting to mess up the moment or the night ahead. "Oh, my God! Maceeee." I jumped into his arms and started kissing him all over his face. "I can't believe you got my chain! It wasn't supposed to be ready for another month." I admired the iced-out name tag that spelled out "A Unique Piece" in cursive. Kal was one of the coldest jewelers in the Midwest, if not the coldest, so I knew my piece was gonna be hitting hard.

"I know, but I got with Kal after you ordered it and changed up that game plan."

"I am glad you did. I love it so much." Now I was the one loving on him with kisses.

"That's the reaction a nigga wanted to get."

He pulled his phone, money, and personal stash of weed from his pocket and set it on the nightstand, then unclipped his pistol from his waistband. "I got some grade A's today. You wanna take a few tonight and slang 'em like old times?"

"I wasn't planning on it, but you can slide me a few. I'll put them in my purse just in case one of my old custos come looking to cop. They'll sell themselves." I took the sandwich bag of pills and examined them. "And okay, I see these really are some grade A's. When did ol' boy start getting officials?" I was used to Mace's pill plug having generic brands, but these were all straight from the pharmaceutical mill.

"A'ight, li'l Nina Brown. I see you eyeballing the work. Just remember to flip them to your birds for ten more since the cut is more pure."

"I'on need no reminder on how to hustle, hater." I tossed the pills in my purse, then tossed a pillow at him. "You just worry about hurrying up so you don't get left."

"Chill, girl, I'm about to hop in the shower now. You wanna join me?" He stripped down and headed into our on-suite.

"Nope. You already messed my hair up once today. It took forever for me to fix these curls."

"Have it your way now, but I'm wrecking 'em later." The shower popped on, and I was tempted to go get a li'l dick before we left. But instead I hopped in the mirror, admiring my latest gift and hoping it wasn't a token of apology for some shit I'd yet to find out about. With Mace, you never knew.

Gia

"Here you go, Ms. Fran." I handed one of my patients a Dixie cup with two over-the-counter Motrin tablets in it. She was supposed to be taking one Norco at night for her arthritis pain, but she was one of the residents Dr. Basheer was using for a come-up. He would bill the insurance company for the real medications but have me giving them over-the-counter generic pain pills or vitamins that we got from the dollar store up the street.

Ms. Fran didn't have any living family members we knew of besides a cousin who lived down South, and she never had any kids. She was sent here from the hospital after they diagnosed her with dementia and said it was unsafe for her to live alone. It was New Light Nursing and Rehabilitation Facility that was really unsafe though. Dr. Basheer targeted men and women like Ms. Frances who didn't have anybody checking in on their well-being.

She was one of twenty-five in-house residents at New Light receiving improper medication that would, of course, worsen their health conditions and result in needing more scripts. She was one of twelve patients receiving injections of steroids that would weaken their immune system so they could be more susceptible to developing another disease. I felt bad being a part of Dr. Basheer's scheme, but I wasn't about to pass up the opportunity to bring home an extra few grand every other week. I never really wanted to be a certified nursing assistant anyway.

I'd just busted my ass doing a double and was hella exhausted. I couldn't wait to get home, smoke a fat one, and then climb in bed with my li'l fat man. I'd been missing his chubby-cheeked happy self for the whole sixteen hours I'd been here grinding. His grandmother was at my house babysitting and had been sending me pictures and videos all day. He reminded me so much of his father. Not a day passed when I didn't wish Omari was still living.

My baby daddy was hustling hard trying to ink a rap contract with a major label but ended up getting murked by a nigga as they were leaving a rap battle. He hadn't even won the battle, but niggas knew he was on his way out of the mud with a mic in his hand. In the dirty D, a muthafucka would get bodied for having potential, and that was exactly why my son wouldn't ever meet his father.

Had Omari's mother not begged me to stay in Detroit so she could have a close relationship with her grandson, I would've gotten out of this city. It was too hard for a person to have a dream in this gloomy-ass place. As soon as I stacked enough bread from this scheme I had going on with Mace and Dr. Basheer, I was going to make Ms. Spencer bounce with me and Junior whether she liked it or not. I was 'bout overdue for a fresh start.

"Hey, Ma. I just punched. Do you need me to stop for anything before I get there?" I crossed my fingers that she'd say no because I was exhausted.

"Nope, we're fine. I just ordered some pizza, so you don't even have to stop to get yourself food if you haven't eaten."

"Aww, Ma. Thanks! I swear you be coming through for me. I appreciate you so much." I sincerely meant it.

"It's no problem, sweetheart. This is the least I can do to help you out. I know my son would have spoiled both you and Junior rotten." I heard the pain in her voice and got teary-eyed. I knew my grief for Omari wasn't as heavy as hers was. I wouldn't wish the pain of losing a son on anyone.

"All right, Ma, don't cry or get me to crying." I already had the sniffles. "I'll be home in a few, and maybe if you feel like it, we can watch *Golden Girls* or *227*." She had every old-school TV series on DVD that was made. I was super exhausted and ready to tap out, but I didn't want her sad and lonely.

"Ohh, child, that TV will probably end up watching me. Junior has been up and on the go since you left for work," she laughed. "If it's true that kids keep you young, I'm sure I lost five years of my old age today," she cackled.

I wiped the tear that had fallen about Omari and smiled. "Let me hurry up and get out of here so you can get some rest. I've gotta be back here first thing in the morning." I yawned, kind of regretful that I'd picked up extra shifts. But the more hours I worked, the more bill-able treatments Dr. Basheer got to send to the insurance company, meaning my check would be fatter on payday.

"Okay, baby. Be safe driving, and watch your back." She hated me working late hours but knew I had to do what I had to do.

"All right, Ma. I promise I will." We hung up, and I pushed for the elevator to come. I then scrolled through my phone to the music application and was about to pop in my earbuds, but one of my coworkers got on, interrupting me.

"Hey, Gia." She casually called me by name, but we weren't cool. I made it a point not to be cool with none of the females up here because they were messy and always gossiping about something. I was trying to leave the catty shit at the strip club. The only bond I wanted was with the doc and my chizeck.

Instead of greeting her, I was about to bid her farewell. I wasn't good at acting fake and friendly. "Hey. Good night," I dryly responded, popping one bud in and thinking she'd get back to her business, but she took a nosedive into mine.

"I saw Sav up here earlier. He got a grandma on your floor?" She caught me off guard with her curiosity, but I was quick with the comeback.

"I don't know." I shrugged. "You should've asked him yourself." I looked her dead in the eyes, letting her know she wasn't about to question me and our interaction was done. And it was a good thing she picked up on my energy because I was vibrating lower than a mutha.

"My bad, and I will next time." She got off the elevator before I did, and I almost hit her nosy ass in the back of the head. She needed to be more worried about her funky ass smelling like a pound of fresh fish than Sav, but whatever. I was more aggravated with him because I told his ass to stay in his car. You know, no face, no case.

Tossing my bag into the back seat, I climbed in the car and called Sav, and as expected, his voicemail came on. We normally didn't talk unless it was about product.

"Thanks for leaving the door open for a bitch to approach me at work about you with yo' celebrity ass. The next pickup can't be at my job because I don't want my spot blown up," I fussed, then hung up and went to start my car, but the muthafucka wouldn't start.

"Argh! Oh, my God! You've gotta be kidding me," I shouted, trying to start it over and over again until it clicked and screeched like I was about to flood the engine.

At this point, I was beyond frustrated and desperately ready to cuddle up in the crib. I truly hated having to hustle the way I was doing. I was tired of struggling, then putting in overtime, just to get a setback off one mishap. If Omari were here, I'd be doing nothing but raising our son. A chick needed a break from being a grown-up.

After calling Omari's mom with the current events and change of plans, I busied myself on Google trying to see what was wrong and if it was a quick fix. I was trying to stack my money, not spend it on incidentals, but it always seemed like there was some random-ass expense popping up from nowhere. It was always something. And today's trouble could've been anything from the radiator to the transmission to the starter. Who knew that when Sav called himself giving me that "pain and suffering" cash, he was burning bread on a bitch? That was the money I was about to spend on the tow truck.

"My bad, Star. I hate that I even had to call you." I got into the passenger seat of my homegirl's car.

"It's all good. I know how shit be." She passed me the blunt she was puffing on. "You wanna hit this to settle your nerves while we wait on the tow truck?"

"Hell yeah! Thank you." I took the blunt and started puffing on it like I'd never had weed before. "Damn, Star, where'd you get this shit from? It's hittin' super hard." I'd been stuck getting basic bags of Kush from the boy who lived near me because he'd always drop them off to me whenever.

"Bop. His set is the only set in the city that's slanging eighths for twenty-five, and the shit be hitting."

"Twenty-five? Straight up? That's live as hell."

"How you ain't know that, sis? You ain't fucking around with Sav no more? Bop works for his set." Star's bluntness didn't catch me off guard. She'd always been the "I say what's on my mind" type of person, but it was never done maliciously, where I took it as digs.

"Naw, not like that. But me and him weren't ever on no kicking it shit. All we did was trick. I threw my ass, and he threw his cash."

"Hm. Oh, okay. I could've sworn . . . but that ain't my business." She zipped her lip and threw away the key like we were in kindergarten. Then she changed the subject. "What's up with li'l man? I see all the pictures you be posting on the Gram, but my nails be too long to tap and like 'em." She waved her hot pink claws around so I could see she wasn't lying. "He's cute as hell, but not enough to make a bitch have baby fever." She burst out laughing.

"Thank you for making me laugh. But he's doing good, just growing. I miss a lot of time with him because I'm always working."

"Ugh, girl, why are you working anyway? I mean, I understood why you sat down from stripping while you were pregnant and big O, but what's your rationale behind working fifteen-hour shifts for less than fifteen dollars an hour when you could make five hundred in less than five hours on your worst day? Make it make sense, sis." Star was being brutally blunt again.

"Wow, you really just shit on me, didn't you? I should've called a Lyft."

"But you couldn't because you spent all your spare cash on a tow truck, which further proves why you should just ride to the spiznot with me and do at least one set. Them niggas will be so thirsty to tip yo' ass since you've been off the stage for so long that you'll have me taking you to the dealership in the morning for a new ma'fuckin' whip." Star was geeking my head up.

The reason I'd stopped stripping in the first place was because my baby daddy wanted me out of the club. He used to rag on me heavy because he hated that his fellas had seen me naked. He hated that shit with a passion, but he loved me too much to let that interfere with our relationship. We were building something real.

But now the only real things were my bills and the tow truck driver saying my car's radiator had gone bad and the repair could be upward of $400 or more. Shit was all bad. Rent and bills were due, I had to of course get Pampers and shit, plus Omari's mom needed a few dollars for Bingo and her day-to-day essentials. I wasn't trying to dip into my getaway stash, but the more I ran back my responsibilities, the more backed into the corner I felt. Or, should I say, slid back up the pole.

"So what's up, girly? I see you over there thinking. Are you in your feelings and mad at a bitch because I came at you? Or are you like, 'Hell yeah, I'm 'bout to rock that stage'?"

"As bad as I wanna tell you to drop me off at the crib, the money is calling me."

"Hell yeah, G-Baby! Answer that bitch! Let's get this bread!"

Chapter Five

Maceo

Me and my girl were fly as fuck, smelling rich, and iced out like the money-gettin' couple we were. I was ready to stunt and have a good night with my baby boo. It had been a minute since she played at the club with ya boy, and I'd really been missing her presence. She made a nigga the best version of himself he could be.

I used to have nothing
But now I got a whole lot of everythang

Jeezy bumped through the sound system, and we rocked our heads in unison. Marley loved hip-hop, but me, I was feeling his words like a mutha. I knew all about growing up poor, making it do what it do with some pork and beans and hot dogs. But now I was about to go lay it out in the club like the street boss I'd become. I ain't give a fuck about a nigga's feelings when it came to flexing 'cause I was a young and hungry nigga who'd just started touching big pape.

By the time we pulled up to the club, Marley had taken damn near 100 selfies and even had done some live videos. I hated that social media shit with a passion. It was like the Feds gave us phones to police ourselves for them. I always did my best to stay out of her videos, and of course I didn't have a page of my own. That didn't mean

I didn't make it to the World Wide Web though. I done got caught stomping a nigga out on a video a time or two.

"Ay, chief, let me hold this spot right here down." I pulled up on the VIP attendant with a crisp $100 bill out the window to get additional VIP treatment.

"You got it, bro. But it's fifty for the lot tonight."

"Keep the change." I upped it another hundred and swerved into the space as soon as he lifted the cone. "I'm going to keep the keys, but have 'em page Mace if there's a problem."

"A'ight, boss. I got you." The attendant placed the cone behind my car, then rushed to the next car that was pulling into the lot. From the looks of it, Kris had brought the city out.

"Let's go live it up, wifey." I grabbed Marley's hand and walked her in.

Marley

The club was swarming with supporters for Krissy. The city had really shown up and out for my girl, but I hadn't expected anything less. She'd been humbly hustling with intent for years with some of the hottest names in the city, so her fan base was popping and through the roof. This brand release party was doing numbers.

Mace was close on my backside as we navigated through the crowd toward all the pink and gold metallic balloons that lined the archways around VIP. He kept grabbing my booty whenever we were in gridlock, always on some frisky shit, but I was all in and living in the moment. It felt good being out with my man. I couldn't even front, school had turned me a little boring because I was always studying or trying to get my rest up. I was about to push everything about responsibility to the back of mind tonight though and get lit how we used to.

Krissy spotted us before we got to her VIP section and started calling me out. "It's 'bout time you showed up!" She was in full party mode with a champagne bottle in one hand and a blunt in the other. Jos wasn't lying.

"Congratulations, Krissy Pooh. I'm so proud of you." I embraced my friend and gave her a big bear hug until we both toppled over. "You deserve all this praise and more. You've been busting yo' butt day in and out, and now it's your time to shine!" I was truly happy for her come-up. And not just because her success meant more success for me. There was enough money out there for all of us to eat.

"Oh, my God, thank you, friend! Please don't make me cry again! You know I've been waiting on this day forever." She was grinning and glowing like she should have been. "Heyyy, bro. I see you back there hiding and shit. Don't be scurred though. I'm not about to curse you out for making my boo tardy to my party." She looked around me to where Mace had sat down and started rolling up.

"Yo' drunk ass is crazy as hell, sis. I'on even know if I should buy you a congratulatory bottle or an ice-cold bottle of water." He waved one of the two waitresses assigned to Krissy's section our way.

"Don't play, bro! I bet' not catch nobody over here with a water." She spun around in a circle, pointing her finger at everybody in her section.

"Yup, yo' ass is lit." Mace licked the blunt and sparked it up. "This is about to be an interesting night fa'sho. I can't wait until my fellas get here." I already knew that he, Shawn, and Rem-Dog were gonna show out, especially when Fresh hit the stage. He was on the ticket tonight to perform. I knew every word of every track that nigga made because Mace stayed bumping his music. Everybody on the east was fucking with Fresh hard because they all grew up with him.

The waitress came over and took Mace's order, which was a bottle of 1738, a bottle of Cîroc, and two bottles of champagne. He was laying the spread out for when Rem-Dog and Shawn arrived. Ain't no telling how much money we were about to blow tonight once it was all said and done.

"Tell this lady what you drinking on, wife." Mace started peeling some bills off his wad of cash to pay her.

"Bring me some Crown Royal Apple, some cranberry juice, and a Red Bull." I knew I could handle dark liquor better than light. Not only would I be on one of these poles like I was chasing a check off some light liquor, but I wouldn't make it to school in the morning because my head would be in a bucket full of vomit. I'd never been able to handle my high when I was buzzing off tequila, vodka, and even some Moscato if I had enough glasses of it.

"Damnnnn, diva! I see you out here shining! Ay yo, DJ, play 'Ice Me Out.'" Jos came up on the mic, hyping me up about my A Unique Piece pendant. "This bitch is niiiice, sis." She got a closer look at it.

"Thanks, boo." I started dancing to the beat of the song as it started bumping through the club. Jos was hosting the event, so she and the DJ were synced up. He even shined the spotlight on our section so we could rev it up with our Rolex watches in the air.

"You got it jumping in here, Jos. I done broke a sweat and it ain't been five minutes."

"I don't even be trying." She blushed and batted her long eyelashes sweetly. "But let's take some pictures and go live real quick. One of the bouncers said we're filled to capacity with a line still waiting to come in. I wanna stunt that I'm hosting a sold-out event." Jos lived her life for social media.

Mace was our photographer until his fellas Rem-Dog and Shawn showed up, and then I went live with Jos's phone so she could entertain her followers. She had over 1,000 viewers and wasn't doing shit but singing, blowing out hookah smoke, and showing different angles of her body. Every now and then she'd shout about Krissy, Unique Pieces, and the venue, but my girl was in her zone and feeling herself to the max. I couldn't blame her though. I saw the comments and her DM jumping with niggas who wanted to Cash App her money just so their timelines could stay looking pretty. I low-key wondered if my girl was trickin' on the web, sending naked pictures and shit.

"What you drinking on? You wanna taste a li'l bit of this Jossy-Baby Jungle Juice?" She swirled her cup around in my face. "My girl Nita is the bartender tonight and she made me my own special pitcher."

"Ummm, sure. Why not?" I knew I was risking it all with school in the morning but was feeling the need to let go and live.

"Cheers!" She tilted the cup back in my mouth. "Nita ain't light handing none of the drinks coming to this section. We're all about to be fucked up. Period!"

Right on time, the waitress came back with our bottles, and from there it did get lit. Me, Mace, and Jos took a few shots as a trio, and then Rem-Dog and Shawn showed up already on ten and didn't waste time calling some girls over to trick some cash off with. It was a good thing I wasn't insecure, because they were bustin' it wide open for Mace, too. Money was flying everywhere.

"Oh, okay! I see what time it is up in this muthafucka! Moneyyyy time! All I wanna see is green on the floor and in the air. All the broke, red-flag niggas be quieeeeet!" Jos got on the mic and started hyping up the dancers so they could run up a check. She'd gotten so laid-back with the crew that I'd forgotten she was working.

"Ay yo, li'l Nina Brown. I got a few dollars for you to twerk that fatty up on me." Mace waved me over with a devilish grin on his face.

"Oh, naw, playboy, I'on want your few dollars. I'll take the whole sac." I cupped his dick print and jiggled his balls through his joggers.

"Ahh, that's what we doing?" He pulled me down on his now-stiff dick, and I started doing my thang like I was busting it down for a buck. There were at least fifty pretty dancers in here, but he was checking for my attention. I'd be damned if I wasn't about to give it to him.

Jos must've peeped me in action and told the DJ to play my ratchet girl song 'cause Meg's song "Body" rang through the club, and I started bouncing my booty until my thighs ached. I'd even stood up on the bench and was throwing it in his face. Jossy's Jungle Juice must've had something else in it 'cause I was hella lit and couldn't come down off the high.

"Goddamn, girl! Fuck your friend and her fashion show. Let's bounce." Mace pulled me down into his lap and nestled his face into my chest like a baby.

"I caaan't," I whined, "but you better believe I'm going to run all that back on you in bed when we get home."

"Oh, yeah, I'ma make sure your drunk ass don't pass out first," he laughed, and then we started dancing to the R&B mix the DJ flipped to. It felt so good lying against his chest and being chill for a second. I tuned everything out and took in the moment as he held me close like it was just he and I in the room. I loved Mace so much I swore I felt his heart beating inside of my own chest. Something told me this was the calm before the storm though.

"Umm, I hate to break up y'all caking session, but we need to go make sure Krissy is straight. The show is about to start, and she's probably losing her mind."

"I hope not, but I'm right behind you." I kissed Mace, then grabbed my purse of pills and followed Jos to the locker room.

Chapter Six

Gia

The ambience at the club was exactly how I remembered it the last time I was on the scene. My head was spinning as I tried gathering my thoughts as well as my positioning. I never ever imagined I'd be back begging for dollars with my body after Omari retired me. If I went back on the promise tonight by dancing again, I'd never be able to promise him again. That was why I'd started hustling with Sav and Dr. Basheer in the first place. My loyalty was with Omari in a major way. Whatever I owed him, I ultimately owed our son. I was trying to remain ten toes down on my word.

"Damnnn! My eyes must be playing tricks on me. Long time, no see. How have you been, baby girl?" The bartender recognized me off the rip, and she should have. Nita opened the bar, closed the bar, and nursed all of us girls to the mental states we needed to be in, in order to get buck naked and nasty. She gave us liquid courage whenever it might've been lacking. Nita was the first person I saw whenever I worked the club.

"I've been good. I can't complain. Still working the gig at the nursing home."

"I see." She nodded at my scrubs, which had to be smelling like Icy Hot and old piss. I really did do more than pass out dollar store meds and fluff up charts.

I sank down on the barstool realizing I should've asked Star to shoot me to the crib for a quick shower and clothing change. But it was too late, and I probably would've backed out anyway.

"What's up with you tonight? Are you here to model for Kris?" She set a Styrofoam cup of liquor down in front of me.

"Kut 'Em Up Kris, the seamstress? Naw. I didn't even know about it." I took a sip of the drink and damn near fell off the stool. "Damn, Nita! I see you're still heavy-handed as hell."

"Naw, baby girl, you're just a lightweight nowadays. Once upon a time, you'd be complaining over a watered-down drink."

"Well, not tonight. Throw a few ice cubes in this." I wanted the edge off but wasn't trying to misplace the mental discomfort I was feeling for a physical one. I hated being sick to my stomach off a hangover and having my body spaz out like in *The Exorcist*.

"Let me know if you ever finish this drink, and I'll check the back to see if we've got a Capri Sun or something." She was laughing so hard she could barely finish the sentence.

"Ohhh, you ain't right! But I got you, and I'll check for you in a few." I laughed along with her, then tipped out before making my way to the locker room so I could check off into Star for putting me in a trick bag. If Kut 'Em Up Kris was throwing a party, I knew her entourage was in the building, and that included Sav and his bitch.

"Um, excuse me, but you could've told me who was having a party tonight." I walked up on Star, clearing my throat.

"Girl, good the fuck bye! Since when are you worried about somebody's bitch? And from what you said in the car, you and Sav wasn't on nothing but some trickin' shit, and that's been over. Now unless you were lying, I don't see what your problem is." She stopped talking and side-eyed me. Star knew nothing about me plugging Mace with pills.

"I wasn't lying. I just think you could've said something since you brought Sav up. But whatever." I got my outfit from the vending machine, then headed for the shower instead of taking an Uber home to my kid like my gut was telling me to do. Nothing about tonight felt right, but I downed Nita's drink, hoping it would drown all my anxiety. The water was cold since it was late in the night and had been in use all day, so I was in and out real quick.

"Okay, damn! My bad, G. I admit I didn't tell you intentionally. But why not let that nigga see all your sexy thickness and wanna trick that cash-cash off on you again? It ain't like you don't need the money. And besides, it's not like he's the only man up in here with pape. Hell, there's some bad bitches out there with purses full of cash trying to trick as well. That CNA shit done fucked up your head when it comes to your hustle, because worrying is the last thing we do up in here when it comes to gettin' to the money."

"Awww, ho, shut up! I see you got jokes! You're not about to keep ragging on me about my job."

"Oh, yes, I am." She burst out laughing, then poured half her cup of liquor into mine. "Now hurry up and get sexy. His bitch just came in here, which means it's the perfect time for you to prey on him." Star walked over to where Kris was sectioned off with her girls getting ready for the fashion show she was having.

It was then that I realized Star was actually walking in the show. She stayed chasing paper just as much as she did being on messy shit. I was at least happy for the heads-up that Sav was unattended to though.

Mace

The club was going up, and me and my crew were living it up. We'd come a long way from being in juvie together, and it was only right that we got to flash our wealth. Kris had us in VIP, but we were laying out our own spread. I wasn't about to drink, smoke, or mingle too long with any of my wifey's friends because I wasn't cut like that.

I was buzzing like a muthafucka and ready for Marley to get back from fuckin' with her friends. She'd clown if she caught my hands slipping in one of these dancer's G-strings, but I was about ready to get off or get home so she and I could make a porno.

Rem-Dog had a honey he'd been on all night who had a bad-ass body that didn't seem like it would break after a hard night, but Shawn was off into every chick in here. He wasn't even giving one dancer a chance to finish her song before he was on to the next, and he was dropping fifties per dance.

"Fam clowning tonight." Rem-Dog sat down and took a drink.

"I peeped. What were y'all hitting on the way here?" We'd all been smoking the same weed and drinking the same liquor, but he was off his shit.

Remy chuckled. "Not a damn thang! We rode clean to this bitch 'cause my L's ain't right. I got this ticket I forgot to pay, and they suspended 'em today at midnight."

"Awwww fuck, Rem-Dog! Why you ain't handle that shit, bro? You know you can't get on the highway without yo' L's being tight." I threw back a shot because that was not the news I wanted to hear.

"I know. I know. And I'm going down there Monday morning."

"Yeah, a'ight. But sit still until you do. The last thing we need is for you to get caught up on some dumb shit and fuck ya license up for real." I was dead-ass serious.

We took a few more shots, and then Rem-Dog lit the blunt he was rolling. "Sav, yo, ain't that ol' girl we were just talking about earlier?" Rem-Dog low-key pointed in the direction he wanted me to look, and my eyes followed.

"In the flesh," I quickly dug my phone out of my pocket and took her off my block list. I didn't want her doing no dumb shit and coming straight through on my line like she'd done earlier.

Me: Yo, wtf you here for? I shot her a text and watched to see how she was gonna play it.

A few seconds passed, and then she finally looked down at her phone, then looked right up at me, which confirmed she already knew I was in the building.

Gia: Trying to make some money. Wtf it look like? I could see her eyes rolling from across the room.

Me: Get your dumb ass over here now! I threw her back on block and put my phone back in my pocket.

Gia

"You're so sexy. Where've you been all my life?" The dude I was giving a lap dance to was all over me for his $10. I couldn't wait until the dance was over. I'd gotten chosen as soon as I exited the locker room.

All the money was in VIP, the main floor by the stage, and the sections where people paid for tables by the hour. Wasn't shit popping in the general admission section, and there never was. I hated working in that area, especially when I couldn't be the goddess girl I usually was. I used to own the titty club when I was in the game. That was why my baby daddy wanted me to sit down. I was about my bread, and being about love humbled me. I couldn't even fall back into the groove of how I once was because I was lurking in the lame section, trying to stay out of Mace's way. His bitch's bestie had this place slapping. I hated when somebody counted my bag, but I knew Star was about to be bragging in the car about her come-up.

I kept trying to busy myself with the dances I was giving, but I couldn't help but watch Savage and how he moved. I knew he was rude as hell with it at all times, but I couldn't help but be attracted to that same rudeness. That was why when he hit my inbox up telling me to get my ass to his section, I was on it.

Marley

"Hey, superstar! Are you all good back here, or do you need some help?" I walked in on Krissy fussing while doing some last-minute alterations that seemed to have her frazzled.

"Oh, my God, I'm so glad y'all came to help a bitch out. I 'bout need to pop one of them pills I know you got in your purse." She put me on blast, but I let it slide because since I knew she was stressed. Also, because there were probably more pill poppers than OPPs within earshot.

"What do you need me to do?" Jos asked.

"Be my end man and make sure they're ready to hit the stage. And, Marley, please help me stitch up this last costume. You're the only one who doesn't have long nails." I was only getting manicures because it was easier to type with short, natural nails.

"Okay, I'll try my best to get it right. But a chick's been drinking like I need a meeting." I grabbed a bottle of water from the cooler Krissy had underneath her station and started sewing where she'd left off. I was concentrating hard as hell but couldn't keep the thread from tangling up, and when I did, the threaded line was not straight at all. Everyone has a knack, but sewing wasn't mine.

"Um, sis, I did my best, but I don't think you're going to rock with me too hard after you see how this ended up." I hesitated when I handed her the lingerie piece but knew I didn't have a choice. "I did the best that I could."

"Kris bitch! I know you don't think I'm 'bout to go out there with some ol' mammy-made-ass outfit on. I've got a reputation to uphold." The dancer the outfit was for jumped loud.

"I feel you, Star. And it is jacked up, Marley," Krissy said. "But there's nothing I can do about it at this point. The show is about to start."

"Wowwww, Krissy! So it's like that? I ain't made a slug all night because you wanted us all fresh and shit for this li'l lingerie line or whatever. And now I've gotta miss out on making even more paper?"

"It's not my fault yo' fat ass wouldn't lay off the crab boil bags and loaded potatoes for a week or two, Star. I wouldn't have needed to add more fabric to your outfit in the first place."

"Don't front me off, Kris. We both know you don't wanna do that for real. And you are indeed wrong, because you should've never let your ditzy friend play like she's a seamstress."

"Whoa, ho! This ditzy bitch'll dog walk you through this club and sit you down for days." I got ready to box.

"Ohhh, okay, I get it. Today's letter of the day at school must've been D just like that dick you've been sharing."

"Hell naw, Star! You ain't have to take it there. You're out of fucking line." Krissy jumped fast and started pushing ol' girl back and out of the locker room while Jos was trying to back me into a corner.

Some of the girls watching started amping up the possibility of a fight, while others were complaining of missing out on their money. Even though I wasn't trying to hate on their come-up of course, I wasn't about to back down behind Mace. Her wack ass wasn't salty over no flimsy-ass lingerie. Naw. Her beef was off some legit shit I was most definitely gonna find out about.

"Don't you dare drop your hand, Marley baby. All ol' girl wanna do is get in your head and out of position. We've been flexing all night, and you're iced the fuck out. You think these hoes ain't jelly of you? They want your spot. This is not even your beef." Jos was trying to talk me down, but I wasn't trying to hear one single, solitary word.

"I'm far from stupid, and I'ma air this bitch out once you let me go. Plus, you said yourself how Mace be purped out at the club when I'm at school. That scavenger ain't come up on my business by accident." I'd sobered up and run back her comeback ten times already. Ol' girl said what she said from her chest. She'd meant what she said to me from the heart.

Her and Krissy's impromptu beef was simply the bridge she needed to get at me. Me flexing as the pretty bitch I was was the icing on the cake that had her dropping her mask. That was what this was.

"Bro ain't checking for these throwaways, sis. You took that the wrong way earlier, and this ain't the time to apply that conversation anyway." Jos was stuttering over her words, then gave up trying to interject her opinion altogether. "Aww, damn! This is all too much, and it's blowing my high. Come on." She let her weight off me but only to interlock my arms with hers. "Back to your boo you go. Ain't nobody gonna be able to calm your crazy ass down but him."

"Wrong call, sis. I'm even more lit now." I spotted Mace as soon as we stepped out of the locker room with some stripper ho in his face, and I damn near knocked Jos's guts out of her back, getting free from her grip.

My blood felt like it was boiling. We were just out here cuddled up and caking, and now he was grinning in ol' girl's face like I wasn't in the building. I felt disrespected and played. After the slick shit ol' girl just said to me, I wasn't asking questions or giving passes but about to shut shit down.

"There's been a slight delay, but the show will be starting in a minute, y'all. Until it does, the shot girls are on the floor with two-dollar shots. Who about to bring they boy a blue muthafucka?" the DJ announced just as I grabbed one of the bottles of Moët that was on chill and cracked ol' girl smooth across the back of her head. I hit her with so much force I cut my own hand.

"Awww, shit! Marley, no!" Mace jumped back as her body smacked against the floor. "What the fuck tip is you on?"

"Naw, nigga, what the fuck tip have you been on? You got hoes checking me about you in the locker room, and then I come out here seeing you grinning in a throwaway's face. I saw that dusto hugging all on you, Mace. You got me fucked up and she do too. That's why I was trying to knock some sense into her dumb ass." I was about to start stomping ol' girl just because my adrenaline was pumping and I was mad as hell, but Mace scooped me up and tossed me over his shoulder. I settled for laying haymakers into his back. Wasn't none of my punches fazing him though. So I settled for kicking anything and everyone around me as he power walked me out of the club. Bottles, ice, and scraps of food were flying everywhere.

"Calm your nutty ass down, Marley." Mace tightened his grip on me. "Yo, Rem-Dog, make sure ol' girl is straight, then hit me up. I gotta get her wild ass to the crib."

"What the fuck you care for if that ho is straight? Put me down, Mace!"

Continuing to hold me over his shoulder, Mace kept trucking through the club not responding to one word of my rant. He didn't release his grip from my waist until tossing me into the back seat like a kid. That set me off even more. I caught my breath until he slid in, and then I started laying haymakers into his ass again. I was tagging Mace all on the side of his face, the jaw, chin, and ear, until he swung back and knocked the wind out of me.

"Quit putting ya muthafuckin' hands on me, girl, damn! Ya shit is leaking! What if yo' nutty ass need stitches? I can't believe you started all this bullshit over a trick. The fuck are you for real? Fuck yo' event? Fuck yo' girl? Fuck the fact that we've got dope, guns, and money on us? Huh?"

"Naw, fuck you! Fuck you and ya nappy-headed mama for having you." I was trying to burst his eardrum from how loud I was yelling. "And my hand wouldn't be leaking if you weren't out here disrespecting me. But I got you. I can't wait to grin in a nigga's face on purpose." I was fuming and in my feelings, which was a dangerous combination.

"That'll be the last day you smile. Make a nigga turn around and knock yo' teeth down ya throat right now if you want to," he threatened.

"Yeah, whatever. Both my hands will be leaking if you put another hand back here, bro. My suggestion is that you get me the fuck hoooome." I leaned into his ear and yelled a migraine into his head.

I wanted to make Mace as mad as I could make him so he'd slip up and tell me the truth. As long as he stayed cool and collected, he could control and manipulate the situation, and I'd had enough of him creeping around this muthafuckin' city making me look stupid. It was about time I showed Mace what my loyalty was worth.

Gia

Clutching my bag of prescription pain pills, I stormed out of the urgent care with more of an attitude than when I walked in, partly because I had a li'l more energy thanks to the pain relief shot they administered. Sav's bitch really tried taking me out of the game tonight.

"Drive me straight home, and don't make no stops. And here's my bill. I want my cash within seven to ten days." I tossed my hospital bill at Star as soon as I got in the car. I was mad as hell. I went to the club to make some extra cash and ended up in the urgent care, cashing out for some stitches. This day felt like a setup from Satan.

"Aw, naw, bitch! This ain't my bill. You might wanna holla at Savage for that."

"I ain't got two words for that sucka." I was openly in my feelings.

I'd blocked Mace from messaging me when I was in the waiting room. He wasn't blowing me up. But he'd sent a few messages asking me if I was straight and saying that he'd hit me up in the morning. I knew he was busy catering to his girl and that his normal routine was to hit me up around her school schedule, but I was feeling extra alone in urgent care. They were taking forever because it was packed and the idle time left my idle mind wondering.

"Okay, so you might not have two words for him. But we should slide past ol' girl's boutique and slide that bill in her mailbox." Star was always up to start some drama.

"Girllll, bye! Like I said, take me home, and don't make no stops. All I wanna do is curl up with my baby and forget all about today." I was pouting, damn near on the verge of tears.

I'd never been super emotional, especially in front of chicks from the club, but it was hard tucking my feelings since my baby daddy died, especially because they were often heightened or exaggerated. I missed him badder than bad and was mad at myself for even being in the streets getting jumped when our son was at home with his mom. This was why he wanted me out of the club as soon as I told him I was pregnant. He was trying to groom me to be a good girl. Shit could've gone worse for me tonight.

Star must've picked up on the vibes, because she backed off. "A'ight, boo. I'ma get you home to your baby."

Chapter Seven

Mace

The Next Morning

"Yo, what it do, chief?" Dex came through my line.

"Slow motion and a late start. What's good?" I sat up from the cramped position I was in on the couch and cracked my neck. There wasn't a way in hell I'd be on this couch another night.

"The early bird gets the worm, and I'm coming in hot. I took care of business last night."

"Well, congrats on stepping into some Tims, nigga. It's about time. I'll get up with you on that in a few. The fam good?"

"Yup yup. These hungry muthafuckas are walking through the door with some Coney Island right now. I'll put you a plate up if you come through with some dessert." He was talking in code for some more product.

"Most def. Say less. I'm about to hop up and get smooth right now." I wasn't about to miss out on no money.

"Bet. See you in a few." We got off the phone, and I instantly hit Gia's line to see where her head was at.

After beefing with Marley for hours and getting locked out of the bedroom, I crashed on the couch trying to see where Gia was at, but she wasn't posting on social media or responding to my texts. And this morning was no different. My call went straight to her voicemail. Hopefully I didn't have to pull down at the nursing home on lit shit to get a response, but I would.

Dex's call saying he needed another stash of work was confirmation the fiends were going crazy over the pills Gia and her connect supplied, so I wasn't about to let her ghost me. Even if it meant breaking her off with some "pain and suffering" cash and getting her whip fixed. I could admit I owed shorty at least that much. It was cocky of me to have her up in VIP with Marley only a few feet away, basically a setup for the chaos that unfolded.

I hit the shower for damn near thirty minutes because my head was banging, but then I jumped fresh and left my house, headed for the trap. Although I didn't hustle where I slept, it wasn't too far away. I couldn't see myself living in some uppity-ass suburbs that required me to stay looking over my shoulder for a racist neighbor. I'd take a hooked-up house in the hood around my cousin's any day.

My and Marley's house was off Linwood in the Boston-Edison District and big as hell. We had five bedrooms, three baths, a full-size eat-in kitchen, dining room, and a huge backyard we stayed hosting cookouts at in the summer months. It was a fixer-upper that of course Marley found, bid on, and titled in her own name to keep my name off the radar. My flips off the street funded the deal, top-of-the-line renovations, and the furniture that filled the big muthafucka up.

The trap I ran was on a street called Ford a few miles down, still off Linwood but closer to Twelfth Street. That put us in line for custos in walking distance from even Highland Park. Plus it was right off a main road, so a custo coming in off the freeway could easily pop in and out with ease.

Pulling up, Dex hopped in so we could kick it about Blue without the many ears that were around. We might've all eaten off the same hustle, but I didn't share my business as such. That was why Blue had to go. He was disloyal, dishonest, and too fidgety, all characteristics of a rat. I wasn't about to get me or my crew hemmed up by a cop or another hustler on the come-up because Blue was giving up our game.

"I caught him leaving Ace's last night." Dex ran down the details of how he caught Blue slipping.

"You kept it low-key so can't nobody ID you, right?" Ace's was a li'l hole-in-the-wall pool bar that got major traffic after hours. I ain't really fuck with it because it had been known as a death trap since my mom was running in the streets heavy.

"Yeah, of course I was smooth with it. In and out. We're not gonna have no pushback on this one fa'sho." He sounded confident in himself, so I let it roll.

"Cool. Still, stay out the way with your eyes open and your ears to the ground just in case somebody comes around snooping. And let the fam work the block." The last thing he needed to do was get picked up on even something unrelated and have the two possibly linked. I didn't want Dex serving time on a body I sent him to hit, but following orders was all a part of the game. There were levels to this shit. I was gonna do my best to protect him though.

After I gave him a few more rundowns on how to run the day and collected the cash from the last batch I put in his hands, I dropped him back off at the trap with a fresh batch he could distribute to the crew. I didn't do hand-to-hand deals or work the block. I was Dex's boss, and he was theirs. Again, there were levels to this shit, and every man had to play their position with loyalty or get sent up outta here like Blue.

"Yo, let me get fifty on pump twelve." I grabbed my change from the gas and my snacks, then headed back to my car.

One of the OGs from back in the day approached me. "You want me to get that for you, Sav?"

"Aw, naw, Popps. I'm good. But here's a couple dollars to work with to get you something to eat." I peeled off a few bills and passed them over without wanting a thing in return. "And you can probably fall through later on for some work around the house. Marley probably got some jobs at the boutique." I stayed plugging him with side gigs. The whole hood looked out for Popps. Even though he had an addiction, he didn't rob for his hits but worked for them or would simply ask you to break him off for a Baggie.

"Thanks, neph. Good looking out. You always take care of unc." He stuffed the bills in his pocket.

"It ain't no thang. You've been around since I was a young buck, OG."

"I be telling these suckas around here that I'm Linwood official, the grandfather of this avenue." He was laughing with glee, showing the few tattered teeth he had left. "Oh, and speaking of old school, you know Sturtevant's son is out of the joint, right? I saw him over at Frog's house a few days ago."

"You what?" I got amped, ready to whip my heater out on Popps, and he wasn't even guilty of anything. Jinx was the name on the floor. Sturtevant was his father and the first body I caught.

Popps nodded like he knew exactly why I was amped up though, which didn't surprise me because Popps knew the secrets of this hood and the skeletons in everyone's closet better than everyone.

"Yeah, nephew. I saw him over at Frog's house a few days ago. It look like she got him living there." He was quick to give me the pinpoint on his location and even what ol' boy was wearing.

"Good looking out, OG. You be safe out here." I passed him a twenty, thankful for his information but also conscious that my informant's loyalty lay with his addiction, which was fueled by the almighty dollar.

Hopping in the car, I dropped my head for what I was about to do. Then I pulled off and bent the block, meeting Popps coming out of the alleyway, skipping up rocks and broken glass, giddy as hell off the money I'd just given him. He hadn't a care in the world until I called his name, and he looked up to the barrel of my gun staring at him. I sent three shots into his chest before he could beg or question my motives, and I pulled off before his body finished hitting the pavement. OG or not, I wasn't letting nobody drop the dime back to Jinx on where I laid my head.

Gia

I saw Sav calling, but I wasn't fucking with him. He was wrong as hell for letting his girl get at me. Matter of fact, he didn't have to call me over to his section, trying to be thirsty, having his cake and eating it, too. I was cool, in my feelings or not, chasing a check on my own terms. But I already knew he was gonna bring his ass up to my job. He was the most unavailable nigga with terms I'd ever known. I hated that shit got messy with us.

I'd been up and at work though I really didn't want to be. Even after getting home from urgent care, I was up with my son, cranky and going through the motions. He normally wasn't a fussy baby, so I didn't know if he was picking up on my vibes, but he cried all night to the point where I left him in the crib and smoked a fat blunt in the shower while my tears flowed down the drain. I missed my baby daddy with my whole entire soul. Struggling would've been the last thing me and mine would've been doing.

Work was finally slowing down, and I was happy about it. It was late afternoon and about time for my lunch, and I was starving. I hadn't gotten a chance to eat breakfast because the midnight shift consisted of a bunch of lazy CNAs who didn't do shit but collect their hourly pay. I came in changing beds, diapers, giving late meds, and even giving showers to those patients they'd left pissy all night. Sometimes I hated working this job, but I was really trying to stay out of the club to honor my baby daddy's wishes. I knew he was rolling over in his grave at the way my life was turning out.

"Hey, Gia, Doc wants to see you in his office right quick." My coworker leaned over the desk, breathing her dragon-like breath in my face.

I sighed with an attitude, more than ready for my break, but I didn't have a choice but to meet with him. I grabbed my cell off the desk, tucked it in my purse, then rushed to his office. I froze in my tracks when I saw the Detroit Police though.

FBI Agent Thomas asked me almost a billion questions about Dr. Basheer and why I worked on so many of his cases. At first, I was playing it dumb like I was only doing my job, but then they dropped printouts on the table of his billing statements that had the injections I'd been administering all over them. I damn near fainted when they told me how many years I'd be facing for illegally giving patients shots when I didn't have a license to give shots in the first place. I wasn't certified in the State of Michigan to do nothing but wipe shit and give sponge baths. I was so fucking scared. I had a baby to think about. With his daddy dead, he couldn't have a mother in prison.

Chapter Eight

Marley

"You won't become successful by accident or overnight. It takes a lot of hard work, perseverance, living many hours within your craft, and sacrifice." My business marketing professor preached to us about not giving up while I was busy trying to stay awake.

Downing a big gulp of the coffee Lance brought for me, I was also happy he was passing along subtle nudges every few minutes when he caught me dozing off. I felt like a zombie. Last night was wild as hell, and the argument didn't end when me and Mace got home. I would've boxed with him if my hand weren't messed up.

Lance kept trying to press me for details on why it was bandaged up, but I kept it simple, lying that I'd gotten caught in the middle of a club fight. I realized it was bigger than me not wanting him or my other classmates to know my real backstory. I actually cared what Lance thought.

Fighting off a big yawn, I narrowed my eyes at the presentation and took notes from the lecture. I was trying my best not to mess up in school.

Buzz. Buzz! Buzzz!

The vibration of my phone interrupted me and every student close around me. The professor's eyes darted around the room to see who was disturbing her lecture, then landed on me. I was flushed with embarrassment, plus I knew she was about to trip.

"Sorry," I quietly apologized, quickly digging into my purse to find and silence my cell. It was Mace calling, but I couldn't answer even if I wanted to, but I didn't.

"Class, when entering my lecture room, give me the respect of having your full and undivided attention. Matter of fact, show some respect for both me and your peers. It is selfish to halt their learning experience. With that being said, refer to the syllabus for my policy on cellular devices."

Professor Eubanks might've been speaking to the whole class, but she'd directed her chastisement specifically at me. Her heavy on the rag acting ass had me on the spot, and I didn't like it. It felt like I was in middle school all over again, and Lord knows I was far removed from having the innocence of a child. It took everything in me to bow out and nod, letting her know it wouldn't happen again. I hated being silenced.

The moment she turned her back to write on the board, I peeked at my phone, seeing a few messages Mace had sent and that were still coming over. He was pissed as hell about me ignoring him, acting like I didn't have a reason to still be mad from last night. I wanted to text him back so, so bad, but I wasn't trying to get confronted by Ms. Eubanks again.

The first half of class went on around me for almost an hour longer. It was beyond hard to focus. I almost wanted to leave, making myself fall further behind, but I fought against that choice. I wanted to stop putting his needs before mine. Though it was hard, I copied all the notes and tried holding on to her words at least enough to write them down. I'd worry about studying and processing what I could recall later.

My classmates rushed from the lecture hall, all needing a break from the many Excel charts, spreadsheets, and graphs Professor Eubanks was using to prove how certain advertising strategies worked better than others. I, however, used ten of those fifteen minutes allotted for break time to take pictures of all the slides.

"Um, excuse me, Professor Eubanks." I hated interrupting her.

"Yes. How may I help you, Marley? I see you haven't taken advantage of break time."

"That's because I wanted to make sure I had all the notes copied down. The call I interrupted the class with earlier was of an urgent matter that I must tend to. I won't be here for the second half of your lecture," I informed her.

She wasn't owed an explanation since this was college and I was free to leave, but it was more beneficial for me to have one-on-one relationships with my professors. My time, money, and future were on the line. Being the rebellious chick I'd been groomed into being by Mace wasn't the right role to play in this case.

"You'll be missing quite a bit of information I'll be lecturing about. You know more than fifty percent of my class is lecture."

"I know, but I'll make arrangements to get what I'll miss."

"Very well, Marley. Just remember, you must show up to be successful and fruitful."

If only she knew that was exactly what I was doing. I fa'sho knew all about the art of showing up. Since enrolling in school, I've been semi-mastering the skill of being in two places—damn, three, including the boutique—at the same time. I might've been attending community college for a degree in business, but I was already a mogul when it came to successfully running an illegal operation. Between the trap houses me and Mace were running, we were stacking Ms. Eubank's salary in a month if not less. Like I said, I, too, knew about showing up.

"I understand, ma'am. And thank you for the knowledge." I left my response short and simple.

"You're welcome. Hopefully you'll be able to grace the class with your presence in a couple of days," she sarcastically ended our conversation.

She was lucky I respected her, because I was itching to let the hood in me out.

Grabbing my belongings, I rushed from the lecture hall as some of my classmates rushed back in, making sure they weren't late. I was pissed that I had to leave because that meant I'd miss out on the study groups that were arranged after every class. This was the wrong time for shit to pop off at home. I didn't call Mace as soon as I hit the door because I didn't want to get trapped on the phone. I still had one more thing to do before I could clear school.

"Hey, you're out of here?" Lance looked up to me walking up on him.

I fed him a story. "Yeah. I've gotta get to the boutique. My worker called off, and I've already gotten some calls from some girls at the door, but it's closed. I don't want to get a bad rep."

"I understand that. And you know I've got you on the notes. So don't even worry about that."

"I swear I'd fail without you." I reached over and hugged him, catching us both off guard.

I didn't know if I subconsciously did it because I was angry at Mace and getting my lick back, so to speak, or if I was acting on a feeling for Lance that I never gave energy to because of my loyalty to my relationship with Mace. But either way I'd felt an instant chemistry with Lance as soon as our bodies touched. I held on to him a li'l too long.

"Oh, wow, my bad." I pulled back from his embrace, looking weird and feeling even weirder.

"Wasn't nothing bad about that." He lifted my chin before I was out of arm's reach, forcing our eyes to lock in. I swear it felt like he could read into my soul. I was sure he could feel me fidgeting.

"Umm, I've gotta go." I forced myself to look away.

"Okay, we'll talk later." From his tone, I could tell he expected the conversation to be more than about the notes from class this time around. And his assumption was right. I just didn't know how to address what just happened because I was confused as hell.

Bzzz. Bzzz! Bzzz!

"Yeah," I answered, highly annoyed and letting it show.

"Ay yo, you gonna have to quit that ma'fuckin' class if you can't answer the phone when I call," he barked. "I ain't with all that send a nigga to voicemail and ignore me shit you keep pulling and thinking is cute. A nigga can't get a lap dance, but you can be MIA? Naw."

Here we go about to repeat the same argument. Since I enrolled in college, Mace's complaints had been the same. He couldn't understand my thirst for a college degree since we were banking a helluva salary from trapping. That was because we were brought up by two different types of parents from two different worlds.

Instead of him voicing his opinion once and letting it go, he was making it painfully hard for me to do something for me. We were already at levels folks in Detroit would never see and that folks in my classes were trying to attain. But another person's goals and pockets had never made me shit. My parents had always told me to have something of my own and to be about mine. No matter how much money we banked from the streets, I still wanted credentials.

"Yeah, yeah, yeah, whatever, Mace. Being that you weren't calling me on no 911 shit, I'll see you when I get there. I'm on the freeway now." I checked back into the conversation, blew the topic of school off, then ended the call.

I ran my blood pressure up the whole ride home. Needless to say, by the time I pulled into the driveway, I was in a hitta state of mind and ready to go to war with Mace for him calling me out of class.

I noticed Mace's ripped expression of anger before I pulled all the way into the driveway. It was evident he was more pissed than I'd thought about me not answering my phone. Seeing that I was still supposed to be in class, arguing with him was the last thing I wanted to do. We beefed with one another each and every day I went to school. It'd been like that since I enrolled. Somehow or another, we were gonna have to stop bumping heads and make amends. Our relationship was doomed to fail otherwise.

Remy was sitting beside Mace, sipping a Heineken. All moves, conversation, and motion ceased when I pulled up into the driveway. My and Mace's eyes were locked in on one another, having a conversation where only he and I knew what was being said. Remy quickly caught on to the tension brewing between us and got on his phone. Homeboy or not, he knew better than to get into the middle of our beef. Everyone knew you couldn't fight a couple.

I walked up on the porch, and Mace and I stared each other down without speaking or mouthing a word. I leaned back on the rail, crossed my arms, and then looked at the Rolex on my wrist like my time was precious. Blinking my eyes, I started sassing him. "Well, you was blowing me up like some shit was popping off. What's good?" My cockiness set Mace off.

"Don't be trying to stunt, Marley. I'm the one who put that Rollie on your wrist. I know what time it is. Yo' ass is the one who needs a wakeup call."

"Welp, time to go! I ain't about to be in the middle of none of the shit y'all about to get started, so get at me later." Remy slapped his hands on his thighs, jumped up from the lawn chair, then darted toward his van without looking back over his shoulder at Mace or me.

"Do me a solid and run that package over to Dex for me, then fall back through here." Mace might've been talking to his homeboy, but he was looking directly at me.

I was mad as hell, biting my tongue and two seconds from ripping his head off his neck. I hated for him to front me off in front of ma'fuckas, family, friends, foes, or even imaginary friends, so I stormed inside the house.

"Bring yo' ass back here and sit down, Mar-Mar. We need to talk," Mace yelled after me.

"Fuck you, Mace. You weren't trying to talk a few seconds ago when you were fronting me off in front of Remy. I swear to God, every time I'm in class, you pick a fight with me. Like you can't handle me doing me. Like you can't handle me getting a degree and running a successful business."

Mace's nose flared, his eyebrows curled into a frown, and his temples started thumping. "What I can't handle is your ass being ungrateful. Not only did I give you that boutique you make money off of, but I also pay your tuition. Fuck out of here with that 'I can't handle you doing you' bullshit. I made yo' ass on every level."

"Yup, you're right, Mace. You made me."

As I took aggressive steps toward him, he straightened his stance up, bracing himself. From many of our previous fights the last nine years, he knew I'd pounce on him like an alley cat. The temptation was strong for me to buck at him, but I didn't. I yanked the blunt he'd put to his mouth out of his hand instead. "The only thing you make me is sick. Believe that, jerk!" Storming off to our room, this time I didn't stop and turn around when he called for me to. "You can kiss my fat ass, nigga."

Mace got on my nerves. That was because I loved him so much. Otherwise, his opinion and the shit he talked wouldn't have mattered so much. I was tired of him throwing up what he'd done for me in my face. In my opinion, I'd earned the boutique, my tuition payment, and even my stripes as a hitta. I'd had his back for so many years that I felt he owed me.

While he was distracted, I used the split second to rush off to the bedroom and lock him out again. Last night it was out of convenience and anger, but today it was out of my anger and my safety. I'd caught a whiff of Lance's cologne a few seconds ago, and I needed to get out of my clothes before Mace smelled it.

Then I sat on the side of the bed and smoked the rest of the blunt I had this morning. I wanted to grab the bottle of wine I started on last night from the fridge but didn't want to leave the room. For all this nonsense he and I were going through, I could've stayed at class and gotten the full lecture. The more I thought about what I was missing, the angrier I got. I couldn't figure out why sometimes things went good with Mace and me, then the next minute things were tart and sour.

Lying back, I stared at the ceiling, trying to let my mind wander off, but it wouldn't. Mace's words were cutting me to the core. Of the two of us, he was the ungrateful one. I might as well have spit in my parents' faces behind choosing him over them and choosing his raggedy mama, who wasn't an equal replacement to mine. Right when I was about to go to his stash to roll a fat one up, he knocked on the door.

"Open this door, Marley." He knocked impatiently. "We need to talk."

"Naw, I'm good. Go talk to that fish-face trick from the club you had in your face. I heard that's been your normal routine since I've been in school. Why the fuck you call me home for anyway? Why you ain't out being a ho still?" I licked my lips, gearing up to talk more shit but didn't get another word out before his foot started coming through the door. He was literally kicking it in.

"Are you happy now?" I looked at him, shaking my head as he walked over the broken wood into the room.

"Yup, I am, as a matter of fact. You keep locking doors, and I'ma keep knocking them down. And I'm not sleeping on the couch again, just so you know."

"You can sleep your ass over at that trick's house for all I care, Mace. But you're not sleeping in this bed. I don't want you around me."

"Don't start that madness up again over no pointless bitch, Marley. I swear I'm gon' end up choking you if you do. Today ain't the day. That nigga Jinx is out."

"What? Oh, shit." I fell back off tripping because I knew the story behind Jinx.

Chapter Nine

Vernelle

If Karma Ain't a Bitch . . .

Jinx being released from prison was a problem—a major fuckin' problem I hadn't anticipated. We were in some helluva real shit behind my decisions from back in the day. I wasn't the type of mother who coddled her son or kept him home at night out of the streets. I pushed him to get money, to protect himself, and to murder the nigga I was sleeping with because he was a savage with deep pockets. We had to eat, and the government's monthly stipend of cash and stamps wasn't enough.

Sturtevant was my provider at the time. And when I tell you he had money on top of money that was stacked on top of dope, I'm not exaggerating or boosting his status. I'd watched Sturtevant grow from a bum to a boss just the same as my son went from a bum to a boss. Funny how shit will boomerang back. Karma. Anyway, Sturtevant started slanging in the eighties, then took off pulling his rank up in the eighties by pushing crack cocaine and heroin. By the time I had my son put him in a body bag, he was pushing that plus pills, weed, and even meth.

He and I were kickin' it strong for almost eight months before I orchestrated a plan to murder him. Sturtevant was giving me money for my rent, but I didn't have no rent, was putting cash in my hand for whatever I asked for, and was upgrading me from a rat to a hood-rich side piece. Sturtevant didn't have a woman or a wife but a bunch of bitches he was fuckin' on the frontline. He tended to all of us and didn't keep no secrets, but I didn't respect his honesty or care how he rolled. I'd always been a woman with my own agenda.

From day one of Sturtevant rolling up on me, talking about he'd look out for me and Maceo in exchange for me to letting him stash a li'l weight here and there, I'd plotted on how to get down on him and come up.

"Damn, V baby. My dick drowning in ya sloppy-ass pussy. I'm about to cum," Sturtevant moaned and grunted on top of me.

"Hol' on, papa. Let me get mine first." I didn't care about cumming. I was only giving Maceo more time to man up and get his ass in this room. I'd told him to come in when he first heard Sturtevant screaming about how good I was givin' it to him. But here we were, two minutes into us fuckin', and Maceo still hadn't shown me the barrel of his gun.

"I can't. Oh, shit, V! Ah." Sturtevant was reaching his climax.

"Last stroke, cocksucker." I heard Maceo's voice followed by his gun cocking back.

Three shots rang into the bedroom, and then Sturtevant fell on top of me and was flopping like a fish as his life seeped out of his body. I couldn't let him die on top of me, and damn sho' not inside of me, so I hurriedly pushed him to the ground uncaringly, only thinking about his money. He meant more to me dead than alive, and I was ready to reap all the benefits.

"What in the hell took you so long?" I yelled at Maceo, knocking him upside the head, then putting on my

clothes while looking for my phone to call 911. The plan wouldn't work if I left Sturtevant's body to be found.

"I was making sure we were good, Ma."

"Boy, you do what the fuck I say when I say it. We're good 'cause I told you we'd be good. Now follow me so we can get this cash and dope before the pigs get here."

I'd been over at Sturtevant's house enough to snoop and locate more than a few of his hideaway spots. He wasn't even the type of gangster who kept his cash stashed in a safe. I took Maceo to all of them. We snatched up what we could in dope and cash, and then Maceo kicked in the door to make it seem like someone broke in. He was gone by the time the cops arrived, and I was in full actress mode, a frantic mess. I told them the masked man ran in and popped Sturtevant and was screaming revenge the entire time. Being that he was a hood nigga with a record who wasn't cooperating, they didn't care about his murder. The cops didn't even take me down to the station for questioning.

I got more backlash in the streets from a few of his homies who threw it at me like I set their boy up, which was the truth, but I kept my face straight each time I lied. I was skilled at manipulation and deception, knowing how to play the game like chess. After the buzz of Sturtevant's death died down, I had Maceo step to the streets with his sidekicks, putting the stolen product to sale. We'd been gravy ever since. But with Jinx getting out, my gut told me shit was about to get shaken up real bad.

Maceo

I pushed the problems between Marley and me to the back of my mind as soon as I stepped out of the house. She had her fallback plan, but I was still knee-deep into the game. And to add several layers of madness on top of it, I murdered Sturtevant to get my start, and now I needed to find and murder Jinx to retire.

"Where to, Maceo?" Remy played like he was an Englishman driver.

"Into war, so load one up top, and have some ammo at ya fingertips." I kept it real, then gave him directions to where Sturtevant and Jinx used to wreck shit at. Rem-Dog pulled off without fear or question.

Thankfully, my left-hand man didn't need a reason to roll out alongside me or have my back without an explanation. Rem-Dog, of us three, had the least to lose. He didn't have a woman, kids, or a family he gave a fuck about.

"Yo, did you holla at Shawn or hear from him? Is he in Penny yet?" Caught up in my own drama with Jinx and Marley, I hadn't touched based with my cuzzo.

"I'on't know. That nigga ain't like me. I do shifts of ten. Ten to drive there, ten to rest, then ten straight hours to drive back. You know ya cuz likes to pull over at rest stops and fuck with the truck driver prostitutes."

"Man, that nigga's dick just might fall off." I referenced what Rem-Dog said the other night at the titty bar about Shawn fucking any chick walking.

We told a few jokes, caught up about the drama at the titty bar, and then said a prayer for protection from the sins we were about to commit. It didn't take long to get to Jinx's childhood neighborhood. He wasn't from our zone but only a few miles away in another roughed-up area. Back in the day when there were picnics or local activities, our zones would hook up together, but they didn't linger together on a day-to-day basis. Folks from the hood were cut that way.

Rem-Dog drove at a moderate speed, waiting on his cue to aim and shoot. I told him a basic description of

Jinx, but my eyes were roaming enough for the both of us plus Shawn in his absence. I wanted to kill Jinx so bad that I'd imagined it time and time again. Block after block, I made eye contact with every man outside. If Jinx was around, he wasn't making himself seen. And just because I didn't have eyes on him didn't mean he didn't have eyes on me.

I was fidgeting in my seat, antsy to find Jinx and murder him. I was mad at myself for not murdering him the other day when he first popped up on the scene. That shit was an amateur mistake. I wouldn't be miscalculating my steps again.

"Yo, pull over at that store real quick so I can grab a li'l two-dollar shot or something," I said in frustration. As long as Jinx was alive, he was a problem. Sliding my pistol into the waistband of my pants, I was prepped to get out fully protected, but Rem-Dog stopped me.

"Mace man, fuck that liquor, bro. I been on both you and Shawn's team since a nigga was an absconder, which means I know when some shit ain't right with either one of y'all. What's good for real? It don't matter whether you're wrong or right. You know I'ma rock and bust bullets with you, dog."

"Rem-Dog, real spit, if I could kick it with you about the shit, I would." I sounded like I was carrying a ton of weight on my back.

"And you can. Not on no homo-thug shit, but on some 'I roll with this nigga, and he's my brother' shit." Taking a breath and a break from speaking, he slammed his hand on the dashboard, then said, "Fuck it. Look, man, I know I'm the last cat to care about family off the strength of how my mama played me, but that's what makes me value you and Shawn like family. At the end of the day, if we can't rap with each other and hold one another down on all levels, we ain't gonna be shit but some washed-up hustlers."

No matter how tough my exterior was, Jinx's appearance had fucked me up. Rem-Dog and I had history and were like family since he'd been around, and he was seeing through the bullshit and noticing there was something different going on with me. Before Jinx came back blowing up my past or catching me and my crew off guard, I made a decision as a man and told my comrade. Hearing every word and detail, though he'd been deceived, Rem-Dog didn't flex but gave me a play.

The major part I left out of the story though was that the "bitch" who set ol' boy up in the first place was my mom. I wasn't the type of nigga to incriminate another person in my confessions. I was only breaking code by telling Rem-Dog because he was the nigga I rode with hustling and trying to stay in survival mode. If Jinx wanted me dead, he'd kill Rem-Dog and anyone else to get to me. I knew this, and that was why I wanted to clip him so quickly. I was tempted to shoot and kill my own fuckin' self for not shooting Jinx at the trap, or at least letting my man Dex let one off since he was anxious to prove himself.

In the middle of the story, Rem-Dog ended up pulling off from the store and driving around Sturtevant's old neighborhood again. His word was bond, and he was loyal to have a nigga's back.

Marley

Over an hour had passed, and Mace still wasn't back. I was irritated as hell about how he was playing me, and that's an understatement. He'd shown the deck of cards he was playing with by saying he didn't think I'd be his trap queen once I got my degree, although I saw how deeply he loved and depended on me and also showed me he'd do anything to keep me on his team. I hoped he wasn't trying to jinx me into failing so I'd have no other choice than to be his rider.

After I play packed, I chose to use my time more wisely. Pulling out my textbooks and the notes I'd taken in my business class before leaving, I dove right into studying. I even jotted notes down in my private planner that were good ideas to try implementing for my boutique. The more information I processed about marketing plans for my upcoming test, the brighter I believed my future could be as an entrepreneur.

Even though a lot of things would have to change before I could, I'd set a goal of opening up another location. It wasn't an impossible goal to attain either. Hell, real talk, I'd masterminded the game plan to open up trap houses. That was why Mace couldn't let me go.

His mama had him running around making moves and money like a li'l boy, and I turned their operation into something he could stand behind like a grown man. Whenever my mama talked to me about how she met and married my daddy, she'd brag about how she cleaned him up and made him perfect for her. I guessed, in a way, though my mom wasn't talking to me, I was doing the same thing.

Taking a break from studying, I pulled out the notebook I kept for Unique Pieces and went over my to-do list. Since I didn't have a partner, all the responsibilities of making sure it ran efficiently fell on me. My girls, Jos and Krissy, helped by implementing whatever I needed them to and working when I was busy trapping or in school. So I couldn't even act like Kris not responding to me wasn't irking me a tad bit more than I was letting on. I'd lied big time to Lance when I said my employees were incompetent. I was glad they'd never hear the bullshit of a story.

For the week, I had to order merchandise, meet up with a few vendors for a pop-up shop I was hosting, and advertise heavily for my shop's blowout sale that was only hours away from occurring. That was another reason why it was so important for Kristina's party to pop. Ever since Professor Eubanks lectured on branding, I'd been putting a lot of energy toward establishing my name and marking my territory within the fashion industry.

Ring. Ring! Ring!

Grabbing my phone up, ready to go, I thought it was Mace calling in response to my text about him feeling my wrath if he was with a bitch. But it wasn't. My caller ID read Customer La'Nese, which meant it was really Lance calling. Mace would go crazy if he knew I'd given my number to a dude from school. He'd swear all the times I didn't answer the phone was because I was cheating and not getting an education. That was an argument I wasn't willing to waste my time on. Lance wasn't my type. The only thing mean about him was his studying skills.

Quickly peeking out the blinds to make sure the Mace and his boys weren't back, all I saw were kids playing, so I picked up and said hello.

"Hey, is this a good time, or does the boutique have you tied up?" Lance questioned at the sound of my voice.

"Actually, you couldn't have called at a better time. I'm just getting in from taking care of everything there," I lied.

"Cool. That's good you've taken care of things. I know how important that boutique is to you. I'll shoot you over an email of all the notes once I get home and scan them in. Just to give you a rundown though, we covered all of chapter nine, part of ten, and the section of eight she's gonna let us retest on. The grades are posted from the quiz if you haven't checked."

Smacking my lips, my mood checked right back in to where it was when I first realized I had to leave school early: sour. "Wow, I missed almost a whole semester in one half of a class session," I whined.

What that really means is that Mace is gonna have to pull Rem-Dog and Shawn in more often when it comes to running the traps, at least until this semester is over with. I don't care how he feels about it. I'm not making a choice. I've let him have his cake and eat it with me, so he's gonna do the same. Fuck him talking about seeing how real my love is for him. He'd better show me how he's riding for me. Shit is always all good when you're getting your way. It's the compromise that tells if you're in it to win it, at least in my opinion.

"It appears that Professor Eubanks will be flying through all she noted on the syllabus, plus more," he continued. "I can tutor you on a few topics and, of course, look out with the notes whenever you've gotta miss class, but I just got signed up for a hectic schedule at work. I'm about to have a lot of sleepless nights myself."

Completely ignoring Lance's complaints on his issue, I was too wound up in mine. We were only halfway into the semester and strong feelings of anxiety were bombarding me. I wasn't feeling confident that I could pull off the complete 180-degree change that required tons of focus and time, which I lacked tremendously with the help of Mace. A passing grade in this course was required for me to progress to the upper-level ones. Simply put, I couldn't get my associate's degree without passing this class. I felt extra screwed because it was too late to drop the class.

"Hey, you got quiet on me."

"Yeah, my bad. Just wondering if I'm gonna make it to the end of this semester," I sighed, being honest.

"Of course you are. That ain't even gotta be a worry of yours as long as I'm around, sweetie." Something about the tone of his voice settled me to the point of smiling. Lance was always encouraging, but something about this time was different.

"Wow, for real? You've got me like that?" Pushing my notebooks and stuff to the side, I folded my legs Indian style and ended up catching a glimpse of myself in the mirror. My cheekbones were raised and red. Lance's pretty, nerdy ass had me blushing.

"Make no mistake about it, sweetie."

Sweetie? Since when . . . And why am I . . . Confused and twisted up in my thoughts as to when Lance started using pet names with me, because he'd always called me Marley, and more importantly, why I was blushing by him doing so, I hadn't heard Shawn pull back up in the driveway. Mace was already coming through the front door by the time I realized he was back. I was about to get caught doing whatever it was that I was doing, which I couldn't name. *I'm not sure what it is, but I know it's wrong.*

"Marley! Yo, Mar-Mar," Mace called out to me as soon as he entered the house.

"Hey, Lance, I've got another call coming in. Can I call you back in a few?" I was rushing him off the phone, hoping he hadn't heard Mace yelling crazily on my end.

"Yeah, sure. It's no thang, baby girl," he replied. "The email is—"

I cut him off by hanging up. Mace was two paces from the bedroom, and I wasn't about to let him find me on the phone with another nigga. He might've been crowned a cheater, but he'd never accept the same behavior up out of me. Right before he popped open the door, I cleared the call from Lance altogether.

A Hustler's Heart

by

T.C. Littles

Chapter One

Phillip "Doughboy" Hughes

"Yo, Hughes. Let's go, fat boy." Officer Franks opened the holding cell that I and nine other men had been packed in like sardines for almost the entire weekend.

Wayne County Jail was one of the oldest operating jails in the country. I didn't see how the rat-infested, raggedy muthafucka was still standing, let alone housing gangsters, goons, and murderers. It was hotter than a dirty pistol up in this joint, like Satan himself was punishing us for our sins. Damn near all 250 pounds of me was sweating. I thought I was going to pass out last night because it got up to almost eighty degrees with damn near no circulation. I was hoping this ho-ass cop was about to take me down to processing to bond out.

"A'ight, gang-gang. Stay up." I nodded to the men still awaiting arraignment, then stepped out of the cell with my hands in front of me so I could get cuffed. "And don't hate on the big boys, Franks. Ask ya wife about me. I had her begging for mercy the last time I stuffed her with this well-fed dick," I disrespectfully mocked him.

"Oh! Is that so, bitch nigga? We'll see how tough you're talking when the judge sits you down for five to ten. I pray to God you drop the soap on the first fuckin' day." He damn near sliced through my skin with the metal cuffs.

It took everything in my power not to headbutt him or send my shoulder blade through his chin. My hot temper wasn't going to last in jail, which was why my mind raced itself into a migraine over the weekend trying to map out some hustles that could rack up enough cash to fight the case they were building. I'd been holding my head up like a G, but deep down in my gut, I was worried about my fate.

I needed the coldest criminal attorney practicing law within metro Detroit to get all the evidence on my record tossed, and that request wasn't going to be cheap. Going to court with a public defender interested in making a side deal was a no-go with my rap sheet. I'd been fuckin' with the wrong side of the law since I was a young nigga. Plus, I wasn't cooperating with the flip-snitch requests they kept trying to manipulate me with during the passive-aggressive interrogation that went on for hours. They wanted an inside man to take down my boss and his operation, saying it was a pipeline to a cartel in Mexico. The shit was over my head, and I wasn't no snitch. So I was facing some bogus charges that could actually stick.

Franks and his partner swooped down on me almost a block away from my job, and of course I was riding dirty, and they knew it. I worked as a security guard at a medical marijuana dispensary called the Choke Café. I stole their stock and slung it on the side, plus hustled a li'l with one of my homegirls, Paris, who worked there as a bud tender. We got down on a daily basis flipping everything from shake to top shelf. She'd pass me the stash, and I'd slang that shit in the parking lot, the gas station across the street on a snack run, up at the Coney on a lunch break, and of course after hours. On a good day, we'd rip the Choke off for a whole garbage bag of Strongs, then pop out partying. I was happy as hell they didn't ride down on me with that but even happier Paris was trailing me. Ain't no telling what foul moves Franks and his partner would've made on me had she not been on the curb screaming she was recording. Some cops in the city were cool, but Franks and his partner gave the entire Detroit Police Department a bad name for how dirty they got down.

A few hours later, the security gate closed, separating the jail's lobby from its holding cell and general lockup, and I was free to start fucking shit up again for at least forty-five days. After then, I'd be locked up if I didn't go before the judge. They were postponing my hearing for me to retain the legal counsel I'd been demanding. All I used the public defender for was snacks and a McDonald's combo meal he'd had DoorDash deliver there, trying to bribe me to let him defend me. That alone had me playing dumb on his ass, because he was obviously either scum or a bum in the courtroom.

I stepped out with my arms wide to the side and took a deep breath of fresh air. Detroit pollution never tasted so good. It was time to go hard so I didn't have to go back in. I sat on the curb to lace my sneakers up, then powered my phone back on. It was jumping with missed notifications, but none of them had a name attached. I'd hit the master reset when the cops swooped down on me because I wasn't trying to have them use anything in it as evidence against me.

"Yo, come swoop me up. I'm about to start walking, so hit me up when you're close." I didn't give a fuck what my baby moms was doing. I needed to get away from downtown.

"Huh? They let you out on a Sunday?"

"Don't you think they did if I just told your birdbrain ass to come swoop me? Yeah. So hurry the fuck up and quit asking questions." I hung up, mad at myself for even calling Chanel, but I needed to see my li'l man bad as hell.

I wasn't one of those ho-ass, deadbeat types of men (emphasis on men) to leave my seeds to be nurtured by another nigga, so it was fucking me up mentally that there was a possibility I was about to miss out on the first few years of his young life. I was already playing stepdaddy to Chanel's daughter because her father was walking down a fifteen-year bid for trafficking dope. His hustle was how me and shorty met in the first place.

She was buying weight from me for his crew back in their hometown. One thing led to another, and before I knew it I was slipping up in her, then flipping her the product she wanted at a wholesale price. It was harder than a muthafucka denying Chanel's li'l sexy self, especially when she wasn't talking cash shit. Everything about her body was tight, right, stacked, and banging. Plus, she was cool to kick it with and didn't mind that a nigga was gettin' it out of the mud. Our situation didn't start getting shaky until she was six months pregnant with Cash.

Chanel went from needing to stay in a nigga's face and having me on *Dora the Explorer* adventures around Detroit for pregnancy cravings to disappearing for days at a time, talking about she was hormonal or posted up with her homegirl on some "women are warriors" type bullshit. I wasn't as dumb as Chanel was trying to play me, but I let a lot of shit slide because she was carrying my seed and I couldn't beat her ass. Now, though, I was standing ten toes down until she got li'l man out of the system.

He was currently living with her mother until the case was closed, which was another wild story of its own because she and her OG didn't get along. Chanel got in trouble with the State of Ohio's child protective services department when she gave birth to Cash because there was a high level of marijuana in her system, which they said led to him being born at a low birth weight with underdeveloped lungs.

When Chanelle hit me up from the hospital screaming and crying that the social worker was going to take our son, I thought she was on bullshit and lying until I got there four hours later and could only see him through the glass that separated the nursery from the hallway where only passers-by were allowed. I couldn't even boast and brag like every other proud father holding their legacies, because my name was too muddy and I couldn't risk getting caught up in a case that would tip off the law to my lifestyle.

As long as this court case was lingering, everything was up in the air. I was hoping I didn't have to check out as Cash's dad before I really got the chance to be one. I had a whole lot of shit to get straight. I was feeling the pressure like a mutha.

It wasn't even noon, and the sun was already beating down. There were big-ass globules of sweat pouring off my forehead, and I was damn near wheezing by the time Chanel met up with me. She had her music banging loud as hell, per usual, with a blunt of my chronic burning. She stayed choking off my stash. I'd been telling her about taking privileges with me, especially since she wasn't my bitch.

"Damn, nigga, your body odor is on bump! Roll the window down before you choke me the fuck out." Chanel's mouth was as reckless as they came. She was always popping off, and we were always getting into it behind her smart-ass mouth.

"Stinking or not, I bet your thirsty ass will suck my dick if I pulled it out. Now shut the hell up and drive." I took the blunt from her lips as she was hitting it, then took her phone off the charger so I could plug mine up for some juice.

"I swear to God I can't stand your rude ass. I should've sent you a Lyft and gone back to sleep."

"Then I would've given that muthafucka yo' address and slapped you out of yo' sleep. What the fuck you thought?" I looked at her like she'd forgotten who I was in forty-eight hours.

"Boy, please! You know I sleep with my piece under my pillow. I would've put a hot one in your fat ass," she laughed, always wanting to match my gangster.

"Yeah, whatever. Just hurry up and get to the crib so I can put a hot nut in yo' fat ass. A nigga need some pussy bad as hell."

"Oh, first you wanna smack me, and now you wanna fuck me? How romantic." She rolled her eyes. "You're gonna be sick in the guts when another nigga swoops me up." She always got in her feelings over me not putting a title on the li'l here and there fucking we'd been doing, but shit got too toxic with us whenever I did try wifing shorty up.

Chapter Two

Chanel Tucker

I swear to God this nigga gets on my last nerve, but I'ma stick beside him. I was in my feelings, which was crazy as hell because I wasn't pressed over even meeting Dough when my homegirl Reena first told me about him. And once she did link us, I was just fucking around with him so he'd cut me a deal on the product I was getting for my daughter's father, Vontez.

I was six weeks pregnant with Vontasia when Vontez got arrested, three months along when the judge sentenced him to fifteen years, and at the midpoint of my second trimester when I walked some contraband into a prison for the first time. Vontez had me smuggling in pills on a regular basis. The more weight I gained because of my pregnancy, the more stuff he had me sneaking in underneath my maternity clothes. I was Von's mule until I had our daughter, and then I started stripping to keep his books on bang and him blessed with every amenity the prison allowed them to have. Von was so spoiled that he even had me put money on his cellmates' books whenever their loved ones failed to look out.

I graced the pole five days a week, visited Von once a week, and got my rest up the last day of the week so I could do it all over again. By that time, Von was cool with me only using our visitations for visitations instead of transporting weight, especially because he didn't want the guards feeling up on me. My snap-back game after having Vontasia was a beast, plus she'd filled me out in all the places I was lacking. We played cards, laughed about silly shit from our past or people we knew in common, and even planned for our future once he got done serving his sentence. This routine went on for three years up until I got pregnant with Dough's baby and Von rolled out a new game plan.

"Yo, call your moms. I wanna go holla at the kids if you're cool with it." Dough finally passed me the blunt back, but it was down to a nub.

I took that as my opportunity to roll down the window for some air. I always got anxious when it came time to deal with my mother. I really wanted to ask Dough to postpone his request until next weekend and settle for a FaceTime call, but I wasn't trying to deny him even more time with his son. I was already the reason why Cash wasn't in my custody now. That was a big reason I was feeling sick to my stomach. Chantel knew the truth I never needed Dough to find out.

My children lived with her in Ohio and had been for the past few months. I'd temporarily lost custody of them doing some dumb shit but had six more weeks of a parenting program, therapy, and probation to complete to regain all of my parental rights. Although I was enjoying the break I was having, I couldn't wait until the case was closed. I hated having my mother in the middle of my business.

Dough had been getting us rooms at a hotel by my mom's house that had a pool, water slides, a splash pad, and arcade games for Vontasia to play so he could spend time with Cash as well. Dough even catered to Tay-Tay and spent time with her, too. He never treated her differently and always looked out for her whenever he looked out for Cash when it came to clothes, shoes, toys, whatever. I couldn't front and say Dough was a bad father if I wanted to.

Chantel might've taken temporary custody of my kids as a favor to me, but we weren't on the best of terms and hadn't been in years. We had a strained relationship all throughout my childhood because I was always rebellious, so our issues only magnified once I met Vontez and started spiraling out of control in the streets. My heart used to beat so hard for him that I shut all of my emotions off for everyone else in my world, especially if they were against us. My mom, my family, my friends, and people on social media all got the boot because I was mentally and physically stroked by a savage. He had full control over my mind and my pussy to the point where I felt invincible.

Chantel answered on the fifth ring with nothing but attitude in her voice.

"Hey, Ma. How are you?" I was trying my hardest to be polite, but the task wasn't painless.

"Fine." She didn't care to greet me with any pleasantry.

I pushed past all of that because, ultimately, I wanted me and Dough to spend family time together so he'd soften up. We weren't a family, but of course I wanted a title. Tay-Tay would be grown by the time her father got out of jail, so it only made sense for me to try making a family with Cash's daddy. I for damn sure didn't want any more mutts with any more dogs.

"Would it be cool if me and Dough came up there and stayed overnight at that same hotel with the kids?" I came straight out with why I'd called.

She sighed before answering. "Well, I'm supposed to be hosting a card game here this weekend, so can ya so-called baby daddy spot me the money I'm going to miss?"

"For real? Are you serious? You can't just switch with one of the other women?" Chantel belonged to a club of women who gave parties every month.

"Whoaaa! What you're not about to do is pencil more of your bullshit on my schedule. It's already bad enough I've gotta limit who smokes a cigarette up in here when I do host a party because of your son's asthma."

"This isn't a walk in the park for me either, Ma. I'd much rather have my own kids than deal with all the shade you throw my way. I might not say nothing, but I hear the smart remarks you be throwing out when I'm on the phone with Vontasia. Those are my babies, and I don't want you poisoning their brains not to like me because you don't." I hadn't meant to go into the emotional spill like I had.

Chantel started laughing and coughing on smoke from the cigarette I knew she was puffing on. "Daughter, honey, trust me when I say this, the last thing I want to be doing with my time is raising your and that thug's babies. My whole life, house, and sanity has been flipped upside down trying to handle these li'l ruffians you call children. I can't wait to give you your kids back." The hard emphasis she put on the word "your" made my stomach churn. She stayed holding my secret over my head.

"Damn, you be trippin' hella hard on me for nothing, but it's cool. I'm gonna make sure I pass those classes so me and my babies can let you live your life," I shouted, wishing I could hop on the road without waiting.

She burst out laughing. "Awww! Shut your shit up, Chanel! You talk a good game, but you ain't never been no real chess player. I swear to God I wanna see you make it happen so I can get my life back." She wasn't encouraging me but antagonizing me. "If you're at my door a minute after four, you won't get in. And if you come in with this conversation, I'ma expose yo' ass, and we both know you don't want that. Goodbye."

"I'ma expose yo' ass, and we both know you don't want that." I replayed her threat in my mind a few times before letting my cell phone fall into my lap.

"Pass me the blunt and stop hogging it, damn! I swear to God that she wrecks my nerves. I can't wait until all of this CPS shit is over with so I can be done with her for good-good." I took my frustrations out on Dough when he hadn't done a damn thing but support me.

"It's all good, shorty. Stop tripping. That shit'll blow over, and if it don't, you ain't got but a few more months to work those classes out with the State. Keep ya head up and walk that shit down. I'ma be right here holding you and li'l man down once we get him home. You know that, so believe that." Dough tried selling me some encouragement.

Though I tried feeling better behind his pep talk, I couldn't take too much stock in what he was saying because he didn't know how deep my shit swamp really flowed.

Vontez was the muthafuckin' man when he was a free man, known for pushing dope in the streets and flippin' niggas over into their graves for personal gain. My young ass felt invincible by his side when I first started tagging along with him on murderous missions. Within the first month of our relationship, I was partying, popping pills, and helping him hustle. I was his love and his accomplice at the same time, better than any right-hand nigga could be because my heart was tied up in knots with his.

If he needed something weighed, I had a backup scale in my purse. If he needed some prescriptions for cough syrup, mood-altering pills like Adderall and Xanax, or some high-milligram pain pills that were rare on the streets, I'd be the one faking an illness at an emergency room so we could re-up through pharmacies. I could've been a scholar or at least an actress for as much time as

I'd researched symptoms that would require mind-altering pills and practiced for my performances.

I'd been bipolar, a manic depressive who had suicidal thoughts, and I even tried playing like I was schizophrenic once until the doctor started acting like he was going to lock me up in a psychiatric ward for further testing and evaluation. I snapped my fingers and told his script-writing ass that it was magic and I was healed. Vontez thought the cops were after us when he saw me burst through the exit doors running for the car. Later that night, we hit our first lick on another thug for his stash of pills, then kept living off licks. We spent our days casing hustlers and our nights hittin' 'em off for their profits. I would sometimes even use my sex appeal to set the target up.

Once I got pregnant with our baby though, our hustle shifted and I went right along with Von's plan. He claimed he didn't want our seed to start off struggling, so he started picking up packages of dope from Detroit and driving them to Ohio so he could increase the prices of each one of his Baggies. What sold for twenty in the D sold for a fifty spot in our hometown, which meant we were hittin' a helluva lick. We had a good thing going until Von caught his case. That didn't stop me from holding him down though.

We counted on one another like Christians count on Jesus Christ when Von had his freedom, so it wouldn't have sat right with my soul if I'd left him dangling when he needed me the most. It ain't never been a time Von called on me for help and I didn't show up and out, even when I was pregnant with Cash. It was that part that Dough could never find out about.

Chapter Three

Dough

"Phillip, baby, is that you? Doughboy?" I heard my mother's sweet voice calling from the three back of the house as soon as I opened the door.

"Yeah, Ma. The jail was overcrowded, so I caught a free pass home," I lied, not willing to put the worry of my case on her heart. It'd been me and my mom since forever, and though I stayed fucking up as a young nigga, I knew as a man I had to hold her down.

"I'm about to use the bathroom and wash my face so Mama won't see me like this. Give me a sec." Chanel looked just like Tay-Tay did whenever she got chastised.

"Doughboy, what's taking you so long to get back here? Hurry up so I can lay eyes on you and make sure they didn't beat you up behind them bars."

She'd named me after my father, but then nicknamed me after the Pillsbury Doughboy when I was a kid because I was on the chunky side and jolly. She still had pictures all over the house of me dressed in too-small baby clothes, cheesing and chubby as fuck, but I'd been transformed into a big and mean nigga. I didn't go by Phil because my daddy didn't fuck with my family. And I dropped the "boy" part of Doughboy because I'd become a man about my money. Niggas in the street called me Dough, but my mama could call me whatever she wanted and would get an answer. I respected and cherished mine, make no mistake about it.

The shotgun house I grew up in had three bedrooms: a bedroom for her, the den (her chill spot), and my old room was a junk room, but it was now Tay-Tay's playroom and would soon be Cash's as well. All my mom talked about was getting her grandkids running through this house.

Anyway, I found her in the den with her feet kicked up, watching *Perry Mason* on the fifty-inch flat-screen TV I'd just mounted last week. My mother was a big and bubbly old lady. I got my weight from her. I leaned down and hugged her tightly.

"I had the pastor pray for you to come home this morning at church, and look at you standing before me now. Ain't the Lord good, baby? All the time, He's right on time," she sweetly preached as she always did. My mom was a firm believer in and minister of the Word. Even in the face of having a thuggish-ruggish son, she still felt like prayers never failed her.

"He's good to who He wants to be good to, fa'sho," I said, not really wanting to get on the topic of religion. I wasn't trying to come off incorrectly to her or disrupt her peace, but I didn't share the same beliefs she did.

It wasn't that I didn't believe in God, because there's gotta be a good reason for the creation of Earth and whatever. I just didn't understand why folks like my mama, aunt, and the aging neighbor down the street who was struggling with a billion ailments were allowed to live low when they'd helped the community, were in the front row of Sunday service, and led Bible school. I tried not questioning God, but a savage like myself couldn't help but wonder why.

"Son, I know what you're thinking. Don't speak it or think it. Not only are your words powerful, but so are your thoughts. God knows what He's doing. If you'd slow down a little bit, maybe you'd hear His plan." She'd been preaching at me since I started hugging the block.

"Ma, we ain't gonna agree on religion, and I love you too much to argue with you about it. So let me respectfully end the conversation and show you who I brought to see you for a little while."

Chanel came out of the bathroom from fixing her face right in time and fell into my mother's arms. "Heyyy, Mama," she sang, genuinely sounding happy.

"Oh, Lord, hey, sweetheart. Come on over here and give me a hug. I miss seeing your pretty face around here."

With all the petty arguments and fights Chanel and I had, she never acted funny or disrespectful toward my mother, and she always took time to chill with her. That was one of the main reasons I kept shorty around despite us not being an official couple. My mother adored Chanel, even more so since she gave her a grandson, and Vontasia was a jewel to her as well. Sometimes I thought that Chanel loved my mother more than she loved me. My mom filled the void in her heart from the lack of love and acceptance she received from her own mother, or at least that was my take on it. I was happy their dynamic was cool as fuck, especially if I had to sit down. I was confident Cash would have a hella tight relationship with his granny because my family just about stopped at my OG.

"Yeah, a'ight. Y'all can bond and do all that girly stuff without me. I'm about to go jump in the shower. Don't forget what you gotta handle, Chanel." I winked and walked out.

I had a crib by where I rolled, but my home was in the three-bedroom flat upstairs from my mother, Mona Hughes, mainly so I could protect her from the gangsters of the neighborhood who preyed on senior citizens. If these savage-ass bums from around the way knew I wasn't living here, they'd be around this bitch on a daily, begging for homecooked meals and spare change. I done had to pull my strap out on a few rambunctious dopefiends who thought her ministries at church were a mission she served from her front door as well. If she weren't refusing to let me buy her a house because of her sentimental attachment to this one, I would've moved her to the 'burbs so she could leave all this hood shit alone. Until then, I made sure I decked this one out and the property taxes stayed paid up. Mona didn't have to worry about nothing as far as bills, upkeep, renovations, or the tithes she put into the church. I was the man that clown-ass nigga Phillip was supposed to be to her.

After trashing the outfit I'd been wearing for days, I hopped in the shower and started doing my thang. At six foot one, I knew I was smelling loud like Chanel had said. I'd been cooped up in a small room full of niggas. There wasn't any other way to smell. I spent about fifteen minutes washing all the sweat, grime, and jail residue off my body and from within the pockets of my skin with some peppermint Castile soap I was glad Mom Dukes had put me on to, and then another fifteen just chilling underneath the hot water, thinking.

I had forty-five days before my court date, which meant I didn't have more than thirty to get on my hustle and grind harder than ever. I was trying my best not to think about all the time I was missing with my son, espe-cially since there was a chance I'd be locked up by the time Chanel completed her programs and got Cash and Vontasia back. Li'l shorty might've not been my daughter, but she was my son's sister, so that partially made her mine. I wasn't trying to have her drawing pictures and writing letters to another daddy in jail.

Once I ran all the hot water in the water tank cold, I climbed out and trimmed up my hair. I was sick about missing my standing barbershop appointment, because my facial hair had me looking wolfish. I did the best I could lining my beard up, but I didn't even fuck with my fade or my hairline. Cutting hair wasn't a skill a nigga had, and I wasn't about to chance having to walk around sporting a funny-shaped bald head.

I texted Chanel. Fresh. Come drain this dick.

I was ready to work my frustrations out on her pussy.

Chanel

I loved Dough's mama. Like for real. We didn't see eye to eye when I first crept around her house trying to get at her son, but I wasn't bitter at her shade. Not then or now. Once Dough told her I was carrying his baby, she hugged me and told me that if ever me and her son got on the outs, that didn't include her, and I'd always be welcome in her home. I'd had to take her up on her open offer a few times. Despite her checkin' me for calling her son a fool, he was and could be. But I had nothing but love and respect for Ms. Hughes because, at the end of the day, she stood up for her son regardless if he was right, wrong, or indifferent.

"What's wrong with you, child? Why are you sitting over there looking like you're about to cry?"

"Oh, my bad, Mama." I quickly fixed my frown. "I was just thinking about my mother. I called her when me and Dough were on our way here, and we kinda exchanged a few sour words." Ms. Hughes was familiar with how me and my mom operated from being mixed up in the custody case.

She shook her head. "I pray for that woman and y'all's relationship every day, sweetie. The good Lord will work the kinks out eventually. Just give it to Him and stay focused on getting your babies back." Her pep talk didn't come with criticism or judgment. I loved Dough and wanted a family with him, but I clung to Ms. Hughes because she filled a void in my heart that I wished my own mother could occupy.

"How's Cash-Cash and my cutey-patootie Popsicle doing?" She was referring to Vontasia, because every single time my daughter came over here, she'd have a Popsicle in her mouth and be asking for another one. I couldn't even complain about her craving because she'd gotten it honest. All I ate when I was pregnant with her were freeze pops and Bomb Pops because I couldn't keep anything else down.

Just like Dough, Ms. Hughes never treated Vontasia like she wasn't flesh and blood. She'd even framed a few of her pictures and hung them around the house along with Cash's.

"Cash is getting big and bad, and just started day care last week, and Tay-Tay is doing good. My mom enrolled her into kindergarten at my old elementary school, so she's been excited about having some friends." I pulled out my phone and went to the gallery so I could show her the pictures of them I'd snagged off social media. Crystal swore she couldn't stand having my kids disturb her life, but she sure as hell made it a point to post pictures of them all the time.

"I cannot wait to have their little bodies around here." Mama Hughes sounded sad as she looked through the pictures. "Dough was supposed to take me to the store this weekend so I could put together a li'l box of toys and goodies for them, but maybe you can run me there one day this week? I don't want them to think Granny-MaMa doesn't care about them."

"Aw, naw Mama! They know you lovvveee them." I was animated on purpose. "But of course I'll take you shopping. We can go anywhere you want to go."

"Thank you, sweetheart. Those babies will be back home with you and with us in no time, Chanel. Just keep up the good work with those parenting classes and watch God work it out."

"I hope so, Mama. I reallyyy hope so. I sometimes feel like God's forgotten about me."

"Nope. He's just waiting on you to remember Him." She pointed at me with love. "But I won't start coming down on you. I know how you and my son hate it when I get to preaching."

"It's okay. It's good to know you care." I smiled, not wanting to hurt her feelings because I was extra low on hope and lost when it came to religion.

"And don't you forget that. It's important for you young kids of today's society to know you're loved." She winked, then moved off the subject. "Now light this phone back up so I can see some more pictures of my grand blessings. You know I don't know how to work these thingamajigs."

I smiled at her innocence and silliness. "Maybe Dough can give you some money to get you a 'thingamajig' so I can start sending you pictures. That way you can see them even when I'm not over here."

"That's a great idea! You'd have to teach me how to work it though. You know Dough can't sit still and out of the streets long enough for the good of his soul." She wasn't preaching but talking how every old person talked about savages, thugs, and the corner boys.

I laughed. "I got you, Mama."

After changing the settings on my phone so the phone wouldn't lock up after a few minutes, I rushed out of the room and hurried upstairs to Dough's flat. Ms. Hughes didn't say anything, but I knew she saw his freak-nasty text message telling me to drain his dick.

The smells of peppermint soap, powder-scented body lotion, and the lingering fumes of the aerosol deodorant spray Dough used smacked me in the face when I walked through his front door. He might've had some weight on him, but he didn't play about his hygiene, which was why I was cracking on him in the car. Dough took at least three showers a day in the summer and no fewer than two in the winter to make sure he wasn't funky. The neighborhood crackhead who stole stuff like personal care products and detergent made her bank for the month off him alone. He probably had more body soap than I did.

Walking through his house was kind of bittersweet. I stayed with Dough at least five days a week when I was pregnant and even made Cash a nursery. There were three bedrooms, so even Vontasia had a spot to play with all her toys at. There wasn't a doubt in my mind that all four of us would be living here as a family had I not been creeping back and forth to the jail on some dumb shit. I was so busy looking out for my first baby daddy that I jeopardized the good thing I had going with my second one.

Dough was in his bedroom going through his merchandise when I walked in. A friend of his worked in a warehouse that was the hub for a gang of mainstream shopping centers and stores. They housed everything from Nike products to video games, and Dough's homeboy stole it all. In the middle of the night, he'd walk the boxes right out the side door and to Dough's trunk, and then they'd split the profit fifty-fifty once Dough flipped whatever the product was. He could be hustling phones on Monday, gym shoes on Wednesday, televisions on Friday, and computers on Sunday.

His back was turned, and he was rapping verses to Detroit rapper 42 Dugg's tracks. He didn't even feel me watching him.

"See, baby daddy? Doesn't it feel good to be fresh and clean? Now all I've gotta do is get yo' ass in the gym to drop a few pounds." I playfully smacked his big belly when he turned around. It was slightly hanging over his basketball shorts, but all I could focus on was the big-ass imprint his dick was making through the thin fabric.

"I'll drop these few pounds all right." He grabbed the meat I was hungry for. "Get naked."

"My pleasure," I purred, then slithered out of my bodysuit.

Wasn't nothing nice, sweet, or loving about how Dough was fucking me. With my legs spread into a V, he had me bent over the bed and was ramming his hardness into my coochie without remorse. My insides were jiggling like he was drilling straight through to my stomach.

Whap!

His hand flew across my backside, making my vagina tingle and swell up even more. I loved it rough, and he loved giving it to me that way. I begged for him to spank me again. So he did.

Whap!

My body jerked forward, and his dick jumped farther into me. "I swear on my soul this dick is so fuckin' good, bae." I damn near had tears coming out of my eyes.

"Yup, I know it is. It's the only thing that calms yo' crazy ass down."

For us to always end up cursing, arguing, and fighting with one another, we were a perfect match in the bedroom. He was trying his best to stroke me to sleep, and I was trying my best to take it and throw it back so I could take all his nut. I was bouncing, twerking, rolling my hips, and doing the butterfly on Dough, all while he dipped his dick in, out, in, and then out again.

"Flip that ass over, spread them legs, and grab ya ankles," he commanded, breathing roughly. Then he checked the condom to make sure it was still pulled up and secured on his dick. I thought he was about to take it off. I wanted him to take it off. I'd pop his babies out for the rest of my life if he'd put another one, two, or three in me.

Dough's tattoos were dancing all over his body as he stroked my pussy out of commission. Clutching his back with my nails, I scratched my name into it as he built up a sweat on top of me. We were going to end up breaking the bed frame down to the floor from how wild we were going at it.

"Oh, my God! You got it, nigga." I damn near bit a hole in my bottom lip. "I'll swear to God I'll be on my best behavior from now on!"

"You fucking better be." I felt the veins in his dick swelling up and prayed he didn't pull out.

Chapter Four

Dough

Damn, she's got some juicy-ass thighs on her. And that pussy sucks a nigga up each and every time. Maybe I should give her another try. It might be good having her, my li'l man, and Mom Dukes underneath the same roof. I rolled up while Chanel snored. I had just blown her back out and cleared my mind in the process. I was now ready to eat and hit the highway to see Cash.

"Ma, did you eat? I'm about to hook some shit up real quick."

"Boy, watch your mouth. But you know I'm not about to turn down none of your food. Where's Chanel at?"

"Upstairs asleep." I left out that she was sprawled across my bed, freshly fucked to sleep.

"Oh, okay. Well, you better keep her close until my grandbaby is home. I know you don't want to give her a ring, but she's too fragile for you to keep messing around with her head."

"I got it. You ain't gotta worry about that."

"All right. I know that means shut my mouth. And I will. Just bring me a piece of chicken as soon as it comes out of the grease for my peace."

"I got you, big hungry. I got you."

She was the one who taught me how to cook in the first place. When I hit puberty and started getting bigger and bigger eating up family packs of pork chops in one sitting, she put me to work in the kitchen alongside her. I hated the chore then but appreciated the skill now. It was because of her that I didn't press none of the hoes I fucked around with to even touch a skillet. A bitch ain't gotta feed me if she could fuck and suck me good.

I commenced getting down in the kitchen. Seasoning the wings to perfection, I let them marinate while I cut up damn near a pound of potatoes and a few onions for some homestyle fries. The chips, Ramen noodles, and soda pop I had in the pokey hadn't hit on shit in my big belly. Junk food made a weighted nigga like myself hungrier.

All four eyes on the stove were lit. Two of the piping hot skillets of grease were for the wings only, one was for the potatoes, and the other was for a doctored-up can of Glory greens. Just as she taught me to cook, she taught me to eat my veggies to stay strong and healthy. I couldn't wait to cook for Cash and teach him the same things.

Once everything was on and cooking, I fixed a big bowl of cereal, then flopped down on the couch in front of the big-ass television I'd put over my mom's mantel. I had the whole crib decked out. The first few thousand I made off the streets went straight to the Chaldean-owned furniture store a few miles down to get my mom together. Mom Dukes got a new bedroom set, living room pieces, a La-Z-Boy reclining chair and a television for her lounge room, and a dining room table to entertain her church-going friends with Sunday tea and cookies.

The more licks I hit, the more I stepped up. I made sure the roof was patched and the furnace was replaced, and I fixed the electrical work that had our lights randomly going on the fritz. It took me a good minute to get my crib upstairs together, sleeping on an air mattress for months with my big ass, but I slept like a baby knowing my mom didn't worry about shit. Whether she took my dirty money in her Christian hand or not, I was the man of this house, and I rocked as such.

Chanel

Today is about to be on point! I thought as soon as my eyes popped open for the impromptu cum-slumber Dough rocked me into. There was never a time his dick strokes didn't put me to sleep and have me drooling. Von might've been controlling my mental, but Dough was the master of my body.

Squirming around, I hugged his pillow tighter, loving his scent, but felt my stomach starting to grumble from the smell of food cooking downstairs. I already knew Dough went crazy in the kitchen whippin' up some grub since he'd been away from food for a couple of days. My bae didn't play and probably went crazy in the county having to miss meals.

If his mama weren't home, I'd have taken my freaky ass into the kitchen completely naked and let him have his way with me on the counter before getting my plate. He kept me fed so swell when I was pregnant with Cash that I was overweight. But I wasn't complaining. Dough was giving me the fairy-tale pregnancy I wanted with Von but was robbed of. I couldn't wait until my CPS case was closed so maybe he and I could be a real family with Vontasia and Cash.

Rolling out of his bed, I tiptoed to his dresser and went through all six of the drawers. I was looking for condoms, sex toys, and what I hoped not to find: another female's clothes. I knew I wasn't the only chick climbing on Dough's dick, but I'd feel worse if I knew someone else was lying up over here. I didn't want him messing with anyone seriously, only on some hit it and quit it type shit, especially since I didn't want any other girls around my son. I knew how bitter and funny females could act toward their boyfriend's kids when the kid wasn't theirs, and I didn't want Cash caught in the middle of a feud. Well, at least not theirs. He'd been birthed into this world eight weeks too soon thanks to my and Von's drama.

Dough

"Doughboy! Is a piece of chicken ready yet?"

"Yeah, Ma, I got you," I yelled back. "I'll be back there with a plate in a second."

"Okay, baby. Don't forget to fix me a little taste of something." She was referring to a drink.

I laughed. "Yup, Ma, I got you on that, too."

Any kind of whiskey, my mom would drink. Her ass would be sitting back there watching television, buzzing like a muthafucka but swearing she wasn't. It was all good, though. I fixed her a drink, fixed her a lady portion of food and myself a big, hungry-sized portion, left Chanel a plate for whenever she got up, then retreated in the den to chill and grub with Mom Dukes.

Ring. Ring! Ring!

I looked up and around for the ringtone I knew so well.

"Oh, straight up? Who calling you?" I playfully questioned my mother as it startled her from the plot unraveling on television.

"What? Boy, stop playing," she laughed, waving me off. "You know I ain't got no cell phone and that ain't nobody but church folks call me. That's Chanel's phone. It's been going off ever since she left it with me, but I didn't want to disturb y'all from doing the nasty." She shook her head with a sly smirk on her face. "Yeah, I know what y'all was doing up there. And I seen how yo' nasty behind talks to her, too. I see how y'all done made a baby. But here, go give her this phone because I'm tired of hearing it." She pushed it in my hand and dove into her plate of food.

"A'ight, Ma. I got you. Let me know what happens at the end though, okay?"

"Boy, bye. Get on out of here. You don't care nothing about my program, but thank you for spending time with me. Another thing you can do for me is bring a few more pieces of chicken in here if there's some more left. Give me Chanel's even. She ain't gotta know you cooked no food." Rocking back and forth and giggling, she was cracking herself up. "Oooh, that's so dirty."

I laughed again. "Yeah, Ma, you know I got you, and I won't tell her until you decide to team up with her again against me."

"Oooh, don't be no snitch. Ha-ha-ha," she laughed so loud that tears came from her eyes. "G'on and get my chicken before I keep telling jokes and end up peeing my pants messing around with you."

Mom Dukes was right about Chanel's phone jumpin' off the hook. The phone rang while I was fixing my mother a plate, and then again when I was handing it to her. I ignored it both times and then a third but was tempted to see what was up now that it was ringing again.

Chapter Five

Dough

The screen read Von, which I knew off rip was Vontez, the same Vontez I forbade Chanel from communicating with until I got my son in my custody. "I told this sneaky-ass bitch not to be talking to this nigga!" I stormed out of my mom's crib and rocked the house as I ran up the stairs. I was about to pop Chanel's neck off her body. Here I was with a million things I was worried about, and her dick-handling ass was lurking behind my back, about to cause more problems.

Ring. Ring. Ring. Ring!

He hung up and called back, then hung up and called back again. I wasn't even the type of nigga to go through a female's phone or answer it, but ol' boy's persistence had me hot.

"Yo, what up?" I answered.

"Whatchu mean, what up, nigga? Who is this and where's my bitch at? Where's Cha-Baby?"

"Unavailable like I told her to be, nigga. And this is Dough. You got a problem?" I wasn't trying to argue with a nigga I couldn't reach, but I wasn't about to let the nigga take the lead on the conversation like I was a ho-ass nigga.

"Ohhh, hey, Big D. I see you made it out the county. I was hoping they sat yo' fat ass down and you ended up getting shipped my way. I swear to God I can't wait to meet the cocky muthafucka who's been keeping my bitch's pussy wet while trying to fuck up my hustle at the same time." I heard the hurt on his heart, so I let the nigga know.

"Awww, Von man, keep it savage and stop coming at me all in your feelings about Chanel. You can have that ho, and she can be back to shoving pounds up her loose coochie once I get what's mine." I stormed in my room and snatched Chanel up by her throat and collared her against the wall. "You've been pillow talking to this muthafucka about me, but then begging me to wife you. Tell this nigga Von that whatever y'all got is d-e-a-d until further notice. Now!" I applied pressure to Chanel's neck and slid her up the wall to where here feet were dangling.

"I . . . I can't fuck with you like that no more, Vontez." Her lip was quivering more than her body was, and I was the one she should've feared the most. Her body language told me that that nigga had her heart and mind and I wasn't doing shit but keeping her afloat so she could hold him down.

"You heard that right, my nigga? Yo' bitch will be back on your roster when I'm done with her." I was exploding.

"Yeah, a'ight. We'll see about that, big fella." Vontez cockily disconnected the call, and I dropped Chanel to the floor right after.

She started scampering around the room, getting her clothes and putting them on.

"Get a Sprint representative on the phone, and change that muthafuckin' number right now." I started pacing around the room so angry that my vision was blurring in and out. "How long you been back to talking to that ho-ass nigga behind my back?"

"I swear I stopped when you told me to. It hasn't been nothing but a few weeks. One of his friends saw me at school when they went to pick up their daughter and ran word back to him that I was living in Ohio. I had to tell Vontez what was up, Dough. He has a right to know what's going on with his daughter." Her dumb ass thought her rationale made sense, but all it did was make me snap harder.

"Bitch, quit playing me for a joke." I clotheslined her down onto the bed, then gripped her throat again. "I've been buying every undershirt, gym shoe, JoJo Siwa bow, school uniform, and toy that Vontasia has had for the last two years. I'm her father, and I know that nigga don't care enough about her to be blowing you up like he was. You're back being a mule for that nigga. I ain't dumb. I swear to God you better put your shit in order before I put you in a body bag."

"Please get off me, Dough." She clawed at my back, gagging and struggling to breathe.

Nothing in me wanted to, but I saw how flushed Chanel was becoming, so I let go and rose off the bed. I was going to need an attorney to get me off for murdering her disloyal ass if she didn't get dressed and out of my crib with the quickness. "Hurry up and get yo' shit on and bounce. I swear to God you better not even think about that nigga Vontez until I get my son back, or I'm gonna send my son and Tay-Tay to foster care for good because I'm going to go to jail for murdering yo' stupid ass. And I put that on Mona Hughes. Your scurvy ass got me wondering if Cash is even mine." I'd never questioned his paternity, but Chanel's messy-ass moves were making me question if she'd been playing me all along.

"Oh, hell naw, clown! Don't play me like that. You can go to hell and take ya mammy with you, Dough!" She suddenly came to life when the paternity of Cash came into play. "And since you want to play like you don't know the truth all of a sudden, don't hit my line up begging can he see you. As of right now, you're dead to Cash. Just like I got Tay-Tay a stepdaddy, you can be replaced." She smacked her lips right before I grabbed them big muthafuckas and tried twisting them off her face.

We went from tussling all over my bedroom to all over the house and eventually down the stairs. After "bitch this," "bitch that," threat after threat, and a few blows were exchanged, we were on the porch and drawing a crowd. That was when Chanel figured she'd really start showing out and going buck wild on me.

"Phillip Hughes, get your hands off that girl." My mother limped onto the porch, yelling with her finger lifted in the air and very badly shaken up. "I don't know what she's done or why y'all are mad and fighting, but I didn't raise you like this. Stop it, and bring your behind in this house!"

"Ma, please make him stop so I can talk to you. Please," Chanel cried and begged, prompting my mother to start praying.

Not willing to be tag teamed, I slung Chanel to the sidewalk. "Ma, go back into the house, and I'll tell you what's up and what happened when it settles." I wasn't trying to be disrespectful by cursing, but I didn't want her in the middle of my mess at the same time.

After gaining her composure, my messy baby mama lit off with her mouth one last good time. "If you don't want your mother gettin' in the middle of your drama, then maybe ya grown ass oughta move up outta her house. You ain't nothing but a grown-ass baby out here faking like you're big," she said, disrespecting me, then sprinted for her car.

"Yeah, whatever. You better g'on and get up outta here before I bust one at you."

"I hope yo' cocky ass gets caught slipping today." She pointed her finger at me and motioned like she was sending a hot one my way.

"Fuck all this nice guy shit." I flicked the cigarette to the grass and hopped over the porch's rail.

Mona was complaining about the yellow tulips I'd crushed coming down off the porch, Chanel was sprinting to her car, and I was right behind her ready to shut her mouth once and for all. It was obvious that she had me pegged as a fuck-boy, and I was about to beat some sense back into her, fa'sho!

"I hate you, Dough! I swear to God I do." She hopped in and floored the gas pedal.

"You hate that a nigga'll dump off in you but won't wife you! Don't bring your trifling ass back around here until you got my son, ho." I tried reaching my hand through the tiny opening so I could snatch her head to the window by her hair, but she jerked to the side and threw the car in drive and tried running me over as she whipped away from the curb. All I could do was raise my size-thirteen boot and stomp the brake light out of her shit.

"Your son? What son? You're dead to me, Dough! D-e-a-d, dead." Her words rocked the ground I was standing on, because her vindictive ass really did have all the power in the world to X me out of my son's life. I wasn't on his birth certificate or any other paperwork that could link me to Cash. He didn't even have my last name.

Standing in the middle of the street with my mom praying behind me for all the madness to stop, I threw my hands up like I didn't give a fuck when I was really pissed as hell. Somehow, someway, I had to get custody of my son, even if I had to do a bid.

"Son, I know I done told you I'd do less talking and more praying when it came to your relationship with that girl, but I can't be a woman of God and allow you to put your hands on another beautiful creation the Lord has made."

"Ma, you know good and damn well Chanel's ass ain't saved. Hell, she don't believe in the image of that white man any more than I do."

"Blasphemy! Shame your tongue for speaking those vile words and your brain for thinking them. Our Father has no color, just like you have no faith. Maybe that's why you've been making all the wrong decisions in life, because you don't know the Lord."

I threw my hands up and dusted them off. "A'ight, Ma, I'ma let you chill in peace with ya shows. The last thing I wanna do is disrespect you, so I'm not. You know we don't see eye to eye on religion, and quite frankly, with all the shit you go through on account of me, not to mention watching your best friend die of cancer, I don't see how you're downing me for doubting. I'm out here doing dirty daily but not dying. That ain't from me praying." My uncertainty about religion ran deep.

"It's from me praying, Phillip. I ask my Father to protect my son each time you step your foot out of my house doing the devil's deed."

"I guess He'll be hearing from you in about thirty minutes then. G'on and get back in the house, Ma. I got some stuff to handle."

Chapter Six

Dough

I was still hot about Chanel, but I couldn't let that shit slow my hustle or game plans. I had moves to make. I threw on my boxers, some Nike joggers, and a Nike T-shirt from the hanger. The only clothes I kept in my dresser drawers were boxers, socks, wife beaters, and "chill around the crib" wear. All the 'fits I wore out of the house got dry-cleaned and hung up, even my T-shirts. I was a VIP customer at the cleaners and at the corner liquor store where I copped my $5 white tees weekly. I don't care how much bleach you throw off into the washing machine, a white tee ain't never as white as it is when you first pop that boy out of the plastic.

The police still had my main car impounded, so I had to push the hooptie. It was my mom's old car from back in the day, an '83 Grand Prix I'd gotten the engine rebuilt in. I was cool with riding low-key though, especially since my name was popping. I was riding dirty over to my homie Lu's house to sell him some weight.

"Ay yo, Lu!" I whistled for him on my way up his walkway. His real name was Luke, but he never went by that shit.

"Come in, Dough."

I stepped into his crib to a cloud of smoke but still pulled my leaf up and blazed it. Me and Lu always chopped it up over greens and a good drink. He was cool people I'd met back when I was a shorty in juvie and then ran into a few years ago.

I got into a lot of trouble when I was a teenager because li'l skinny niggas taunted and bullied me in school because of my weight. They'd call me Fluffy Phil, never picked me in gym to play on their teams, and even mocked me at lunchtime when a nigga was supposed to be eating. I couldn't win for losing, even when I starved myself at lunch as an attempt to stop the jokes. I was expelled and sent to juvie for thirty days for snapping and breaking the nose and jaw of one of my classmates.

"What up, big D?" He passed me a bottle of D'Ussé and a glass. "I got at Paris the other day when your phone kept going to voicemail and she said you got flicked by Franks. You straight?"

"Hell naw, bro." I poured my shot, took it back, then poured another one. "You already know I had my heater on me, so of course they talking about sitting me down for a double." That meant two years. It didn't matter if your record was as clean as a whistle. If you got caught with an illegal firearm, you were on the chopping block from society, point blank period. A nigga like me, who'd been in trouble with the law since I was a young'un, was worried for real.

"Shhhh! Damn, D! I know that's stinging." He dropped his chin to his chest, then poured himself another shot. "That puppet-looking muthafucka Johan ain't coming through like Jay-Z and looking out for you on a lawyer or a slip out the back door? I know he's got some peoples who are well-connected." Lu was spitting the truth.

"I didn't holla at him about it yet." I threw my shot back and slid it back across to Lu for another one.

"Why in the fuck not, yo? The only reason Franks is probably putting pressure on your neck is because they really want Johan and his affiliates. There's a dispensary on almost every corner, but that musty muthafucka is the only owner parking a Porsche Panamera Turbo in front of their building. He's making that whole zone hot with his flashy ass, and real talk, I'm surprised the gang over there ain't shut that spot down." He wasn't lying.

Lu knew all about the Choke Café being a front for a more intense and illegal drug and money-laundering operation. There weren't many in-the-mud type of niggas who didn't know what the dispensary's purpose really was. Johan drove a different extortionate, flashy car every day of the week, flashed his money for no reason all the time, and was gaudy as hell when it came to rocking jewelry and diamonds. This fool would wear a Rolex on each arm just to flirt and floss on all the pretty bitches who came through the door. Johan was the type of cat who would make you pay him attention when he wasn't even on your radar, which made him an easy target I was surprised none of the goons in that area had got at yet.

"You ain't lying. Franks and his partner had all kinds of pictures of him and his people on yachts, still shots of them living in luxury within their mini mansions in their gated communities, and a few of them hopping on private jets."

"Meanwhile, can't none of our black asses swim, the only gates we have are bars across our windows, and the only privacy most of us are going to get is the face-recognition crap on our phones that's secretly set up for the Feds. Don't be no dummy and take no charges for that nigga, D. I'm not trying to tell you what to do, but there ain't no bro code with niggas who don't look like you." Lu was talking from experience. His older brother Damien called himself being cool with a white boy from across Eight Mile and ended up getting set up and then killed by the cops.

When I first met Lu, he was 14 years old and getting dragged into the juvenile detention center with blood all over his clothes, hands, and face, mixed with tears and snot. The blood was from his older brother Damien. Damien was 19 and running around with this wigger named Oliver who went by O. Nice. O. Nice swore he was black by the clothes he wore, the way he talked, and how much he hung in the hood with the crew, but he was quick to play the white-privilege card when it came down to it.

O. Nice and Damien used to hit houses up all day and night for anything of value. They'd mainly hit the houses in Nice's neighborhood because the homeowners and renters were usually at work, plus they had nicer things. All they saw was green as they stole and either pawned the items or sold them around Damien's hood. Nobody was questioning where Nice and Damien were getting PlayStation systems, flat-screen TVs, expensive music equipment, or laptops. All they knew was that they were getting a hot item for the low-low, and that was considered a blessing in the hood.

Then Damien pulled Lu into breaking and entering so he could steal stuff like clothes, shoes, and food so they could survive and stack the money they'd gotten off the flip for themselves. One night, O. Nice called Damien over, saying he had a house they could run up in, but it was a setup, and the police were waiting to arrest Damien and Lu when they walked through Oliver's door. While Lu was putting his hands up and complying, Damien took off running, and the police used his body for target practice.

The social worker let Lu say goodbye during a private viewing before the family hour started, but he wasn't allowed to attend the funeral. You couldn't pay Lu to play nice with white people, period. And he was iffy around redbones.

"Ay, nigga, did you hear me or do the liq got you spent?" He went to reach for the bottle again, but I pulled it back.

"Naw, I'm good. You've got my attention and got me thinking." I took another shot. "How would you handle the situation if you were in my shoes?"

"Oh, that's easy. I'd take what I needed from Johan and lawyer up. And then do whatever the lawyer says to do to stay out of jail for your family."

I hit the leaf hard and let Lu's advice sink in. It wasn't necessarily a bad idea.

"I got this young Black Panther type of cat's number who's fresh out of college and a beast. His pops used to be the man back in the day, but now he only works as a consultant for his kids. I can put you on to him, but that muthafucka is going to want a deposit before he even speaks to you."

"I swear I picked the wrong side of the line." I thought about how much bank criminal lawyers made off retainer fees alone. "What's his numbers looking like? Have you ever used him?"

"For a gun case I wouldn't hit ol' boy up until I was ready to part with about three grand. He's going to want that off the rip to even affiliate his name with you, and then at least another three to show up in court and keep your black ass out of cuffs. And have I ever dealt with him? Hell yeah. That's why I'm able to go spit on Oliver's grave once a week."

"Whoa! I didn't even know you got at ol' boy."

He smiled widely and proudly. "That's because I robbed Peter and paid Paul to keep my black ass out of jail. I don't give no advice that ain't followed myself." He matched my shot. "And because I fucks with you the long way, I'll advise you to also let Paul know you're planning on robbing Peter so he'll be an accomplice to your crime and work extra hard to keep you free."

"Whoa! On the real? You trusted that nigga with that info before you went in on O. Nice?"

"Yup. Who you think told me how to get away with murder? I got linked up with these Muslim brothers who introduced me to him and have been A1 ever since."

"Yeahhhh, I most definitely need that man's contact info." I pulled out my phone and unlocked it. Six racks wasn't too much to spare to remain free, but I had to get up on it. The money I had stashed away wouldn't be enough for me to retain a lawyer plus maintain my livelihood, and I was just keeping it a buck. I'd just hit my spot for a tally when I got out of the shower.

"A'ight, Big D. I just texted you ol' boy's name and number. Hit me up if and when you ride out on that clown Johan, and I'll hop in the passenger seat as your shooter. It's about time he gives you your just due. You done held that clown's hand long enough while he bled the hood dry without having to look over his shoulder. You might as well be the one to humble the nigga, 'cause if you gone, it's going to happen anyway." Lu was spitting facts.

I leaned across the coffee table and shook his hand. "Good looking on the advice and the offer of assistance. Either way it goes, I'll let you know fa'sho."

"Make sure that you do, D. We might not rock and roll with the shits on a daily basis, but I fucks with you the long way."

"Same here, fam. Same here." We threw back a few more shots, finished the leaf, then got down to business.

Chapter Seven

Chanel

"Ms. Hughes's old, messy ass is going to end up having a heart attack trying to break you and Dough up from fighting one day." My homegirl Reena was cracking up laughing as I broke down what happened earlier.

"Girlll, don't claim that, but who you telling? She was about to hit Dough over the back with her cane if he didn't let me go. I wanted to laugh, but Dough really had me scared like he was about to give me my first golden shower."

Reena slid off the couch with tears in her eyes from laughing so hard. "Bury me in any color but purple, bitch. I'm dead!"

I snatched the blunt out of her hand before she burned my cushion or my area rug. "I didn't call you over here so you could burn off some calories laughing. I called you over here so you could help me figure out what to do about Vontez and Dough." I was sitting Indian style on the floor, playing with a roll of electrical tape. Dough's bigfoot ass had the passenger side of my car looking like I'd run into a garbage can or a pole.

"Girlll, you better call your li'l police friend to see if he can get you into a protective custody program or some shit like that, because you're going to need it whenever the truth of all truths come out. Vontez might be cool with you if you get that pipeline back flowing with his drugs, but Dough isn't going to be nonchalant or forgiving when he finds out how you really lost custody of Cash. Or maybe he will." Reena knew the ins and outs of both of my relationships with Vontez and Dough.

Reena was my homegirl, my partner in crime, and if it weren't for the term "sis" being synonymous with snake-ass bitches, I would refer to her as that. Reena held me down when my life with Vontez blew up. She and I met through Von when he was getting weight from this dude named Scoop. Reena was Scoop's main chick at the time, but he was now doing time courtesy of Reena. She was bitter about him breaking up with her to be with the next chick and put the law on him out of spite. That's a different story though.

Anyway, right after Vontez went up to do his bid, I paid a moving company to pack our apartment into a U-Haul and then drove it straight to Detroit. I couldn't live in Ohio with all the enemies I'd made alongside Vontez robbing them. He wasn't there to protect me, and I didn't have any friends because I'd cut everyone off because it was all about my relationship. Reena was the only person I could call. She let me stay with her until I found a place.

My homegirl got me all the way together and made me over as soon as I hit her doorstep. She plugged me in with her clothes and shoes booster, introduced me to this African cat who sold legit-looking knockoff bags he got from his brother in New York, and taught me how to apply makeup. The whole first day of my move to Detroit was learning how to be a D-Girl. And the first night of me sleeping on her couch was my lesson on how to play the cards I was dealt.

Reena claimed she wasn't rushing me out of her house, but that me not having a nigga meant I needed to learn how to firmly stand on my own two feet. That was when

I started stripping alongside her in this li'l club that let dancers work without dance cards. Anything went on in that hole-in-the-wall, and to get off craps and ready for my baby, I got strange for change too.

It took me two months of stripping, pregnant pudge and all, to get my money stacked and off her couch. I got a two-bedroom flat a few blocks from her, cashed out on a li'l car from the auction, and had gotten hooked up with some food stamps and cash from the State. My life was gravy living off State-supplemental income and by the fat of my ass.

Being that most of the chicks dancing were out of shape, I fit in without anyone ever questioning if I was pregnant. It just looked like I had a li'l flab to work off until my fifth month, damn near sixth. That was when I went on maternity leave to give birth to Tay-Tay. Had the smoke not bothered me so much though, I probably would've delivered her at the bar. Swooping up bags of money had become an addiction, so I was elated about my snap-back game once I had her. I didn't have any stretch marks but all the juicy fat I'd needed to fill me out in all the right places.

I rocked the fuck out of the stage my first night back from maternity leave and every day thereafter until Dough made me quit the club. He didn't want me stripping while I was pregnant with his son, but little did he know, I wasn't necessarily sure if he was Cash's father.

"A'ight, Reena. I really want to know the truth on how you feel about Dough. You've known him since he was a kid. What's his problem? Why can't he simply settle down with a bitch? All I want is for me, him, Tay-Tay, and Cash to have our own li'l family."

She shrugged her shoulders, then looked at me like she was second-guessing speaking her thoughts. We'd hung around each other long enough for me to know all her quirks. As hardcore as she was, she always tried treating me like her little sister.

"Don't hold me up. I need to know what you think." I braced myself for her spill.

She exhaled a deep breath as if to say, "Here we go," then started reading me and my situation. I couldn't do shit but take it. "Well, Cha-Baby, I think you're giving that nigga too much of your time. You're too accessible for him. Whenever Dough says jump, yo' ass don't ask how high—you jump straight to the moon. Whenever he calls to fuck, you start playing with ya'self before he hits the door so you'll be dripping wet when he gets to you. When he wants a passenger, you're a rider. Hell, you told that crazy-ass nigga Vontez he was dead to you for Dough. Only for Dough to turn around and dog yo' ass. Catch a clue, boo. That nigga don't be willing to jump, fuck, and ride for you. He got you chasing that dick he dangling in ya face because you're his baby mama and his baby mama only. If it weren't for Cash, we wouldn't even be talking about a 'you and Dough.'" Though I'd asked for her honest opinion, I was still like, *damn*. Reena was blowing the lid off all the shit I'd been ignoring.

Truth spoken or not, it was hard to hear. Especially since I'd just heard Dough scream the same shit about cutting me off completely and only wanting to deal with Cash. "Wow, for real? Straight with no chaser, huh?" There was no sense in trying to defend what she, I, and the hood already knew.

Reena was in rare form to check a bitch. "Yes, Cha-Baby. Straight with no chaser. I tried telling you Dough wasn't the type of nigga to wife a bitch because he's busy taking care of his ol' scripture-screaming mammy, but you didn't want to listen. Now you've got a kid by the nigga and are stuck. Are you listening now?"

I sighed, feeling sorry for myself and my entire situation. "A'ight, bitch. Whatcha got on a bottle? I need a drink after talkin' to yo' ass."

"Naw, naw, you ain't gonna put that on me. You need a drink because you've been fucking with an ol' teddy-bear thug. We used to call that nigga Pillsbury Doughboy back in the day 'cause he was so damn fat and cuddly. Trust me, he's not the end-all and be-all like you think. You better quit giving that nigga all your power, energy, and time," she preached.

"I guess," was all I could say, not knowing what else to say.

"Guess and learn, boo. Guess and learn," she nonchalantly countered my response. "In the meantime though, maybe you should make your way to that new beauty bar, get a full makeover, then hit the streets tonight looking fucking fabulous. After my set at the club, we can roll to the after-hour together. I bet that nigga start acting right when he see you're up to livin' ya life again and not sitting around sad about his fat ass. The only reason you're not wifey is because you can wait." Tapping her foot while looking up to the ceiling with twisted lips, she was trying to do an impression of me waiting for Dough to get serious about us being a family.

"Damn, I can't stand your edgy ass sometimes. You sho'll get a bitch together when she's all emotional."

"You know it, boo. Just like you know there's no sense in you thinking with your heart when it can break. Use ya brain. You ain't never heard of that bitch breaking." Reena winked, making me burst out into laughter. "Now about that beauty bar. Can we go? A few hours of being pampered might be the remedy I need to take the edge off."

"Well, in that case, hell yeah, let's go. And it's my treat."

Chapter Eight

Dough

"J mannnn, it's really fuckin' me up that you're a ho-ass nigga. You know who this is. Holla at me ASAP, and quit dodging my calls." I left my third voicemail on Johan's phone, then sent Paris a text to hit me up whenever she went on break.

I was getting antsy about this muthafucka not answering my calls. If I didn't know Franks was posted around the dispensary, I would've pulled down on him so I could get a face-to-face going. My mind kept going back to my conversation with Lu and his proposition. I wasn't about to sit down and suffer without at least getting financially compensated.

"Ay yo, what up, Dough? You got a dubb on you?" One of my homeboys, Gooney, walked up.

"Yup yup. You know I stay with some light work on me." I went in my pocket when I saw the $20 appear.

"Damn, this shit smell funky." He popped the top of the container and held it underneath his nose.

"Come on now, Goonz, you know I only pass out gas. I swear to you that shit is straight fire." I'd gotten down with over 100 grams off some platinum cookie the day before I got knocked and was happy I had. My bags were usually $10 a gram like the dispensary did, but I was shorting all the Baggies down to .7 until I got my bread stacked to retain a lawyer.

Gooney and I had been running around in this same neighborhood since we were kids. Unlike a lot of new-comers to the hood, we helped build and tear down this community. His mother wasn't a church-going woman like my mom was, but she worked like a slave every hour of her days. She was retired now but doing part-time work because the bare minimum that social security added up to wasn't paying for her cost of living.

When I talk about women struggling when all they did their whole lives was sacrifice, work, or devote them-selves to making someone else's life better, I'm talkin' about Gooney's mom, too. She should have been living on a Florida beach, enjoying a summer sky every day of her last days. Anything but the grime and grit of the hood. Life had a way of fucking over hard workers, at least in the reality I lived in.

Gooney had the buds broken down a back wood rolled within sixty seconds. Smoking was like a second nature thang to us. We'd been blowing trees and cigarettes since fifth grade on the playground. Gooney's mom smoked cigarettes to supposedly help her cope with stress, and he used to sneak them out of her purse for us. We wasn't doing shit but trying to look grown and fly to the li'l hot hoes we wanted some attention from.

"Damn, this shit hittin' hard." Goon took a hard pull of the back wood, then started coughing.

"All day, every day. You know I keeps that fire, Goon."

"I know, fa'sho. I was looking for you Saturday night. A nigga had a bitch with a fatty swerve through here with a few more girls built just like her. I ended up having to get at Nutty for a few Baggies, and then him and his wack-ass li'l brother posted up for the freak show." Gooney hipped me to one of the things I'd missed over the weekend.

Shaking my head, I took the blunt he was passing and hit it before responding. "Naw, man, I wish I had been caked up with baby moms. The boys flicked me leaving work and sat me down the whole weekend. I just walked up outta that bitch this morning."

It was his turn to shake his head. "Damn, homie. That's messed up you had to sit down, but you're doin' hella good if all you had is their foot on your neck for the weekend and then got released. Them boys out here putting bullets in black men, then playing like all lives matter."

"Hell yeah! You're right!" I thought about all the times that cops had gotten away with bloody murder. "They are bodyin' 'em and justifying the shit later by pulling out their criminal record."

"Yup, and if I'm ever on the wrong end of the barrel, they gonna have a field day saying I deserved to die."

There was a moment of silence for the truth we'd just dropped and for knowing racist cops weren't done using black brothers as target practice.

Similar to me, Gooney had his run-ins with the boys in blue as well. He'd been in raids, thrown in the paddy wagon several times for being caught on the corner purchasing drugs, and even sat down for a year right after we graduated from high school for stealing cars and breaking them down for parts.

Gooney could rip a nigga's rims, sound system, catalytic converter, tires, steering column, and anything from underneath the hood within minutes, seconds even. He was making a killing as a kid. Although my dude didn't brag on it now, I knew he still stole from time to time. I'd never heard of him having another hustle besides some light industrial or factory work. Goon could never keep a job 'cause the nigga couldn't keep a blunt out of his hand.

We got caught up in another conversation over another blunt as I served a few custos who pulled up. Not only did I keep a variety of buds on me at all times, but I flipped my Baggies for the same price the dispensaries did: a dollar per gram. I was pissed about not seeing my son but was in my zone making money.

Ring. Ring. Ring! It was Paris calling me back.

"Damn, D! You stay ringing and serving. Put ya boy down with a gig."

"Sit tight if you ain't playing, buddy. Real talk." I popped off the porch and answered my phone. "Paris, my baby. Tell me what's good."

"I'm so glad you're out, D! You know I was worried about you. But ain't nothing good to report on. Ya boy been acting hella funny since I called and told him you got hemmed up. It's tight as hell around here. He's got us checking IDs, medical marijuana cards, and even turning newbies away. Plus, two of his brothers are up here working the bud rooms instead of me. I'm 'bout ready to quit. You know how disrespectful them muthafuckas get."

"Damn, I can't even say I'm surprised at this bullshit you're telling me. That punk ain't answered to none of my calls or messages all day."

"And he's not. He's scared as hell that Franks is going to run up in here behind your black ass getting locked up. He told Nia he might shut down shop and go home with his brothers for a few weeks."

"Naw, that ain't gonna work. Not until I holla at him. Are you off?"

"Nope, on my way to grab lunch. I'm here 'til close. Why, what's up?"

"Holla at me when you're off so we can link up, but don't tell ya boy you spoke to me." I didn't want Johan to start moving differently around Paris.

"Oh, you're good. I got you. I haven't been saying shit to his weird ass anyway. I'll call you when I'm off. Maybe we can get together and blow something."

"Hell yeah. Hit a nigga up and don't forget." I was planning on grilling the shit out of her whenever we hooked up.

As soon as I hung up the phone, I got at Goon to see where his head was at when it came to hitting a lick on Johan and his brothers. I was straight to the point, criminal to criminal. He'd cut into me at the right time about wanting in on a hustle he could make some money from. And I knew there'd be more than enough dough to split because Johan's brother's pipeline ran deeper than his. I wouldn't be surprised if them lion-fed muthafuckas had bricks of gold on 'em. I'd learned a lot about Javier and Jihad as their baby brother's security guard. I never thought I'd be about to run a play on their asses, but it was oh-so-muthafuckin' necessary at this point.

"All you gotta say is the word, and I'll be suited and strapped up." Gooney was ready to get it out of the mud.

"Doughhh." Mom Dukes came out of the house in a panic, her entire body shaking. Both me and Goon were caught off guard.

"Yeah, Ma? Are you good? What's wrong?" I reached for my clip.

"I called the hospital to make sure Leslie was up for company, and the nurse answered, saying I should come down to pray as soon as possible because something happened they weren't expecting to happen, and it's not looking good." She was stuttering over her words and grabbing her chest.

"Ma, be chill and take it easy before you make yourself sick. Goon, do me a solid and help her get in the car so I can get the crib locked down. I'ma shoot her to the hospital, then holla back at you about that situation."

"Fa'sho. I got you, Mom Dukes. Take it easy. Ms. Richton is going to be okay." Gooney was damn near carrying Mona to the car.

Right then and there, I decided to give that nigga an extra 10 percent cut off the lick we swiped from Johan and his ho-ass brothers. If I ended up having to sit down for that pistol, I was gonna get at Goon to look after Mom Dukes as well.

Reena

"I'm here to see Leslie Richton."

"I'm sorry, but her visitation is restricted to her family members only."

"Are you trying to be funny? You know I'm her daughter."

"Oh, I'm sorry. I didn't recognize you because I haven't seen you in a while," she snickered and handed me over a visitor's pass.

"Don't end up in one of these rooms trying to get your midday laugh off me, bitch." I snatched the pass out of her hand and dared her to call security on me. These hoes up here made me sick thinking they were better than me because they punched a clock, but they were gonna fuck around and get their lights punched out. I was already on edge even after smoking with Chanel in the car before dropping her off and then having another blunt on the way here, and I still hadn't gotten my nerves together.

Me and my moms started having it rough when she took my cousin in. I felt like I was forced to live in her shadow as a teenager. My mother went from focusing on me to attending all of her niece's pity parties with gifts. I might as well have run off with my aunt for how alone I felt. It seemed like my mother was putting someone else's child before her own, so I started acting out, being disrespectful, and doing the opposite of whatever she asked me to do.

After a year of me getting suspended every other month, running away for days at a time with this wannabe gangbanger I was calling my boyfriend, and stealing some of my mother's jewelry to flip at the pawn shop, she dropped me off at the hospital for a psychosocial evaluation and made me get therapy. It was then that I went from acting out to get her attention to hurting, embarrassing, and disgracing her every chance I got. If there was a way I could disrespect Leslie, I did it. If there was a way I could break her heart, I tried it. I was hurt, angry, and bitter.

The shit finally hit the fan and she stopped trying to fix me when she found out I was fucking my psychiatrist every Monday and Wednesday. Instead of getting the therapy I desperately needed, I was getting down with a grown man. Dr. Hawkins was actually the creep who turned me out. Instead of him exploring my mind and why I had so many mental issues, he was hypnotizing me and exploring my 17-year-old body. The psychology was more dangerous than the drugs, but by the time I realized I was being abused and manipulated, I was already strung out on the power sleeping with Dr. Hawkins gave me. Or at least what I thought it gave me.

Our all-women household was like a zoo until both my cousin and I graduated from high school. She left for college, and I left for the streets, scamming the community college out of their financial-aid money to get my own apartment and a few pieces of furniture. The rest of my pocket money and my bills got paid by Dr. Hawkins until his wife found out about his numerous infidelities and put a LoJack on his nut sac. The day he called to cut me off, I showed up at his house saying I was pregnant so he could pay me to go away. I got $5,000 to leave him alone, and another $500 to get rid of the baby that really didn't exist. I couldn't tell you how many stupid men I'd hustled since Dr. Hawkins.

I got off on the floor my mother was on and stopped at the nurse's station to get a mask and suit up. No one was allowed to go in my mother's room without either of the two on because they didn't want her getting any sicker than she already was from our outside germs.

"How's she recovering?" I walked in on the nurse checking my mom's vitals and went straight to her bedside. She looked skinnier and darker, and her face was sunken in. I couldn't understand why she looked worse than she did over a week ago when the doctor said she was doing better.

"She's stable now, but we did have a scare a few hours ago. Her body ended up having an allergic reaction to the new medication she was on, and we had to remove the IV. She went from bad to worse, but like I said, she's stable as of now."

Already pissed, I went from one hundred to a million within a second. "What do you mean, as of now? And an allergic reaction to the medicine? How in the hell did y'all not know what her body could handle and what it was allergic to when she's been a patient at this same mutha-fuckin' hospital for years? This sounds dumb as hell. Who dropped the ball and needs to lose their job? I mean, damn, all y'all have been doing is drawing her blood for this and sending her for X-rays for that. I smell a mutha-fuckin' medical malpractice lawsuit." I was going off on the nurse like we were on the block. I wanted answers. I wanted to know who was negligent. I wanted to know who was trying to take away my chance to get my rela-tionship with my mother right.

"Um, let me go get the doctor for you." She stumbled over her words, probably wishing she hadn't given me the update so casually. From the streets or not, I knew a li'l something-something about HIPAA and how the doctor was supposed to be the professional to give you information like that. Not only had I fucked a psychiatrist for years, but I'd also had my share of test results that only the STD-diagnosing doctor could deliver to me.

"That would be in your best interest. It's really not safe for you in here anymore," I snapped at her, then plopped my big booty down onto the visitor's chair.

I held it together as she gathered her cart and exited the room before laying my head into my mother's lap and crying. I knew I shouldn't have been threatening the nurse or the disrespectful bitch at the front desk even, but I was five seconds away from losing my sanity. I was acting strong. But that was an act. My mother was my everything, and I'd wasted a whole lot of time hating her when I should had been telling her where my hate came from. I'd managed to retain bits and pieces of some of the psychobabble Dr. Hawkins was running down on me while he was going down on me.

"I'm so sorry that I haven't been the best daughter to you, Ma. I swear to God that I am, even though it may not seem like it because I've been terrible to you for so many years. And I wish that I could take back everything wrong that I've done to you." I started choking on my apology, wishing I could've begged for her forgiveness years ago or even months ago when I had the chance. I was a fool for taking time for granted.

My heart was heavy with regret, heavy with the truth, and heavy with the worry that I'd have to bury my mom with my apology left weighing heavy on my soul. Even though she was the one battling lupus, I felt like my body was shutting down as well. I'd been blaming myself for her illness ever since I found out it could've been triggered by stress. I didn't know which virus was ripping her apart more: me and my toxic bullshit or the autoimmune disease itself.

Picking my mother's hand up, I rubbed it and wished she'd wiggle her fingers and let me know her mental was awake enough to hear me. Maybe, just maybe, if I knew she'd at least heard my apologies and knew I was present to check on her, I'd stop hitting the drugs as hard as I was. I couldn't keep my mouth off a bottle since the ambulance brought her in here a few weeks ago. Shit ain't never been this bad, and she'd never been admitted for so long. A pill to take my mind off everything would've felt so good coasting through my bloodstream now. That was the only thing I really missed about my relationship with Dr. Hawkins, besides the sex and money. I kept a bottle of Xanax.

"Oh, my goodness, Reena honey! Bless your heart." Ms. Hughes's comforting voice filled the room. "Get up and come here. It is going to be all right." She pulled me from my mother's lap into her arms.

As my mother's best friend for over forty years, Ms. Hughes saw me come into this world and had been watching me take leaps and bounds in the wrong direction heading out of it. She knew more about me than I knew about myself, even with all my disappearing acts.

I let the mask I'd been wearing fall off, exposing the vulnerable young girl I pushed down over ten years ago. "Are you sure, Ms. Hughes? Because it sure doesn't look or feel like it. Look at all those machines she's hooked up to. I can barely even hear myself talk for all the noise they're making." Now that the tears had started, I couldn't stop crying.

"Looks can be deceiving, but only God can have the final word, not these doctors. What you need to do is pray and pray over your prayers, not lose hope and stop fighting while your mama is still fighting. Those machines are helping her live, not living for her, which means we've still got work to do."

Wiping the tears from my face, I took a few deep breaths but didn't pick my head up from her chest. I'd been hugged by a whole lot of men who claimed to love me over the years, but not by anyone I knew had my best interest at heart like Ms. Hughes. She felt familiar, safe, and comforting, especially since she smelled the exact same way as when I was a kid. I used to play with her perfume instead of with her son whenever she'd babysit me.

"The nurse told me she had an allergic reaction to the new medicine, so they stopped it. Did they put her on something else? Or go back to the old meds? Please tell me what's going on!"

"Oh, honey, I'm so sorry." Ms. Hughes dropped her head, then lifted it up with tears running from her eyes. "The trial is over, and her insurance doesn't cover that medication under normal circumstances. They don't have an alternative treatment for Leslie right now but have promised to keep her comfortable while they work on researching one."

Her words temporarily paralyzed me and snatched the breath from my lungs. "B . . . but, if they don't give her any medicine, she'll . . ." I kept pausing and stuttering because the words were too hurtful to say. "And keeping her comfortable sounds like hosp . . ." I couldn't even finish the word. The shit was too finite.

Ms. Hughes pulled my head tighter to her chest in a loving way and rubbed my back. "Shhh! Don't breathe existence into that thought, sweetheart. Our words our powerful, so we mustn't speak anything but positivity over this situation and our lives as well." She lifted me off her bosom to stare into her eyes. "You have got to trust in the Lord, Reena."

I knew she was trying to tell me something without telling me something, but I was too full of anger and frustration to hear it.

"If praying really worked, Ms. Hughes, my mama wouldn't be sick in the first place." My words were cold because my heart was cracked. "The last time you all's beloved pastor was at the titty bar, he made sure to brag about his faithful servant not missing a Wednesday night Bible study or a Sunday worship service." My bitter voice filled the room. "The same muthafucka y'all got sending up y'all prayers be stuffing y'all hard-earned tithes and social security checks down my thong. That nigga is the biggest trick at the bar, and everyone knows it. In other words, you better put your sincere prayers in the hands of a real ordained pastor."

"Um, well . . ." She clutched her Bible bag, completely caught off guard by how verbally aggressive I was being.

I couldn't help being mad at God. I couldn't help telling Mona about the man in cloth she praised like he was really God. My mother knew the Bible so well that she had a hand in rewriting one of the new-age editions. I'd never seen her eat a bag of potato chips without praying over them first. If anyone deserved to be having their organs shutting down and their body attacking them, it was my selfish, sinning ass, not my mother.

"Um, well, what? Why aren't you preaching the gospel and reciting Bible verses now, Ms. Hughes?" I kept badgering her because she was available for me to attack. I was taking my hurt and anger out on anyone and all the wrong people.

"Because I'm too busy trying to pray the devil up out of you, girl." She finally pushed the words from her mouth, which sounded more like judgment than pity.

I dropped my chin to my chest, took a deep breath to ease the pressure that was building up within my gut, and bit down as hard as I could on my bottom lip all at the same time. I was trying my best not to give my mama's best friend the fade she was poking at me for.

"You know what? Instead of you wasting your time praying about me and my shortcomings, why don't you try sprinkling some of that damn holy talk around your own kid? The last thing I heard about that nigga was that he had his dick out and was trying to piss on Chanel on your front porch. What type of woman raises a heathen like that?"

"Um, excuse me, ladies, but I paged the doctor, and he's in surgery with another patient."

"How long is that going to take? And you better make sure you're not lying for him so he can stall for your fuckup." I rolled my eyes.

"No, ma'am, and you're free to check with the front desk to see if I'm telling the truth. The operation is scheduled to take two hours, but it could be longer or even less. I really can't give you a time."

"Yeah, all right. How fuckin' convenient." I waved her out of the room, then turned to Mona. "Make sure you call me as soon as the doctor is out of surgery. I'll be back up here to check on my mama."

"Quit banking on a lawsuit, and start putting that energy into praying that your mother's organs start perking back up." This old hag couldn't stop coming for me.

"If and when she dies, y'all can have a double funeral if you don't stop fucking with me, Mona. Like I said, call me when the doctor is out of surgery." I grabbed my purse and walked out of the room before I ended up being dragged out of the hospital in handcuffs by Detroit's finest. I didn't care how much I did to my mother and how in debt I was for forgiveness to her, Mona didn't have shit coming and had better stop coming for me.

"Oh, you're leaving already?" The front desk clerk had something smart to say when I dropped my badge into the basket and turned to walk out through the metal detector.

I'd peeped her staring at me with a smirk, but I wasn't going to give her the justification of saying anything, plus my mind was on my mother and everything the nurse told me. I wasn't even thinking about Ms. Hughes.

"Maannnn, damn! What time do you get off? I want to make sure I don't come back up here while you're on shift." I was banking on her to be dumb enough to tell me, and once she did, I walked out without saying another word but with a grin on my face. If I wanted to, I could be back up here at eleven tonight and follow her home. She didn't know how ruthless or heartless I was or money hungry. I'd get that trick for her iPhone 11 she kept flexing in my face, that Rolex watch on her wrist, and those Tiffany glasses on her face.

As soon as I got to my car, I dug my bag of nose candy from the glove compartment and scooped enough out to feed both of my nostrils. I knew the powder was only going to intensify my anger and rage, but I didn't care about nothing but getting high to numb the pain I was feeling. I couldn't wait to get to work and in my zone. Whenever I was in the club, I was in control, and nothing outside of those walls existed.

Chapter Nine

Chanel

Today had been crazy as hell. I was spending the rest of my evening blowing on some Mary Jane, sipping on some wine, and cleaning up, going back and forth with whether I should call Mama Hughes and apologize. Although her son made me go crazy, I felt bad for cursing and acting a fool in front of her. I wouldn't be able to forgive myself if she had a stress-related heart attack or a stroke while trying to break me and Dough up from fighting. You could see the heartbreak through the wrinkles on her face when he and I were spitting venom at one another.

To break up the silence and perk up my mood, I turned some music on and found my nail polishes so I could hook my nails and toes up real quick, as well as my beauty kit so I could arch my brows and put on some lashes. I wasn't sure if Reena still planned on going into work tonight, but I wanted to be ready just in case she called.

We didn't stay at the beauty bar after Reena got an emergency call for her to get to the hospital about her mother. I'd offered to go with her for support, but she was real private with her emotions about Ms. Richton, and I wasn't one to push.

Halfway through cleaning the dirt from underneath my toenails and cutting them down, the alarm on my phone started going off. Every limb on my body froze because it was a reminder of the video visitation with Vontez in thirty minutes. Dough would've stomped my computer to pieces if he knew I was communicating over the webcam with him at least once a week.

It only took me a few minutes of going back and forth with myself about how Dough would feel before I started getting dressed for the video visit. I didn't want Vontez mad at me, no matter what story I tried selling the world. Before Reena, Dough, and even my kids, it was me and him against the world.

I decided on a cute burgundy cropped-top jogging suit that was lightweight and clung to my curves. I was able to show some sexiness without being too risqué. There was more leniency for what we could wear during a phone visit than an in-person one, but I still had to walk a fine line. I spent the remaining few minutes making sure my concealer was doing its job. I still had bags underneath my eyes from crying about my and Dough's argument.

My computer stayed in ready mode, so I was just one click away from the site we used to communicate on as soon as I opened the laptop. I was happy as hell Dough upgraded me to a computer with a seventeen-inch screen when his plug got a Best Buy shipment in. The larger Von's picture was, the closer I felt to him.

I didn't feel all that giddy about being up close and personal with Vontez once I saw how ripped his mug was though. I was sure I would've caught a backhand had we been in each other's presence, guard around or not.

"I'm sorry about earlier, and as soon as I get a few extra dollars, I'm going to get another phone so you can get in touch with me," I said, trying to smooth him over.

"Save all that sorry shit, Chanel. That nigga called a spade a spade, and I'm going to take that shit to heart and accept it. You're his girl, cool. Congratulations. But you're still my bitch. I don't care what you two have got going on out there. Me and you have our own thang cracking that you better not let him get in the middle of," he threatened me.

"But, Vontez—"

"Nah, shorty. We ain't fuckin', so don't call my name out. You already know what it is and how I'm feeling behind what happened earlier. That coward-ass mutha-fucka don't know me, and I'm tired of him stroking his ego off me." His nose flared, a sign that he was getting angry and about to explode. I was actually happy he wasn't in a position to put his hands on me because Von would've beaten my ass.

"Bae, calm down. Me and him aren't back together. He only exploded because he doesn't want me getting into trouble until I get li'l man back. I swear he's not trying to step on your toes." I didn't want Dough and Vontez having beef. At the end of the day, I had a child by each of them I'd eventually have back. And for Von's sake, I didn't want him upset with me or getting into a fight with another inmate. The last time he and I got into it over me dropping the ball on something he needed done, he ended up cracking a nigga's nose wide open. The no-snitch policy was what kept him out of the hole.

"Fuck that nigga and his son," he growled. "I popped that pussy out of place first, and you weren't supposed to be out there giving it away, especially making kids with a clown. You were supposed to be my bitch. You're lucky I didn't send yo' disloyal ass to the chop shop with that bigheaded bastard. Had you not agreed to do what you did for a nigga, I wouldn't even be dealing with yo' ass now."

And with that outburst, I stopped giving two shits if Vontez made it through the day without having to guard himself from getting shanked. I wasn't about to keep letting him act like my baby boy wasn't a living and breathing person.

"Whoa, you just dropped your hand like a rookie! I already knew you had your dick in your ass about me moving on, but I had no idea your heart was this heavy, boo. You need to be thanking me for busting it open for Dough and helping him have a li'l man to carry on his name, nigga." I was purposely gunning to piss him off. I was saying the most creep-foul shit I could think of to have him snapping on everyone around him and end back up in the hole. I was feeling spiteful, bitter, and hurt.

"Oh, for real? You out here signing checks and cashing 'em." He called my bluff, wanting to see if I'd start back-pedaling behind the bass of his voice.

"You're the one who took it there first." I refused to back down.

"A'ight then, li'l gangsta. Let's see where else I can take it. I'll be in touch." He abruptly disconnected the video visit, leaving me with an attitude and, more importantly, a wandering mind.

"Oh, my God, he gets on my last nerrrrrve!" I wished I had never decided to take the video visit in the first place. Between him and Dough acting like they were two emotional bitches on the pad, I now fully understood how niggas felt when they had a gang of babies by a bunch of different women yapping in their face about this, that, and muthafuckin' nothing! The last thing Vontez needed to be mad about was me doing my thang. Since the last day he was free as a bird he was doing his thang.

Vontez left home on a lie that he was about to meet up with his boys for basketball, but he slipped up the highway to the D. Vontez was gone for hours, but I wasn't blowing him up or nothing and hadn't even thought about him being on no sneak shit because I was happily pregnant with a ring on my finger behind a marriage proposal. Vontez had me fooled, but Reena made sure I was schooled.

"Ya baby daddy is in my driveway with some funny-looking bitch. Who is she, and why ain't you with the nigga? I walked outside thinking we were about to go shopping for my godbaby."

"Well, damn! You know a lot more than I do, because I didn't even know that scurvy bastard was outside of the city, let alone in the D! Are they still there? How does the girl look? Send me a picture. I'm about to call and blow this nigga's cover, so bye." I'd blurted out a bunch of questions but didn't give her a second to answer.

I didn't care if Reena cared that I was throwing her underneath the bus. I called Vontez's phone back-to-back until he answered. I couldn't believe he'd lied his ass up the highway to Detroit without me and was ultimately cheating on me. I got madder each time he sent my call to voicemail, knowing exactly how scummy his ass got down with whoever he was with on the ride up there. Although I was nauseated from carrying our baby, I hopped out of the bed and went straight for the kitchen for a butcher knife. Vontez didn't answer my call until I sent him a video of me cutting up all of his jeans, shirts, and sneakers. I was on a roll and not close to done.

"Chanel, what the fuck?" Vontez yelled into the phone, panting like a damn dog.

"Don't 'what the fuck' me, nigga. You better be glad I don't have a car, 'cause if I did, I'd meet you at a rest stop and give it to you and that bitch." I was fuming while slicing more of his sneakers up because I couldn't do shit else.

"Oh, hell to the naw, ho! I know they say carrying babies and shit makes you dumb, but don't get fucked up behind that mouth of yours. I advise you to sit down

somewhere and continue waiting on this good dick to get back home." Ol' girl was going in on me from the background.

After I finished catching my breath from laughing erratically, I got to going, letting homegirl know that I was the wrong type of bitch to test and that I'd have her bodied by the time she crossed over into the state of Ohio. I wasn't playing either.

I started pulling a pair of leggings up over my juicy thighs so I could see if my neighbor would let me borrow her car. I was never the type to be shaken, nervous, or afraid to buck with a bitch, and this one, I wanted her head because she was impeding on my home. Vontez was more than my boyfriend. He was my baby's dad. I was intending on wrecking her before she wrecked my home.

"Ay, shut the fuck up," I heard Vontez yelling at ol' girl.

"Ah, naw, muthafucka! I'ma lay my hands on yo' dirty-dick-having ass too. You better hope I don't even think I'm itching around my coochie, nigga, or it's gonna be snip-snip time around this bitch! You've got me twisted, Vontez. Straight twisted. Oh, my God! On my unborn seed, I'ma serve it to you raw when you pull up. And bring that bitch with you. Please, please, please, bring her with you. I'm begging you to." I was an emotional mess, stumbling over my words and repeating myself, madder than I'd ever been.

My li'l baby was a rider and wasn't even out of the womb. He or she (being that I didn't know the sex of Vonesha at the time) *was going on a helluva roll-er-coaster ride with Mommy. I actually felt the blood in my body surging throughout it, making the organ I needed for life feel like it was about to jump straight out of my chest.*

"*Bae, chill! You already know this ho don't mean nothing. She wasn't nothing but a last-minute tagalong 'cause you ain't feel good this morning. Quit with all this muthafuckin' rah-rah bullshit before something happen to my baby and I really fuck you up,*" Vontez said, trying to calm me down.

I got ready to curse Vontez out. I was seconds away from telling him I wasn't buying his bullshit when he cut me off. I wondered why ol' girl had gotten so quiet. The whole explosion between us had leveled.

"*Ain't this some shit! Fuckin' arguing with yo' ass got me flicked.*"

"*What? Oh, my—*"

Click.

The phone went dead.

I didn't know how many times I called Von's phone back before it stopped ringing and started going straight to voicemail. By the time I heard his voice, he was locked up and waiting for the judge to determine his future. There was so much weight hidden all over that car that ol' girl had to sit down too. Had his eyes and attention been focused on the road instead of the argument with me, there was a chance Vontez wouldn't have gotten flicked. But more importantly, had he not been doing his thang with that shorty he was so pressed to spend time with, there wouldn't have been a reason for me to be popping off in the first place.

My cell phone snatched me from my thoughts. It was Reena calling.

"What's the word, boo? Are you good?" I answered in an upbeat mood, deciding not to tell her about the video visit or argument with Vontez. I already had enough on my mind and didn't need her opinions swirling around, too.

"Naw, not really. I went to the hospital to check on my mom, and shit took a turn for the worse. I need to get to the club sooner rather than later so I can get my mind off everything. Are you still riding out with me?"

"Of course you can swoop me up, boo-boo. If you're rocking, I'm rolling." My loyalty lay with Reena-Ree because she'd done nothing but have my back since we'd met and gotten cool. "And it goes without saying that my prayers are with your mom. I'll even go with you to visit her the next time you go to the hospital if you want me to." Supporting Reena and her mom needed to be higher on my priority list.

"I'm going to hold you to that tomorrow, sis. But tonight, just hang with me until the wheels fall off and help keep my mind off my mom."

"Say no more. What time will you be here?"

"About ten thirty. I've got a set at midnight."

"Okay, I'll be ready."

Chapter Ten

Dough

Lu's recommendation was on point. Mr. Malek had plaques lining his wall of all his degrees and accolades, even of his affiliation with well-known black organizations. Instead of procrastinating and letting time catch up to me, I was trying to get my affairs in order. And since Johan still wasn't answering my calls, I knew he wasn't going to save my black ass from the time the law was threatening me with. Thankfully, after dropping Lu's name as who referred me, his secretary pushed another one of his appointments out so I could see him immediately. After dropping my moms off to see about her friend, I'd shot to the crib and changed into a pair of slacks and a polo-style shirt. I wasn't trying to show up handling business as the thug I was.

I sat, kinda fidgeting in front of him, as he reviewed the particulars of my case. I didn't even know lawyers were able to pull the DPD records, but bro knew about every run-in I had with the police back to my juvie days. I already knew he was about to tax the hell out of me, but I wasn't worried about the ticket not one bit. Johan was gonna foot every dollar of it whether he wanted to or not.

"No time in jail is going to cost you, my brother." He looked over the rim of his glasses, then slid back in his chair and folded his leg like we were about to kick some real spit. "They want you to be an informant, but without your cooperation, they are going to sit you down for the gun and the drugs you had on you. That's firm because you've got a record. However, I can get this case thrown out as well as a sweet deal for you if you hire me." He was strategic to keep his winning game plan to himself, but he also grabbed my full attention.

"My freedom is worth it, sir. What's the ticket looking like?" I was ready to cooperate.

He penned the number down, then slid it across the table. "Half up front, twenty-five percent twenty-four hours before the case, and then the final balance before we walk into the courtroom. Motions are extra, new evidence I have to cross-examine later is extra, so make sure you're straightforward with me right now within this meeting." I read his note of $8,000 while listening to his terms.

"With this amount of money, I'on want even probation. I want this case tossed to the wind and a clean slate to fuck up all over again." The thug slipped out of me.

He casually laughed, then took his glasses off, commanding my attention with his stare. "I do not take cases I cannot win, Mr. Hughes. Your freedom is on the line, yes, but so is my reputation. And I'm overly protective when it comes to my career. I won't be fucking that slate up for nothing." He was confident, firm, and straightforward, and he looked me dead in the eyes, all qualities I wanted in an attorney representing me. I couldn't stand behind a man resting my freedom on his shoulders if he was too weak to carry it.

"G'on and draw up the contract then, boss. You've got yourself a client." I laid his retainer fee on his desk, then leaned back in my chair, way more relaxed than I was initially.

For the next hour, he went over his plan of execution, then damn near interrogated me like the cops to know what he was up against. And though I wasn't a snitch, I didn't hold back the info regarding Johan and the dispensary. It was imperative that he separate me from the Fed charges they were trying to tie me to. I had to look out for me and mine since that clown Johan still hadn't hit me back.

"Stay away from that dispensary and keep a low profile. No contact with the police is the route I need you to travel. If you do get caught up with them, the only thing you need to say, over and over again if need be, is that you need your one phone call to contact your attorney. You'll have my direct cell. The case we're building can give you leverage against the force because I'm gunning for harassment. If you are to get caught, be clean as a whistle. I can't help you if you double up on cases before this one is settled. Am I making myself clear?"

"Crystal." My mouth said it, but my mind was already on the lick I was 'bout to put in motion.

My cell rang, and it was my OG. "My bad, but I need a sec. This is my moms." I picked up.

"Doughboy baby, I need you to bring me down an overnight bag with some food and snacks to keep me for overnight. I'm going to stay down here at the hospital."

"Aww, Ma. You tripping. I can come get you, then take you back in the morning. You don't need to be sleeping down there in all them germs and on a raggedy cot. I know you love your friend, but you have your own health issues." I knew it was hurting her feelings to see her best friend sick and in a coma, but she didn't need to get sick in the process of trying to support her.

"Don't you dare tell me what to do or what I'm gonna do, boy. I'll still go upside your head. I don't know what's gotten into you or Reena, but y'all both done forgot how I got down in my heyday. Don't test me because I'm saved. All that means is God is gonna forgive me even quicker because I'm His child and He knows my heart."

"Whoa, Ma. Chill. You got it." I wasn't about to start getting preached to, but I was a little curious what happened with her and Reena. I made a mental note to ask about it later. "I'll swing down there in about an hour, Ma. But I'll call you at the house to make sure I get everything you need."

"All right, son. Now you're talking like you've got some sense. I'll talk to you in a few." She hung up, and though I didn't agree with her spending the night at the hospital, Mona wasn't about to keep chewing my head off. I didn't know what my no-good-ass father was like, but my headstrong personality most definitely came from her.

"It's admirable that you look after your mother the way you do," Mr. Malek commented on my conversation, and then we finished going over some additional key points before he finally called the consultation.

"Thanks for all your help, advice, and taking my case. My fate now rests in your hands."

"No, it's up to both of us. You do your part, and I'll make sure to hit the home run."

"I got it. Fa'sho. And I'll be in touch with your next payment." We shook hands.

"That's what I want to hear. Take care, Mr. Hughes."

I walked out of his office and had Luke on the line before I finished getting to the car. "Yo, your referral is the truth. As well as your advice. Is it cool for me to fall through in a few? I wanna continue our conversation from earlier."

"Fa'sho, I'm here all night. Me and my homeboy on pause right now. And I'm glad that connect worked out for you. I told you he was a beast. But hit me up when you pull up. We're with whatever." We disconnected the line, and I rushed back to the hood to get Mona's overnight bag and swoop Gooney.

It was time to plan the ultimate hustle move.

Vontez

"Yo, bro, you good?"

I sat on my bunk and tucked my head in my lap, rocking back and forth with murder on my mind. I couldn't wait to get out of this muthafucka and start setting shit off. My baby mom and her li'l Detroit flunky had me twisted. I wasn't about to sit on my anger neither. I was itching to have one of my homies drive up to the D and touch some shit. And I ain't give a fuck who got caught in the crossfire. It could be his saint-singing mama for all I cared since his titty-fed ass wanted to talk big. Jail or not, my gangster was still in rare form.

"Yeah. I'm solid, G." I was careful with what information I gave up.

In the years I'd been incarcerated, I'd witnessed more than a handful of these same "aww, are you good, bro?" bunkmates put their counselors or guards hip to the shit that was going down among the prisoners, getting time knocked off their sentences and more added to the culprits'. Feelings? Naw, I kept every single tingle of emotion close to my core and let my heartbeat keep me living.

I'd been taking it easy on Chanel having another nigga cater to her womanly needs or whatever, but it was clear he didn't understand the terms of our relationship. I thought he knew I was the one pulling strings wit' that ass since I was the real reason that li'l bastard he knocked her up with came slippin' up outta her too fast.

Not only had she pierced her placenta bag or whatever the fuck it's called stuffing some product up her snatch for me, but one of these correction officers she was fuckin' on gave her an STD the day she went into labor, and it ran right up in her system. Had she told me his dirty-dick-dipping ass was giving her a hard time, I would've shut all that nonsense down before he'd gotten the chance to violate. Guard or fellow inmate, I demanded respect, and that same level of respect had to be doubled for my girl even if she did wanna be out here playing like she was someone else's lady.

The gangster in me wouldn't let that CO walk another block, rape another inmate's girl, or send another one of us to solitary to help the warden pad our already-extensive sentences. It angered me that he had one-upped me, been in the guts of my bitch, and was walking around here smirking like he'd do it again without consequences. And I hated cocky muthafuckas who lacked spunk. Ol' boy wasn't shit without his badge or outside of these walls, and the jail was full of guards just like him. But now he was pushing up grass. I sliced his dick straight off his body without thinking twice or blinking from the blood spatter, then left him dangling from the pipes in the storage closet. I'd kill any man walking this green earth behind Chanel and my baby girl Tay-Tay. They were my family. They were all I had.

And no matter how my baby moms was trying to play it, I knew she was still strung out for my thuggish ass way more than she was for dog. I was spinning like a muthafucka off my feelings but was gonna keep it chill until I walked these next few weeks down. I hadn't told a soul but my unc I was coming home 'cause nobody needed to prepare for the house visits I was lining up to make.

Dough

It was just a little bit shy of one in the morning and Gooney, Luke, his boy Scales, and I rode in a black Cherokee rental toward Johan's West Bloomfield home. There was a full moon that cast a weird glow beaming from the sky.

And although most of the residents of the upper-middle-class block were asleep, that was far from the case at Johan's house. There were cars lined up the suburban block and in the driveway. I was sure that, on a normal night, nothing could be heard but crickets, but tonight's blasting music was just the distraction we needed to be in and out without being noticed. This was like an all-or-nothing mission for me. If shit went south and I was caught and apprehended, I'd lose my case plus the new one automatically. With the thought of possible witnesses, I went from wanting to rob everybody at this party to wanting complete bloodshed.

It had already been decided who would be the lead through the gated doorway. Lu was the smoothest of us all. He was and always had been trained to go. He was the only one of us four with no woman or kids to worry about returning home to. Scales rose up from the passenger seat, placing one of his dark Timberland boots onto the pavement, ready to put in that work.

"Okay, so we all know our positions, correct? Ain't no getting inside and fucking up the game plan, correct?"

"We ain't gotta keep spinning what we doing. We got it," Goon chimed in, overly ready to get to the mission. He was the hothead of the group, but I hoped that didn't mean he was about to get in here and drop the ball.

"Nigga, slow your damn roll before you fuck around and throw us all off our square," Lu firmly ordered before putting one up top and placing his pistol in the left side of his waistband.

The rest of us followed his lead and did the same with our firearms. Dressed in all black for the occasion, zero fucks were given. It was game time. As we moved toward the driveway, face masks now fully secured, Lu motioned for us to fall to each side of the huge oak front door as planned. Even though the dark emerald green drapes that hung from the windows shielded a view of what was actually taking place behind them, I could hear the sound of laughter and those having a great night. In a matter of mere seconds, all of their carefree smiles would be no more.

No more high-stakes gambling. No more women of the night offering up their bodies for cash. No more free-flowing uncut drugs, and the top-shelf spirits, drink as much as you like bar was about to cease operations. What visitors thought would be the surefire night of their lives would be one for the history books of mayhem. It was said that crime didn't pay. But tonight, we was 'bout to get paid.

I tugged down some on my face mask, and then tapped on the door using a sequence of knocks. A few seconds after the knocks, we heard the sound of the lock being clicked and watched anxiously as the doorknob turned. Without an ounce of hesitation, when the door was slightly opened, chaos ensued. Scales used great force, shoving it all the way back and causing Paris to stumble backward, and then he grabbed her neck and rammed her against the wall. I already knew she wanted to pop off because that wasn't part of the plan.

"Fuck that bitch." I got him up off her, not wanting to air her cover.

All three of us were just plotting everything out in Lu's living room, down to her sketching out a layout of Johan's crib so we'd be smooth with the invasion, but that nigga needed to stay in line for the rest of this lick or else. Splitting the come-up four ways didn't sound as bad, 'cause P definitely had a full cut coming.

She was the key to the house and even gave me the heads-up where Johan and his brothers were partying in particular. The party was spread throughout the entire house, with them in the backyard pool. It was icing on the cake when she revealed that Johan made sure each visitor was thoroughly searched for guns and phones, with neither being allowed inside. He damn near had muthafuckas signing NDAs, which made me know for a fact his freaky ass was doing some unimaginable things off in his crib.

Guns drawn, the crew rushed in. Immediately, Goon got on his wild shit. He made an example of some random guy, slamming the side of his gun directly down on the terrified guy's forehead. With that huge open gash and blood pouring out, the rest of the occupants knew we meant business by his brazen move.

"The only way you're going to stay living is if you keep this music muthafuckin' blasting, do you understand?" I put my heater on the dome of the DJ's head. And the smart guy turned the volume up louder. "Good boy."

"Okay, okay. Let's make this bullshit fucking easy. All of y'all get up and stand against that wall. Raise your arms above y'all's heads and lock damn hands," Scales demanded with fire in his eyes. "And hurry the fuck up! This ain't no damn game!" Scales was holding court, and then he and Goon went around the gaudy room, stuffing the two medium-size duffle bags they'd brought with money. And though we were only there for cash money, Goon swiped off the table coke and pills, making me look at that nigga sideways. I didn't want to body my boy right here and now, but I made a mental note to double back around to it.

Me and Lu rushed to the pool area with guns blazing, and instead of robbing Johan and his brothers, I was murdering them. "It's an invasion, you sand bitches!" we announced, then sent gunfire into the air.

He, his brothers, and a few bad bitches were all squirting out blood by the time we were done. We didn't care about sparing lives. It was the dead presidents we were feenin' for. I went straight for Jihad, stripping him down to his drawers 'cause I knew he kept bands all over his body. Then Lu and I did the same with his brothers and other men because we figured they all rolled the same. These muthafuckas were paid like kings but paying fifteen petty dollars an hour. I couldn't help but haul off and kick the shit out of Jihad before I ran off.

Within just under ten minutes, which seemed more like ten hours to the victims, the crew and I were out the door, rushing back to the Jeep. As we exited the affluent community, our adrenalin was at an all-time high because our duffle bags were overflowing. I couldn't wait to pay Mr. Malek off to secure my freedom, then boss up on my whole life. *After this case is closed, Chanel should have her son back in her custody, and then I'm gonna pay that bitch to bounce so I can raise my son solo-solo. Then I'm going to move us all out of the hood to a house very similar to the one I just created bloodshed in.* I was daydreaming about a whole new life all the way back to the chop shop, where the rental was broken down to melted metal. We had enough money to pay ol' girl who'd put the rental in her name to cash the car out with the rental company.

"A'ight, y'all good with what we snagged or y'all trying to go count this shit up and divvy it up equally?" I asked.

"Shitttt, I'm square as hell with this right here." Lu clutched his bag, followed by Scales.

"I'm not greedy or a fool. It's been good hustling with you fellas." Goon dapped everybody, and then we all broke off.

Finally pulling my phone from my pocket, I saw that both Chanel and my moms had been blowing me up back-to-back. Before I could even call either one back, Chanel came through screaming and crying.

"Oh, my God, Dough! I'm glad you answered me. Get down to the hospital now. Mama had a heart attack."

Super Nova

by

Blacc Topp

Part One

Chapter One

For the third time in the past week, Nova's car stalled on her. It hissed and sputtered, smoke billowing from somewhere underneath the hood of the car. Then it started chugging, goosing itself forward until it stopped altogether. "Shit!" Nova cursed. She put the car in park and shouldered her way out the door. *I gotta get this shit fixed,* she thought, rubbing her shoulder. She walked around the car with her hands on her ample hips, staring at the vehicle as if it might magically start. To make matters worse, she was right across the street from the auto shop that she was trying to make it to in the first place. "Okay, breathe, Nova, it's not the end of the world." She breathed in through her nose and out through her mouth, willing herself to calm down. "Having a panic attack now isn't going to do you any good. Fix the car, that's step one. Everything else will fall into place," she said. Even if she didn't believe it, she had to at least say it, right?

"Move that piece of shit out of the road, lady. Some of us have shit to do!" a pudgy white man screamed. His fat, round face with its rosy cheeks and snow white hair made him look like Santa. Not the jolly old Saint Nick most were used to, but an angry, deranged anti-Santa. His pudgy pink hands, with their sausage-like nubs, gripped the steering wheel, spittle flying from his lips as he hurled hateful insults in Nova's direction.

Probably just found out his wife has been cheating on him with her yoga instructor. Nova took a deep breath

and smiled before she extended both of her middle
fingers and mouthed, "Fuck you, Santa," to the fat man.
"You act like I want to be out here! How about being a
gentleman and try helping a lady instead of adding to her
stress? Go around if you're in a hurry. I'm sure the light
at Krispy Kreme will still be on when you get there, dang,"
Nova said as she got into the driver's seat.

She said a prayer. "Please, God, please," she chanted
repeatedly, each time turning the ignition key. On the
fourth try, the car revved to life, and she hurriedly threw
it into drive. It hesitated for a second but didn't stall, so
Nova gave it gas. It limped across the light and into an
open service bay. As soon as she touched the brake, the
engine stalled again.

"I owe you one, Jesus." She blew a kiss toward heaven.
She got out and surveyed her work. She had coasted into
the bay with precision. She was having a proud moment
when her thoughts were interrupted by a short and
stocky man, who, she guessed by his attire, must have
been the mechanic. He looked like God had stuffed as
much muscular man as He could into the mechanic's
short, squat frame. His coveralls were greasy, as was the
towel that he used to wipe his hands.

"Can I help you with something, little lady?"

Little? "Um, yeah, my car has been making these funny
sputtering sounds. Like, if I'm sitting at a red light, it'll
just jump and sputter, and when the light turns green
and I give it some gas, it wants to die on me."

He regarded her, letting his eyes wander over her curvaceous frame. The dark blue scrubs clung to her ample
ass, and her shirt hugged her ripe breasts. He licked his
lips and smiled. "Okay, it's going to be a minute before I
get to it. I'm working on one now, but I'm almost done.
Gimme a half hour and I'll hook it up to the diagnostic
computer."

"Okay, do you have a waiting area with vending machines or something?" Nova asked, looking around the drab shop. The owner was most definitely not into aesthetics. Open toolboxes revealed oily tools that Nova was sure couldn't be safe. In the bay next to where she had parked, a new car was suspended on a hydraulic jack. It looked more like they were stripping the car rather than fixing it.

"Yeah, let me show you." He beckoned for her to follow him.

They snaked their way through an obstacle course of car tires, tools, and shop vacs. Nova walked on her tiptoes, like that would somehow keep her from stepping in the oil and grime that caked the shop's floors. When they reached their destination, the waiting room was nothing more than three chairs set along the wall adjacent to an elderly Spanish woman, filing her nails behind a puke green desk. A small handheld radio crackled with static during whatever Mexican ballad she was singing along to.

"Have a seat here and I will get back to you shortly. There's coffee on the file cabinet and some doughnuts here if you want them," he said, shooing a fly trying to alight on the pastries.

"Thank you, Anthony," Nova said, making a mental note to not touch the doughnuts.

He looked shocked that she knew his name. He studied her face as if trying to recognize her and where he might know her from.

She didn't speak, but rather pointed to her own chest, forcing him to look down and notice that his own name tag was pinned to his shirt. Embarrassed, he looked up at Nova and quickly averted his eyes. There was something about the intensity of her stare that made him uneasy. He smiled and retreated through the door.

Nova pulled out her phone and went to her messages. Chino still hadn't called. He always dodged her calls and texts when he knew that he'd fucked up. As far as Nova was concerned, he didn't have to call or text. She was over it. Over the lies, over the cheating, over it all. If she wasn't dealing with some thirsty-ass female calling her phone, trying to tell her about her man, then she was dealing with another one of Chino's get-rich-quick schemes. The latest just might cost Nova her job.

She didn't deserve half the shit that she let Chino get away with, but she was in love with a memory. They had been together off and on since she was 13, and the allure of familiarity kept her coming back for more. She was tired of starting over, going from relationship to relationship. She always overlooked the red flags, hoping that she could fix whatever imperfection the man she was dating had. This time was different though. She wouldn't fall for his empty promises or his crocodile tears. On too many occasions Chino had made Nova feel like she was crazy for even assuming that he might have cheated on her. He never really confirmed or denied it, choosing instead to layer his deceit with conjecture, smooth words, and good sex. She hated the way he made her feel, like one minute she was the luckiest girl alive to have a good-looking man who was good in bed, and the next sinking so low into depression that a tow truck couldn't pull her out. She had done things for Chino that made her feel stupid, like stealing OxyContin and fentanyl from the hospital because Chino said he had some white boys from Wichita who would buy whatever he came up with. Turned out the white boys with all the money were meth heads who beat Chino out of the whole stash.

The bright red nail polish was a stark contrast to the dull powder blue muumuu that the old woman wore. She stared at Nova while she blew on her freshly painted nails. Shorty appeared, bringing both women's attention to him, and he smiled at Nova, who in turn gave the lady a look that said, "Don't be mad at me because he smiled at me and not you."

"Let me show you something." He ushered her to her car and sat inside. "This computer is hardly ever wrong, and from the looks of it, I'd say this engine is about shot. I can . . ."

Nova tuned him out as soon as he said that the engine was shot. All she needed was another expense on top of all the other bullshit that she had going on. "How much is it gonna take to fix it?" she asked.

"Normally for a job this size, you're looking at about two grand. Give or take, of course."

"Two grand? I only paid a thousand for this piece of shit, ugghhhh. Do I have to pay it all at once?" she asked, trying to regain her composure.

"I can take five hundred now, and we can work out a payment plan for the rest."

"Be honest with me, is it even worth fixing?"

He shrugged.

The last thing she wanted to do was have to cough up $500. If she did that, she would have to short her aunt Tootie, and that was a conversation that she didn't want to have. Truth be told, her aunt Tootie should be willing to give her a break considering it was her boyfriend Roosevelt who sold her the hooptie anyway.

"Can you give me a few days to come up with the money?"

"Yeah, I can do that, but just so you know, I have a storage fee, thirty dollars a day, until you come up with the five."

Nova agreed and was led back to the office/waiting room and made to stand before the old lady as if she might pass judgment on her at any second. Shorty rattled off something in Spanish, and the old lady smiled in Nova's direction. "Come, *mija,* sign *por favor.*"

Chapter Two

Nova sat at the back of the city bus, watching the raindrops dance across the slickened asphalt. As soon as she'd left the mechanic and made it halfway across the busy intersection, the sky opened, so by the time she made it to the bus stop she was drenched and done. Her only solace was that the bus was pulling up when she made it to the stop. There was an assortment of characters on the bus: a few maids, a cholo who chose to stand even though there were seats available, a mother struggling to keep her toddler still, and a brother who looked like he had just gotten out of prison minutes ago. His scowl was permanent, and badly healed cuts zigzagged across his ashy face. His eyes were slits of pure hatred, and when they locked eyes, Nova felt her heart drop to her stomach.

"Find you something else to focus on, bitch. I ain't in no mu'fuckin' zoo."

He could have very well been in the primate cages with his low, sloping brow and brutish muscles. They all looked like extras from some type of urban-decay film where they show you what life is going to be after adulthood. Most of them looked tired and worn out, workers who had been overworked and overlooked.

Just in front of her she heard the fladadap of butt cheeks cutting wind with no shame. He or she hadn't even attempted to ease it out. They had gone full duck mode. The putrid bomb exploded in Nova's nostrils, and she wretched.

"Come on, mane," someone shouted.

"Gooooodddamn!" yelled another.

A bell chimed, and the bus began to slow down, brakes creaking, air brakes hissing, announcing its intention. "You need to hurry up and get yo' stankin' ass off the bus," a man said. He removed his beanie cap to cover his nose.

The culprit only smiled as he made his way to the back exit. The bus came to a stop, and before he stepped from the bus, he paused and looked back as if he might say something. It wasn't until he had exited the bus and it began to roll that everyone realized that he'd let out a silent but deadly and left the rest of the passengers to deal with the aftermath.

"Nasty ass," Nova said as she pulled her shirt up over the bridge of her nose. Not only was she wet, but she had already had to endure the smell of warm piss emanating from somewhere near where she sat. Now she had to deal with smelling gas that had obviously passed a turd on the way out. She hated public transportation, but she didn't have a choice. If she called her aunt Tootie, she would have to hear her mouth all the way home. If she called Roosevelt, she would still have to hear it from him, too, but there would be the bonus of gas money for his rag-gedy-ass gas-guzzling piece-of-shit car.

She stared out the window, looking for something familiar. They were passing Good Luck Burger on Second Avenue, which meant she only had a few more stops before they reached her stop. It was no longer raining, so Nova pressed the stop bell. It would be a nice walk, and with the smell still lingering in the air, a walk didn't sound half bad.

The bus hissed to a stop, and Nova got off. She had gotten off at the corner of Scyene and Second Avenue and was walking across the parking lot when she saw a familiar face. He was leaning against a black-on-black

Range Rover, smoking a Black & Mild cigar. "What's up, baby girl?"

"Uncle Tedddddyyyy!" she said excitedly, running to him and throwing her arms around his neck.

"Been a long time, huh?" Teddy said, not really asking a question.

"Too long! Last time I saw you was when my daddy got out of Coffield."

"Speaking of your old man, when is he supposed to get out again?" Teddy asked.

"If everything goes well, he should be out by the fall."

"That's like four more months, right?"

"Yep, something like that. Can I ask you something, Uncle Teddy?" Nova said.

"You can ask me whatever you want."

"If you and my daddy are supposed to be like brothers, why don't you ever come around?"

"Oh, you want me to come around more?" Teddy asked.

"I mean . . ." Nova said, shifting nervously from one foot to the other.

"You don't need old Teddy around. I'd just cramp your style, plus I'd be running all of them little niggas away." Teddy grinned. He pursed his lips when he smiled, exposing his two front teeth, making him look like a sneaky, little beady-eyed rat.

"Boys aren't thinking about me, and I'm not thinking about them."

"Shiiiitttttt," Teddy said, rubbing his hands together as if he had just come up with a master plan. "If they not thinking about you as fine as you are, they must be blind or gay."

"I don't know about all that now. I'm just saying I need to get my shit together, and these little lame-ass boys are just a distraction."

"Maybe you need to stay away from these boys and get you a real man." Teddy's voice had become deeper, more serious.

Nova was at a loss. Was this man she affectionately called Uncle Teddy hitting on her? "And I suppose you're that man, huh, Uncle Teddy?" she said, emphasizing the word "uncle."

"I'm just saying, we family, right? If I can help, I will help," Teddy said, pulling her closer to him but not invading her space.

"I can't take any money from you."

"Money ain't shit to stepper, baby. What you need I might have," Teddy said, leering down at Nova.

She pulled away from his clutches and said, "Unless you have an extra car lying around, I doubt that you have what I need."

"You don't have a car?"

"I have a piece of a car. I just had to put it in the shop, and they say it's going to cost two thousand dollars to get it fixed. I didn't even pay that much for the car."

"Oh, no, that will never do. I can't have my little niece walking. How about I come and pick you up tomorrow, and we will go find you a car? That's the least I can do for my brother's daughter."

"For real? I will pay you back every dime. I promise. Well, things are shaky on my job right now, but I'm a hustler, so it still won't be a problem," Nova said. She screamed with glee, jumping up and down. The scrubs were unsuccessful at holding down her perky breasts, and Teddy's eyes greedily drank in the view. She threw her arms around Teddy's neck and whispered softly, "Thank you, for real for real."

For a minute after she removed her arms, Teddy didn't speak. He just stared at her, drinking in every curve of her body. "You eat yet?" Teddy asked.

"No, but I'm sure Aunt Tootie has cooked."

"Damn, I ain't seen old Tootie in a long-ass minute. How is she doing?"

"She's fine, still with Roosevelt, old shade-tree mechanic ass. Wait until I tell her I saw you."

"Both of them niggas are made for each other. Say, looka here, since it's my birthday, you might as well join me for dinner and then a little nightcap," Teddy said, changing the subject.

"It's your birthday? How old did you turn?"

"Old enough to know better and young enough not to give a fuck."

"You sound like my daddy when you say that." She giggled.

He opened the door to his Range Rover and stepped to one side, silently inviting her in. If Nova needed to know Teddy's intentions, all she needed was to look into his eyes. Lustful thoughts danced in his head of bedding the young chocolate thoroughbred. A libidinous rush swept over him, and he involuntarily massaged his crotch as Nova climbed into the passenger's seat. She smelled like honey and shea butter. *Goddamn, this little bitch done got fine as fuck,* he thought, feeling his nature swell in his hands. Once she was inside, he closed the door and scurried to the driver's side for fear that she might change her mind.

He cranked the vehicle, and the soulful sound of Mary J. Blige's voice wafted through the Meridian speakers. He lit a half-burned blunt, and the smell of burning citrus and cherries filled the air. "You smoke?" Teddy asked, trying to pass the blunt to Nova.

"No. I'm a CNA, and they give us random drug tests. I don't want to lose my certifications, but it smells good."

Teddy only nodded but kept his eyes on the road with the blunt hanging loosely between his lips.

"You ready for your old man to come home?" he asked.

She regarded him in the dim light of the SUV. He was a handsome man, and if he was close to her father's age, then that would put him between 38 and 40. His skin was a warm chocolate, and his goatee was immaculately trimmed. The gray streak in his hair only served to make him appear more distinguished.

"Yeah, I guess so. I haven't seen him since I was nine, so it'll probably be awkward. I don't know. I just hope he stays out this time."

"Yeah, me too. The streets lost a good soldier when your pop got knocked. The shit me and that cat used to get into is legendary on these streets. But say, on another note, I can't believe how sexy you got in these past few years. Last time I saw you, you were built like a twelve-year-old boy. Now you got ass and titties popping out everywhere, I was like, 'Shiiiiit, li'l Nova done got all thick and shit on Unc,'" he said, letting his hand drift over to her thigh.

She removed his hand politely and squirmed nervously in her seat. "Soooo, what restaurant are we going to eat at?"

"I'd rather be eating you," Teddy said seriously, but when he got no response, he tried to play it off. "Nah, I'm just fucking with you."

She ignored him and redirected the conversation. "You know what? We should go to my house so you can see Aunt Tootie. I'm sure she would love to see you."

"Nah. Like I said, it's my birthday, so I'm getting into something. I always end up spending my birthdays by myself. I'm used to it. It's cool," Teddy said, pouting. It wasn't even close to Teddy's birthday. He used that same tired line on countless women he'd either given drugs to or liquored up. The way he saw it, women would be more giving, more liberal with their bodies, if they thought that it was his birthday.

"I'm sure you have more than enough of these little thot pockets ready to do whatever you want them to do. I said I haven't seen you. That doesn't mean I haven't heard about you."

"What you hear about me?" Teddy asked, feigning contempt.

"Just stuff. It's just talk, so I don't listen."

"Yeah, don't listen, because most of these li'l hoes are just mad 'cause I ain't fucking with them like that. When's the last time you seen Tara?"

"My mama don't fuck with us at all. Last time I talked to her was last Mother's Day. Auntie invited her over for dinner, and she wasn't there five minutes before she started begging."

"She still fuckin' with that dope?"

"Yeah. She doesn't smoke crack anymore though. Now she's strung out on oxy and Roxy. She doesn't even look like my mother anymore," Nova said. Her mood had turned solemn, and she stared out the window, quiet.

"I didn't mean to upset you, shawty. Let me give you my number. Call me in the morning and we'll take care of that issue, okay?"

Chapter Three

Teddy was a south Dallas thoroughbred, born and raised in the heart of Dallas. He wore his hood stripes like a badge of honor and embraced every vice that the streets had to offer. When most people talked about south Dallas, words like "dangerous," "treacherous," and "cutthroat" came to mind, but Teddy didn't see it that way. South Dallas was an illegal entrepreneur's dream. Dope dealers, car thieves, murderers, pimps, whores—they were all there in the streets, and he wanted to carve out his niche in this American dream.

When he met Roland Toussaint, they hit it off instantly and became fast friends. They were the same age, and Roland was just as roguish as he was. Roland was from the boot, as he called it, and that was all he would say. He would never commit to a city even after Teddy had named all the cities that he knew.

"New Orleans?"

"Nah."

"Baton Rouge?"

"Nah."

"Shreveport?"

"Nah."

"Where then, nigga?"

"Pass the weed, wodie."

Roland was of average height and build and would have probably gone largely unnoticed had it not been for his uncommonly dark skin. He was eggplant purple, but his hair was thick and wavy. If you dared to get close enough to look at his face, you saw that he sported a five o'clock shadow. It was awkward to see a boy barely 16 who could grow a full beard for men to envy if he wanted. Teddy himself had a white streak running from his edge up to the crown of his head. He looked like a human skunk. The boys were like salt and pepper: you never saw one without the other. In fact, they were together so much that some people mistakenly believed them to be brothers, and the duo never corrected them.

When they were 18 and fresh out of high school, they had gone into Little World convenience store with the intention of grabbing a bottle of Cisco, some rolling papers, and some cigarettes. Every weekend they got wasted and went to Lady Love 2 strip club. It was little more than a juke joint with one way in and one way out. The stage was directly in front of the door, giving thirsty patrons an eyeful before they paid their $5 cover charge. Lady Love 2 boasted the kind of strippers with stretch marks, sagging titties, and maybe a stab mark or a gunshot wound or two.

But they never made it to the club that night.

"Pull over!" Teddy said.

Roland followed Teddy's line of sight and saw a light-skinned kid with long cornrows named Puncho. They didn't call him that as a play on his half-black, half-Mexican lineage. They called him that because he was brutal with his hands. He would pick fights with grown men just to humiliate them, especially the ones who were mean to their wives. Puncho would see the interaction and just happen to bump into the abuser and his old lady. He would give them an ass whipping to remember and then tell them, "If I see you mistreating her or she tells me you beat her, it will be worse next time."

The problem with Teddy confronting Puncho was that Teddy couldn't fight, and it was sure to ruin their night. Besides, Roland had lined up a couple of freaks from Oak Cliff who went to Carter High, and they were down for whatever.

"What you beefin' wit' Puncho fo'?" Roland asked, but he already knew the answer.

Puncho was standing inside the bus stop with his hand underneath the skirt of Tara King. It was dark outside, and they were pushed into a corner of the bus stop, but from the look on Tara's face and the placement of Puncho's hand, there was no denying what the beef was.

Teddy thought that Tara was his by default because they had basically known each other since birth. She was a hood chick, just like he was a hood dude, and Puncho was an implant from east Dallas. What the fuck did she see in Puncho that she didn't see in Teddy? He was a hustler, he had a car, he had a little apartment, and he had a little money put away. Puncho still stayed with his mother and caught the bus everywhere. How dare she choose this broke-ass half-breed over him?

"You don't see this nigga finger fuckin' my bitch?" Teddy screamed.

"Man, leave that girl alone. I heard she's a fun girl anyway," Roland said.

"Fun girl" was a term used to describe the easy girls in the neighborhood. Tara was super fine, there was no denying that, but she wasn't worth all the trouble, plus he just wanted to enjoy his night.

"Man, circle back around. This nigga gotta see about me!" Teddy barked.

Roland slowed to make a right turn on MLK to circle back, but as soon as he stopped at the light, Teddy bolted from the car, headed for the bus stop. Roland took the *last swig from the Cisco bottle and tossed it to the back seat. By the time he rounded the block, Punch was knee-deep in Teddy's ass.*

"Get up off him, bruh," Roland said. Then he added, "Ain't no sense in dyin' over a reputation that you already possess. Move away from 'round him 'fore you get burnt with this toaster."

"Your homeboy approached me with the bullshit, homes. So you can either let me finish handling my business with Teddy's sucker ass, or I can take the rest of my frustration out on you," Puncho said. He looked over his shoulder and noticed the .38-caliber pointed at his head, and he laughed.

"That's your toaster? I ain't never been scared of no gun," Puncho said. He had turned his attention to Roland and stared him down. "I been shot five times, and I ain't dead yet."

"That's because you ain't been shot right. I don't wanna shoot you, but I will," Roland said.

Puncho let his eyes roam over Roland, weighing his options for war. Roland was smaller than Puncho, but something in the smaller boy's dull black face gave him pause. He could try reasoning with him to make him see that Teddy was just a loudmouth lame who couldn't back up the shit that he talked. Or he could just rush him, beat his ass, take his gun, and then sell it. He'd beaten up grown men, taken the dope that they were selling, and then sold to their competition wholesale. Roland was too small to pose a real threat to the bigger Puncho, but he still had a gun.

"Let's beat his ass, Ro!" Teddy shouted.

Without warning, Puncho lunged at Roland, who, with no hesitation, fired three shots in Puncho's direction. Puncho's body crumpled at Roland's feet. His body was in such an awkward position that his chest was flat against the sidewalk and his head was turned back, staring at Roland, but he wasn't dead. He struggled to breathe, his breath coming shallow and labored.

"Come on, man, we gotta go!" Teddy said, tugging at Roland's sleeve.

"Hold up." Roland kneeled and put his hand close to Puncho's mouth and checked for his breath. He reached into his back pocket and removed his cell phone.

"911, what's your emergency?"

"Somebody has been shot," Roland said.

"Is he alive, sir?"

"I think so."

"What's your location?" the dispatcher asked.

"What are you doing, dawg? Hang up!" Teddy said, reaching for Roland's phone.

"Location, sir?"

Her voice was a flat, monotone mess that said she'd rather be anywhere besides at what she deemed a boring job. Roland regarded her nasally voice and pictured her as a fat woman with ornately decorated nails sitting in a cubicle, snacking on hot Cheetos between calls.

"Sir?" she droned.

He considered hanging up at Teddy's prompts, but he was nobody's murderer. If they left Puncho like this, he could possibly die. On the other hand, if help arrived and he made it through this, he could snitch on Roland, but that was a chance that he had to take.

"He's at the bus stop on the corner of MLK and Malcolm X Boulevard." As he mouthed the words into the cell phone, he felt a twinge of pain and regret. He had just shot another brother at the intersection of two prolific black men.

"Okay, sir, stay there. We've dispatched a unit to your location."

Roland ended the call and tossed his phone into the storm water inlet beneath the bus stop.

"Let's go, bruh. We did our part," Roland said, and as an afterthought, he went to Puncho and turned him over on his side. Maybe by repositioning him, he could help Puncho breathe a little better.

"P, if you can hear me, blink," Roland said.

Puncho blinked twice.

"Help is on the way, my nigga. We gonna charge this one to the game. You send them people after me and I'm gon' finish the job, you hear me? Blink if you feel me," Roland said.

Puncho blinked twice.

It had taken the authorities almost two years to track Roland down, and by the time they did, he was only weeks away from becoming a father. His court-appointed attorney was able to plead to a lesser charge of criminal mischief and unlawful possession of a firearm instead of the attempted murder charge that they wanted to charge him with. He would be eligible for parole after serving eight years—not too bad considering that Puncho would have to wear a colostomy bag for the rest of his life. Roland's bullets had ripped through Puncho's guts.

Teddy thought about his childhood friend. If he was being honest with himself, there had always been a hint of jealousy with him toward Roland. He resented the fact that Roland was looked at in the hood as a stone-cold killer whose name rang through the streets like Christmas bells, while his name had been relegated to a mere hustler. He felt like a lowlife for preying on his friend's daughter, especially with so many available women at his beck and call. She was a grown woman though, and who better to help break her into her new-found adulthood than her uncle? Besides, it wasn't like Roland had been there to raise her, so he had no right to hold their relationship over his head. There was no way that he was going to pass up fucking Nova's little fine ass. She had stepped into womanhood, and he would be there to christen her cherry.

Chapter Four

After Teddy dropped Nova off, she stood downstairs, staring up at her apartment window, and exhaled deeply. She loved her aunt. Tootie had always been good to her, but she still had her ways. She wasn't in the mood to play twenty questions. Besides, if Roosevelt hadn't sold her the junker in the first place, she wouldn't be going through the shit she was going through. Roosevelt and Tootie had a comically toxic relationship, but their love was real. They both talked shit to one another, but no one else could do it. If the average onlooker saw their interaction, they would assume that the couple hated each other, but that couldn't be further from the truth.

"Girl, where the hell you been? I was worried sick about you. Your phone is going straight to voicemail," Tootie said.

Nova cut her eyes at Roosevelt and turned back to her aunt. "I had to drop my car off at the shop." She turned to Roosevelt. "They say it's going to cost two thousand to fix."

"Sheeeeeit, it don't take that much. They tryin'a get over. Tell you what, buy your own parts and I won't charge you but five hunnit and a case of Heineken. I'll have that mu'fucka runnin' like a new Benz," Roosevelt said, turning up the last of the beer that he was drinking.

"I shoooo' hope you didn't use the rent money to pay for that raggedy-ass car, because the landlord don't give a shit about no personal problems! I told you not to buy that shit from Velt in the first place."

"I haven't spent anything out of my check yet. I wanted to get with you first before I spent anything to see if y'all could take me back and forth to work for a couple of weeks until I get my car fixed," Nova said.

"You better get a bus pass, Nova Jade! I'm not breaking my sleep to take you to work. What's wrong with riding the bus? You can get a bus pass for a hundred dollars for the whole month," Tootie suggested.

"I just experienced the bus for the first time since school, and I can't do that for a whole month."

"I don't know what to tell you," Tootie said.

"Auntie! You're not going to help me? Uncle Roosevelt?" She always added the "Uncle" part to Roosevelt's name when she wanted something.

Roosevelt opened his mouth to speak, but before he could get the words out, Tootie cut him off. "I am helping you. It's called tough love. Whatever you decide to do, I'm going to need that five hundred for the rent because a car won't do you no good if you're homeless."

"Leave that damn girl alone, Tootie. Tough love? Your ass just lazy and don't want to get up an hour earlier. If my niece needs a ride, then I can drop her off on my way to work. That saves her some money and gets me away from yo' mean ass."

"Fuck you, Roosevelt! Every time your ugly ass hear Nova say 'Uncle Roosevelt,' you melt like a damn teenage schoolgirl, grinning like a cat licking shit out of a hairbrush," Tootie said.

"Who you calling ugly? I know plenty of women who would love to have all this man. Matter of fact, since you think I'm ugly, I'ma go down here to Pam's house and see what she thinks 'bout my looks."

"I better be the only bitch who you ask about your looks. Why you like playing with me, daddy? You know you're my sexy man. I better not catch you sniffing around

Pam's thirsty ass. This is mine," Tootie said, stepping to Roosevelt and grabbing a handful of his manhood.

"All right now, you gonna make me put a curve in your back! Keep fuckin' around and I'ma have you 'round here speakin' in tongues," Roosevelt said, throwing his hands into the air, gyrating as if he'd caught the Holy Ghost.

"Okay. Y'all are too much for me. Y'all do know you're too old to be carrying on like this, right?" Nova said, covering her eyes like a frightened child.

"Girl, bye! Stella ain't the only one groovin'. You know like I know, you'll find you a love like this. You better tell her, Velt. How you kids say it, relationship goals?"

"Anyway, chile, what you cook, Auntie? I'm hungry," Nova said, not waiting for a response before slinking into the kitchen. She lifted the first lid and the steam from a pot of smoked neckbones caressed her nose. She breathed in deep. Nobody could cook like Aunt Tootie. She was Nova's father's oldest sister, and after the death of their parents years earlier, she had become the sole guardian of her three siblings. Of all her family members, she and Tootie were the closest. Tootie joked a lot, almost as much as she talked shit, but there was no denying that she loved her niece.

Just as Nova was about to lift the lid on what smelled like cabbage, Tootie eased up behind her and let out a bloodcurdling scream. "What are you doing in my pots before you wash your hands?"

Nova shook violently, every fiber of her being vibrating with fear. The lid that she was holding juddered and clanked loudly against the rim of the pot. Nova felt a trickle of pee escape from her bladder, and she clamped her legs shut to stave the flow as she whipped around to face her aunt.

"You play too much, Auntie. You're going to give me a heart attack one of these days."

"Well, go wash your little nasty-ass hands before you start poking around in my kitchen."

Nova went to the sink, dropped some dish detergent in her hands, and gave them a quick wash. She ignored her aunt's disapproving stare and grabbed a plate from the dish rack. Nova fixed a small plate of smoked neckbones, cabbage, red beans, macaroni and cheese, and hot-water cornbread. She ate slowly and danced in her seat as she did. It was a habit that she had developed as a child, and as she explained it, the food was just too good to be still. With a mouthful of food, she said, "Guess who I saw today?"

"Who, Chino broke ass?" Tootie sneered.

"Who? Eww, no, I saw Uncle Teddy."

Tootie sucked her teeth. "Chile, my mama didn't give birth to no lames, so he ain't your uncle. And he's the reason your daddy is locked up. Every time that nigga opens his mouth and bites off more than he can chew and them niggas in the hood come for his head, your dumbass daddy comes to Teddy's rescue. I just hope when he gets out in three months he stays away from that clown."

"Three months? I thought he had like four or five more months left," Nova said.

"Nope, I got a call from the parole board asking if I would let him stay here. So if he keeps his nose clean and doesn't get into any trouble, he should be home soon."

Nova didn't say anything. Her face was buried in her plate, but she wasn't eating.

"Everything okay, baby?" Tootie asked.

"I'm fine, I guess. It's just going to seem strange having him back home. A lot of things have changed in the past nine years."

"True, but one thing that holds true is that your daddy loves you. I know it may not seem like it, may seem as though he'd rather be in jail than out here being a father, but that's not the case. Maybe you should write him a letter before he comes home. Get the awkward shit out of the way," Tootie said. She was standing over the stove, putting scoops of food onto a paper plate.

"I'm not much of a letter person. I send him money every month, and that should be good enough."

"This isn't about money. It's about establishing a relationship with your father. Now take this plate down to Mrs. Marie's for your mama."

"She's staying at Mrs. Marie's house?" Nova asked, scrunching her face at the thought.

Mrs. Marie was an amputee who had a house on Penelope Street. For whatever reason, she had turned her home into a refuge for the downtrodden. Whether they were dopefiends or just homeless, it made no difference to Mrs. Marie. Nova didn't like going there because the residence always smelled. Moreover, Nova and her mother weren't exactly speaking because Tara couldn't run game on Nova. If she couldn't get money out of you, then she had no use for you, and Nova was sick of the heartache. Every time she tried to get close to her mother, she would do something to ruin their relationship. Tara had done it all, from stealing from Nova to trying to fuck Chino for dope. It was always the same and never her fault.

"You know I hate going down there, Auntie. Her ass is just going to start begging. Blowing her breath in my face, smelling like a bag of dicks."

"Just do what I asked you to do, and you can take my car," Tootie said.

Roosevelt came waltzing into the kitchen. He grabbed Tootie by the waist, spun her around, squeezed Tootie's butt, and then licked her on her neck.

"Okay, here we go again. I'm going to go ahead and take the plate," Nova said. She grabbed the plate and headed toward the door.

"Put some gas in my damn car, and take your time," Tootie said.

"Yeah, take your time," Roosevelt echoed.

Chapter Five

"Jarvis, what are you going to do with your life? You're not finna lie up in this house without a job. You're twenty years old for God's sake!" Angela Lane shouted.

"Yeah, and you're twenty-seven with two kids, so I got you beat, sis!" He crumpled the Doritos bag that he had been eating from and tossed it onto the coffee table.

"See, this is what I'm talking about! Fred is on his way home with the boys, and I just finished cleaning up. Pick that crap up and get your funky feet off of my coffee table!" Angela scolded.

Jarvis stood and adjusted his clothes. He towered over his sister by a whole foot and a half. He bent down and kissed her on the forehead. "Okay, I'm sorry. You need to stop being so stiff, letting that fool run you."

"That's where you're wrong, baby boy. My husband doesn't run me, and I don't run him. It's called love and respect. I know what he likes and expects, so that's what I do. He's a good man who loves his wife and works way too hard to come home to your grown ass lying up in his house sucking up AC with your big-nose behind!"

"Whatever. I know you ain't calling nobody's nose big. Oh, you wanna sco'? Runnin' around here, breath smelling like burnt leaves and Band-Aids."

"Ya mama," Angela said. She put her hands on her hips and mean mugged her brother.

"Yo' snaggletoothed daddy."

They both laughed, and Jarvis pulled his sister close to his chest. "On the real, sis, I'm going to get it together, I promise. Just watch me!"

"I know you will eventually, baby boy. Look, I'm not asking you to conquer the world. I'm just asking you to at least use the gifts that God has given you. You have a mechanical gift, Jarvis, and you're like a surgeon under the hood of a car. Don't let it go to waste. Fred already told you that he would help you open your own shop, but you must be serious. We will invest in you if you invest in yourself. You'd make so much money, I'd be coming to you for loans instead of the other way around. Besides, if you don't do something soon, your black ass will be homeless!" she said, reaching up to mush Jarvis in the face.

"You'd put me out?"

"If you don't do something besides sneaking into the garage to smoke weed and eating up everything, you're damn right. I gave birth to two boys, not your crusty butt."

Jarvis giggled nervously. He had no idea that she knew he smoked. He always kept breath mints, and he was careful to blow the smoke out of the garage window so the smoke wouldn't be in his clothes.

Before he could counter, his brother-in-law, Fred, walked in. His stride was slow, and he dragged like his body hurt. He looked tired and defeated.

"What up, bruh law? You good?" Jarvis said.

"Yeah, I'm straight. Yo, we need to have a talk a little later."

"A'ight," Jarvis said, bending over to pick up his youngest nephew, Martin. "What's up, l'il nigga?" He then turned to his older nephew, Malcolm. "Mal, what's good, gangsta?"

"Jarvis! They aren't niggas and gangstas. They are impressionable boys who happen to look up to their uncle. One day they will look to you for guidance, so I'm going to need for you to grow up."

"My bad, Angel, it won't happen again. I was just talking." His sister loved when he called her Angel.

"That's part of the problem, Jarvis. You're all talk!" Fred huffed.

"Fuck that supposed to mean?" Jarvis said, kneeling and putting Martin on the floor.

"It means you've been talking about getting a job forever. It means I'm tired of busting my ass at work to come home and see your grown ass sprawled across my couch. It means that if you can't be respectful to me and my wife and be a positive influence on your nephews, it's probably best if you move around," Fred said, inching closer to Jarvis. Angela touched his arm lightly to calm him down.

"Bruh, if you don't want me here, I'll leave. You don't have to talk to me like I'm one of your kids." Even in the cool crispness of the air conditioning, the embarrassment caused Jarvis to sweat nervously. His underarms itched, and his mouth felt dry like he'd been eating phone books.

Angela ushered her sons down the long hallway. "You boys go to your room. This is grown folks' business."

Fred waited until he heard Angela close the boys' bedroom door, then turned back to Jarvis. "It's not about wanting you to leave, bro. I'm trying to get you to understand that you only get out of life what you put into it. Hustling and running game won't last forever. What happens when the hustle stops working? Or worse, what if you run game on the wrong person and they do something to you? Life don't come with instructions or road maps, J. You have to have a plan, and I can help you if you let me, but I'm not going to hold your hand. If you want to do better, I can show you, but you've got to want it, bruh law," Fred said, resting his hand on Jarvis's shoulder.

"I appreciate it, but I'm straight! You do you, and I'll keep doing me!" Jarvis said, shrugging free of Fred's claw. He reached into his pocket and pulled out a wad of $20 bills, rifled through them, and peeled off $500. "This should cover me for a couple of months or until I find my own shit, whichever comes first, bruh. Save your lectures for Malcolm and Martin because I don't want to hear that shit," Jarvis said. He stormed into his room, slamming the door in his wake.

"You need to check your brother, baby. He can't live here if he's going to keep hustling. Plus, his ass is disrespectful."

"I agree, but you keep taking the money that he offers you, so that isn't really helping your argument," Angela said.

"These bills don't stop, and if he's going to stay here, he might as well contribute. Money is money, no matter where he gets it."

"If that's your sense of reasoning, then that makes you just as guilty as Jarvis. You guys are just alike. I'll have a serious talk with him, I promise."

"That's all I ask," Fred said, pulling his wife into his arms.

Jarvis lay across his bed, seething. If his sister's husband wasn't complaining about him leaving dishes in the sink, he was running to Angela, snitching about the company he kept. He had saved a little over $2,000, and he would have his own spot soon, but he needed Fred to get off his back.

A light knock on his door pulled him from his daydream. "Come in."

"Hey, Jarvis, you wanna play PlayStation with me?" Malcolm asked.

"I'm getting ready to dip out for a little while, Mal, but when I come back, I'll bang you up on your game." Jarvis smiled. He loved his nephew because even at 9 years old he was more insightful than his parents gave him credit for. He had a penchant for knowing when his uncle was upset or when situations were tense. He knew how to pull Jarvis out of his funk, and he appreciated the young boy for that. Malcolm didn't see his uncle's flaws, only the love that they shared, and he never judged.

"Okay, I'll be waiting, and stop lying to yourself," Malcolm said.

"Lying to myself?"

"Yeah. You know you can't beat me." Malcolm chuckled as he exited Jarvis's room.

He may have been talking about the game, but his statement had hit Jarvis in his chest like a blow from Mike Tyson. Maybe he was lying to himself. He was 20 years old and living with his married sister and her family. The few measly dollars he had managed to save wouldn't carry him far. The days of having a few dollars and a new outfit for the club were over. He sat down with his back against the frame of his bed, pulled his knees up to his chest, and buried his head. He was lying to himself. He knew that hustling was a dangerous game played by dangerous people, but he just wanted the money. He sold drugs, but he wasn't very good at it. He hustled backward, spending his re-up money on nonsense, trying to keep up with the Joneses. When he should have been planning and saving, he was partying and stunting . . . without a car . . . without his own apartment. But Jarvis saw the streets as a short-term solution, not as a career path. He didn't hang on corners or sling from trap houses. He made the majority of his money hanging around Mrs. Marie's house on the weekends. He fixed a few cars around the neighborhood from time to time, so it wasn't like he was a bum mooching off his family.

Yeah, yeah, yeah, you can make all the excuses you want to. You can believe you're not a bum, but you're doing bummy shit, so if the shoe fits, wear that mu'fucka. You need to get yo' shit together, because your parents didn't raise you like this.

Don't listen to this clown. Well, you can listen to him after you sell this pack at Mrs. Marie's house.

Jarvis's thoughts played out in his head like the devil and the angel sitting on his shoulders. He wasn't in the mood to think. He just wanted to walk to Mrs. Marie's and smoke a blunt on the way without thinking, caring, or worrying.

Chapter Six

Nova pulled up to the curb in front of Mrs. Marie's house and sighed heavily. She was not looking forward to trudging through the sea of dope boys and dopefiends who used Mrs. Marie's porch and front yard as a hub for illicit commerce. She walked around to the passenger's side and leaned into the car to grab the plate that Tootie had made for her mother. She heard whistles and cheers.

"Goooooooddamn, l'il chocolate, lemme holla atchu right quick," a voice said.

Nova stood and placed the plate on top of the car. The juices from the food had leaked a little in Tootie's seat, but she would worry about that later.

"You gon' let me holla atchu or what?" Scooter said, repeating his question.

"You don't need to holla at me about nothing, Scooter, so go on," Nova said. She adjusted her T-shirt so that it was over her round butt, but it didn't work. With every step she took, the fabric danced its way back up to her narrow waist.

"You can't hide all that ass, shawty, I don't even know why you tryin'," Dog Face said as he sat on the hood of her car. He was tall and lanky and had a face like a pug. His eyes bulged and wandered in different directions, making it hard to pinpoint who he was talking to. He had a permanent underbite, which made Dog Face the perfect name.

"Dog Face, get your ugly ass off my auntie's shit. You dent her hood, you know she's going to clown you."

"Man, ain't nobody worried about Tootie's ass," Dog Face said, sliding from the hood.

Nova had made it to the door and was about to knock when Mrs. Marie yanked the door open.

"Hey, Nova baby. I thought you was yo' mama. How you been?" Mrs. Marie said, extending her arms for a hug.

Nova knew that Mrs. Marie was kin to Roosevelt, but she wasn't sure how they were related, and neither of them ever elaborated. When asked, they would just say, "We kin," and let the subject fall.

"Hey, Mrs. Marie. Auntie cooked and wanted me to bring her a plate. Have you seen her?" Nova asked, bending to hug the paraplegic.

"I sent her to the store to get me some cigarettes. What your aunt done cooked?"

"Some neckbones and stuff."

"Sho' smell good. That Tootie knows she can cook. How her and Velt doin' anyhow?"

"They're good, still crazy thinking they're young and in love, acting like teenagers," Nova said with a smile.

"Good, good. I knew when Velt got with Tootie she was the one who was gonna calm him down. Hell, 'tween that pistol and that dick, he thought he was a real gunslinger." Mrs. Marie guffawed, slapping her paralyzed thighs, then added, "Sho'nuff did!"

"You're so silly," Nova said, joining in the laughter. The old lady's chortle was hilarious and contagious.

"Anyhow, you can either wait for her or you can put it in the microwave."

Thank you, Mrs. Marie, Nova shouted in her head. The old lady had given her the perfect out to not have to deal with her mother. Whenever the subject of her mom came up, no matter who the conversation was with, it always led to tension. Especially with Aunt Tootie, who for some reason had some type of displaced loyalty to Tara. It was Tootie who had convinced Mrs. Marie to give Tara a place to stay. Tootie believed in Tara and wanted her to succeed. But Nova saw what Tootie refused to see: Tara was playing on Tootie's sympathies.

"She showed up late and high, Auntie. I can't stand her ass!" Nova had heatedly said after Tara showed up at her tenth birthday party high and drunk. She also brought her cousin Bean who was touchy-feely and gave Nova the creeps.

"Ain't nobody saying you gotta like her, but you gotta love her because she's ya mama," Tootie had said, pulling a crying Nova close to her.

It wasn't that she didn't like or love her mother. In fact, she wasn't sure what she felt, but it felt a lot like nothing. How could she have feelings for a woman who had given birth to her but, for whatever reason, didn't have an emotional connection to her only child? According to Tootie, Tara had brought Nova to her on Christmas Day, wrapped in a blanket stained in dirt and milk.

"Tara came in my house slurring and shit. Merry Christmas and Happy fuckin' New Year! I took one look at you and knew that you were going to be special, baby. I knew she was high. Her eyes were glassy, and her nose was running. I knew she had been crying because her eyes were puffy, you know. I got you out of those dirty rags and wrapped you up in one of Roosevelt's sweatshirts and rocked you to sleep. I fixed me and your mama some coffee, and we talked. We talked about how your daddy had made her so many promises and how he made her feel like the only woman in the world. She talked about how Teddy wasn't really your daddy's friend because he low-key hated your daddy because of his reputation and because he had her. She sat right there where you're sitting and told me that ever since she gave birth to you and Roland went to prison, she thinks about hurting you. She said she had shaken you one night because you wouldn't stop crying, but she caught herself before you were hurt. She said she needed me to take you because she didn't want to hurt you, baby. So you see? Your mama saved your life by leaving you with me. I love you, and you are nobody's throwaway. You were my blessing," Tootie had said.

Nova could appreciate everything that Tootie had done for her. Her aunt had gone without at times to make sure that she had everything that she needed and more. Tootie was her mother. Tara could kiss her ass.

"Thank you, Mrs. Marie, that would be great."

The old lady wheeled herself away from the door and allowed Nova to enter. A girl her age named Renee who went to school with her was asleep on a dusty floral-print couch. Her legs, with their crusted-over sores, were bent in an uncomfortable position on the small couch. One of her feet had a dirty sock hanging from it, while the other had no sock at all, just days' worth, perhaps weeks' worth, of blackened grime on the sole of her bare foot. The husk on her heels was so thick that it was cracking, and Nova shuddered. She could remember the kids taunting her so bad that one day she just stopped coming to school. Renee dove into the streets headfirst, and by the time her peers were graduating from high school, she was a full-blown dopefiend.

Two elderly black men sat at a round wooden table playing chess. Nova knew the fat, bald one, Mr. Arnell, but she wasn't sure who the other man was. Probably a new stray Mrs. Marie had taken in. Mr. Arnell was always nice to her. Even when she was in a bitchy mood, he was cool. "Hey, Mr. Arnell. How are you?" Nova said.

"I'm fair to middlin'. I could complain, but hell, wouldn't nobody listen," he said with a chuckle.

"Who's your friend?" Nova asked.

"Nigga ain't no friend of mine. He's my victim. They call him—" Arnell started, but the man cut him off.

"I don't need no country bama introducing me. How do you do, sweet thang? My mama named me Henry, but I prefer Hennessy."

Nova cocked her head to one side and furrowed her brow. She measured this man who was clearly in his late sixties, early seventies. He might have been five foot five, 110 pounds soaking wet, with a voice like Billy Dee Williams. The bourbon-colored wingtips he wore had been polished to a shine and matched his belt perfectly. The corduroy pants he had on matched his fedora's color of brushed copper. To top it off, his polo shirt brought it all together. His skin was almost too smooth for him to be an elder, but she could see knowledge and pain in his orbs of honey.

"Hennessy, huh? Why Hennessy?" Nova asked.

He smiled and did a Sammy Davis Jr. spin. "Because I'm sweet and brown, I go down easy, and I'll fuck you up." He grabbed Nova's free hand, bowed at the waist, removed his fedora, and kissed her hand.

"Henny, leave this child alone. Nova baby, g'on and do what you need to do," Mrs. Marie said.

"Nice to meet you," she said to Hennessy and made her way to the kitchen. She stepped through the door and stopped abruptly. A brown and white pit bull snarled at her but was wagging her tail viciously. The pink collar around her neck was fastened to a chain that was attached to two cinder blocks.

"Her friendly ass ain't gon' bite gnats off her ass. Sheba, sit yo' ass down now. That plate ain't for you. Sorry about that. Sheba think she s'posed to get a bite of everything in this kitchen. Guess it's my fault for spoilin' her," Mrs. Marie said.

Nova opened the microwave and jumped. "Oh, shit!" She was just about to put the plate inside when a roach scurried from the glass tray to the back of the microwave and through the vent of the nuke box. "Um, I think I'd better put this in the refrigerator."

"If you can find room," Mrs. Marie countered.

Nova went to the refrigerator and reorganized the half-empty containers of spoiled milk, orange juice with extra pulp, an unopened bottle of apple cider vinegar, and a pitcher that used to contain Kool-Aid.

"Can I ask you a question, Mrs. Marie?"

"Sho' thang."

"Why do you allow all of these grown people to live in your house?" Nova asked.

"I suppose because everybody needs somebody. Never forget that. Some of these folks are good and decent. They just fell on hard times. I give everybody the benefit of the doubt. I try to give them a place they can get clean and get their shit together. Some do, some don't. Besides, I like the company." Mrs. Marie shrugged.

Nova kissed Mrs. Marie on the cheek and headed for the door. "Tell Tara I asked about her." Nova opened the door to leave, and her mother was standing there about to come in.

"Heeeeyyyyyyy, mama's baby! How are you?" Tara said. She had an uneasy smile on her face, and her front tooth was missing, a new addition since the last time Nova saw her.

"Hey," Nova said dryly.

"That all you got for me? Gimme a hug. Your daddy home yet? How's Roosevelt and Tootie? You still working at Baylor Hospital? You still with that boy Chino? I hope not because that little nigga ain't shit! I asked him to give me a couple of Xanax until I get my check, and he said no, ol' cheap ass. You got twenty dollars I can hold until next Wednesday?" Tara rattled off question after question like she was interviewing Nova for a job.

"I'm sorry. I can't do this with you right now, Tara," Nova said, exiting the house.

"Hold on now. I might be fucked up, but I'm still your mama! You so busy you don't have ten minutes to spend with your mama?"

"No, I really don't have time," Nova said. She was about to read her mother for filth when she saw Chino's car pull across the traffic light, headed in her direction. The car stopped short like the driver hesitated to pull into the spot. Nova saw why when he killed the headlights.

Nova walked to the driver's side and tapped on the window with a manicured nail. Chino turned his back to her and continued talking to the slender, young redbone sitting on the passenger's side. She knocked again, this time with her knuckles and more forcefully.

The girl got out on the passenger's side and stared at Nova over the roof of Chino's Hellcat.

"Damn, thirsty-ass ho. You that pressed?" the girl screamed.

But Nova ignored her and kept her focus on the boy who was supposed to be her man.

Chino stepped from his car and faced Nova. "What up, bae?" he slurred.

Nova took a step back and wrinkled her nose. Chino smelled like he had just had nasty, sweaty sex with the girl, who was her opposite.

"So this is how you get down?" Nova asked, fighting back tears.

Chino smacked his lips and rolled his eyes. "Man, here we go with this bullshit again. Just because you see a bitch in my car, you assume I'm fuckin' her," Chino said.

He wouldn't make eye contact with her, which only made Nova angrier.

"I don't have to assume shit. Chino, your face smells like you ate this bitch's pussy on the way over here. You foul as fuck, nigga!" Nova said, mushing Chino in his face.

"Don't put your fuckin' hands on me, girl!"

"Bitch, don't put your hands on him," the girl parroted.

Without warning, he turned away from Nova and screamed at the girl, "Shantell, shut the fuck up and go home. Talk too fuckin' much, goddamn."

"Fuck you, ol' l'il-dick-ass nigga. And you can't eat pussy worth a fuck either," Shantell said with a wicked smirk on her face. Her rant had been directed at Chino, but her eyes were locked with Nova's.

"Bitch!" Chino screamed and made like he was going to run around the car, but Shantell took off running.

"You better run, l'il trick-ass bitch." He shook his fist in her direction. He turned to Nova with a look of sadness.

"I'm done fucking with you, Chino. I might lose my job messing with you," Nova said sadly. She felt sick, like she wanted to throw up. Her insides felt like she was free-falling from a mountaintop. How could she have been so stupid? Looking at him made her angry, too. He was so fine with his paper-sack brown complexion and muscles popping through his T-shirt. She wondered if his little thot had been the one to braid his hair in such intricate patterns. She had fallen for Chino's looks, nothing more, but hearing the girl vocalize his infidelity made it all too real. The cold part about it was that she had thought the exact same thing about Chino's short-comings. She had to laugh to keep from crying.

"The fuck so funny? You think breaking my heart is funny or something?" Chino asked.

"I told you his ass wasn't about shit!" Tara yelled from the front porch.

Nova had tuned everyone else out when she was arguing with Chino, but Tara's raspy lisp from her missing tooth brought her back.

"Stay out of my business, Tara," she said without looking at her. She was done—with Chino, with Tara, with it all. "I'm leaving, Chino. Lose my fucking number." She had to leave before the waterworks started. Nova chirped the unlock button and headed toward the car, but Chino grabbed her arm.

"Hold up, don't walk away from me."

"Let me go. You're hurting my arm," Nova said, struggling to get away.

"You can't break up with me. Fuck you talking 'bout?" Chino let go of Nova's arm, and she fell to the ground. He moved swiftly to stand over her, fist raised, poised to strike, when Jarvis pushed him violently.

"Say, my nigga, you tryin'a fight a girl? What kinda nigga are you, bruh?" Jarvis said.

"Look out, ho-ass nigga!" Chino said. He was much bigger than Jarvis and contemplated trying to beat his ass, but he liked sure odds. He stood and removed the .40-caliber from the waistband of his jeans and aimed at Jarvis. Nova jumped from the ground and stood in front of Jarvis.

"I'm not going to let you shoot this boy, Chino."

"Move yo' ass out the way, Nova. You willing to take a bullet for this nigga?" Chino sneered.

"And you willing to go to jail for shooting somebody you don't even know? Why can't you just accept that you got caught in your bullshit and move on? You shoot him, you gotta shoot me!" Nova said. She heard the words come from her mouth but couldn't believe that they were coming from her. She didn't even know this stranger who was risking his life to stop Chino from beating her, but if he was shot, it would be because of her, and she couldn't let that happen.

"That's a'ight. Fuck you then, bitch, and I'll catch you another time, homeboy," Chino said, winking at Jarvis. He held eye contact with him until he was in his car and pulling away from the curb.

"Thank you, but that was stupid," Nova scolded Jarvis.

"What's stupid about not letting this clown beat on you?"

"I'm just saying, what if he had shot you? I would have felt so bad," Nova said seriously.

"You can make it up to me by letting me take you to dinner or something sometime."

"I don't think so, but thank you."

"Now why would you break my heart like that, my love?" Jarvis said. He placed both of his hands over his heart and spun in a circle. When he was facing Nova again, he was sporting an award-winning smile. His teeth were perfect, like they had been chiseled from the finest ivory. "Give me one good reason why, and I will never bother you again."

"Okay, if you insist. You're going to Mrs. Marie's house, so I already know what you're about, and I don't want any part of it. I don't want somebody who thinks that it's okay to lie just because their mouth is open. I don't want somebody who thinks new Js and shiny rims are the highlight of his existence. I'm young, but I don't have time for no little-boy games that lead to nowhere, and I damn sure don't need a lifelong dope boy," Nova said. Chino had taught her a valuable lesson. She was finished being the nice, normal girlfriend. She had let Chino talk her into stealing 200 Suboxone tablets from the pharmacy at her job at Baylor Hospital. He had promptly sold them and given her a cut of the money. So she kept stealing pills: Suboxone, OxyContin, Vicodin, and the like. But when she stole the fentanyl, it drew all the wrong attention. Other staff members started watching her like they all knew something that she didn't, and when she passed her supervisor, Jackie, in the cafeteria, she could have sworn she snickered at her. She hadn't been called into the director's office yet, but she was sure it wouldn't be long before she got that call. Not only could she lose her job, but they could file charges against her, all for a nigga who didn't have the decency to take a shower before getting up in her face. Last thing she needed was another pretty boy with commitment issues.

"You think I'm a dope boy?" Jarvis asked, feigning heartache.

"I don't think, I know. I see you around here scrambling. Who even sells drugs anymore?"

"The nigga you was just beefing with," Jarvis said. His words were a little sharper than he intended, but what was done was done.

"Exactly, and that's not what I want. Anyway, thanks for sticking up for me."

It was strange. Jarvis was genuinely sad over Nova's rejection. He had risked being shot, and she hadn't even bothered to give him her name. His palms were sweaty, and his heart thumped like it was trying to escape his chiseled chest. She was not only a beautiful shade of the darkest chocolate he'd ever seen but sexy as hell, too. She was also intelligent, and her words flowed effortlessly, like she had rehearsed repeatedly how she was going to shoot him down.

"My name is Nova, by the way, and you are?"

"I ain't nobody, shawty. I'll catch you later. I do wanna leave you with a thought though. I asked you for one good reason why we couldn't get to know each other better, but all I heard was what you don't want. What about what matters the most? How about focusing on the things that you want from a relationship instead of that other shit? You might start attracting the things that you think about the most," Jarvis said, disappearing into Mrs. Marie's house.

Damn, Mr. Nobody, you give up too easy. Nova cranked the car and drove away.

Chapter Seven

The night before, Nova had driven home and couldn't get Jarvis's statement out of her head. She hated to admit it, but he was right. Nova was a firm believer in the power of positive thought. She believed that the things you focused on the most were the things that the universe allowed to manifest to you. Chino had that effect on her, the ability to make her see the negative side in anything. He brought out the very worst in her until her thoughts were dark clouds of anger and confusion. Not only was Jarvis's personality a breath of fresh air, but his smile was radiant. The way his chocolate skin had glistened underneath the streetlights was borderline orgasmic.

It was already after 10:00 a.m., and Teddy was supposed to be dropping by around noon. Nova was nobody's fool. Teddy threw the word "niece" around, but in his mind she was anything but a familial connection. She stood in the mirror and inspected herself. Tara had given her a curvaceous body and a beautiful face, and that was about it. Nova let her hands slide over her body, the heat from her palms stirring her hormonal honeypot. She knew exactly what Teddy wanted, and if men wanted to play games, then she would be the team owner. She would call her own shots and live her life on her terms.

Most of the girls she knew from the neighborhood were dependent on their men. They put up with bullshit, afraid to lose their support, even if that support meant that they were constantly cheated on, mentally abused, or worse, beaten. Money would no longer be the Super Glue that bound her to anyone. She had had enough failed relationships to see that the level of toxicity between her and Chino was beyond unhealthy. To see with your own eyes your man walk out of a hotel with one of your supposed best friends was heartbreaking, but to allow your man to convince you that it wasn't him was nauseating.

He was high yellow and pretty, with a chiseled body, the kind of man who took longer to get ready for a date than she did. He was the type who stayed in the mirror admiring what he believed to be God's gift to women. As she thought about him, one thing was certain to her: Chino hadn't helped. He'd only hindered. *With his little-dick ass.* She chuckled, thinking about Shantell's insults.

"How you gonna cheat with a little dick?" she said to no one in particular. She wiggled into her jeans, turned her butt to the mirror, and smiled. Nova tied the "Purple Reign" T-shirt that she wore into a knot just above her navel, showcasing her ample breasts. She sat on the edge of the bed and slid one of her feet into a black slide and the other into a black Nike Cortez with a purple Swoosh.

"Which look you like better, Auntie?" Nova said, walking into the living room.

"I like the sneakers. Never know when shit might get real, and you can't get on nobody's ass with slides on." Tootie smirked.

"Um, I know that if I'm too old to be fighting, your old ass definitely needs to sit down."

"Whatever, chile, and where you going, looking like a little ghetto Barbie doll?" Tootie said, slapping Nova on her ass.

"Ouch, and Barbie wishes she had yams like these, homegirl," Nova said as she rubbed her bruised backside. "If you must know, Uncle Teddy is going to help me find a car."

"I want you to be careful fucking with Teddy, Nova. I'm serious. He's a very dangerous man," Tootie said seriously, pulling Nova close to her.

"I'm not worried about Teddy, but I am worried about not being able to get to work. So if he's willing to help me either get my car fixed or get me another one, I'm going to let him."

"Just promise me you'll be careful," Tootie said. She hugged Nova tight. "You're all I got, kid."

The statement held a tone of finality to it, as if Tootie knew something that she wasn't willing to share with her. A forceful knock at the door pulled them from their embrace. "Who the hell is knocking on my door like the damn police?" Tootie said, snatching the door open.

Teddy was standing on the other side, grinning like the cat that had just eaten the prized canary. "Toot, what's good with you, baby girl? I ain't seen you in forever."

"Uh-huh. Come on in," Tootie said, stepping outside and closing the door behind her.

"Why the cold shoulder? We family."

"Yeah, family. Listen, Teddy, I don't know what the fuck you're up to, but you see that little girl in there? She's my life, and if you do anything besides try to help her like you're claiming, I'm going to personally cut you to pieces and sprinkle your body parts into the Trinity River and let the gators fight over your flesh," Tootie snapped.

Teddy flashed the smile that had convinced so many unwitting females to drop their panties. But Tootie wasn't buying it. "I'm serious, nigga."

"I know, I know, and everything is on the up and up. That's my dawg's daughter, and I just want to do my part to help her, you feel me? I ain't got nothing but the best intentions, I swear."

"Whatever, nigga. Just remember what I said," Tootie said, opening the door and stepping aside.

"You got that, Toot. You ready, niecey?"

"Yeah, I'm ready. What were y'all talking about out there?" Nova asked.

"Just family business, baby girl. I hope you're hungry."

Over lunch, Teddy regaled Nova with stories of her father's capers as a kid. "Yeah, your old man was a different breed. This nigga's fuse was so short that instead of calling him Roland, niggas started calling him ZRo because he gave zero fucks."

Teddy wasn't one for small talk, and had she been anyone else, he would've already made his move. The more he talked, the brighter the twinkle in her eyes became. She was mesmerized by the tales Teddy weaved. He made himself sound like a ghetto emperor, doling out justice to wrongdoers, while her father had been reduced to Teddy's short-tempered henchman.

"When your daddy came home last time, how old were you then?"

"I was nine when he came home," Nova said, dropping her head. She loved her father, but she didn't understand why he chose the streets over her. When he came home, Nova couldn't remember a happier time. There was food, fun, and plenty of laughter and money floating around. Roland and Tootie were inseparable. The only time they were apart was when Tootie was with Roosevelt, or her father was with Teddy.

Nova played with the lettuce with her fork, eyes stinging from the tears that threatened to spill. She couldn't let him see her cry, but memories of her father came flooding back to her. She could still remember her father coming into her room the night of her tenth birthday. The day had been epic, starting with them all going to Six Flags. Roland had spent a lot of money, and by the time they left, her 10-year-old tummy ached and she was starting to crash from the sugar rush. Roosevelt's old Ford Explorer was full of stuffed animals and souvenirs. She'd fallen asleep and hadn't woken up until Roland lay her in her bed. Her eyes fluttered open just as he was about to leave the room. "Daddy?" Nova's tiny voice had said.

"Yes, my love?"

"I really had fun today. Thank you for taking me to Six Flags."

"You're welcome, baby, but there's no need to thank me. I want us to do this more often, you know?" he said, smiling.

"Really, Daddy?"

"Yes, ma'am, all of us being together, including your Aunt Tootie and Uncle Velt being together today, really made me happy."

Nova was just about to start telling her father the best parts of the amusement park when his phone rang.

"Hello," he'd said, frustration dripping from his voice. Whoever was on the phone had really gotten up under her father's skin. "Dawg, I'm with my baby. Today is her birthday, and I ain't tryin'a get fucked up with them nig-gas like that." He listened for a while and then nodded as if the person on the other end of the phone could see the gesture. "Bruh, I ain't playing with you. This shit better be what you say or me and you are gonna have a prob-lem." He disconnected the call and stuffed his cell back into the pocket of his jeans.

"Baby, I gotta make a run right quick. But I promise I will be home before you wake up," Roland had said, extending his pinky to pinky swear. The next morning, she'd run to his room, hoping to get him to take her to the flea market, one of their favorite things to do together, but he wasn't there. His bed was made, like it hadn't been slept in. She went to the kitchen, and panic gripped her when she saw Tootie sitting at the kitchen table crying. Roosevelt had promptly shooed her away and back into her bedroom. She would learn later that her father was back in jail.

"You all right, princess?" Teddy asked, pulling Nova from her daydream.

She hadn't realized she was crying until she saw the teardrops puddling in her salad bowl. "I'm good. Just miss my dad, I guess."

Teddy reached across the table and lifted Nova's chin. "I bet you do. Look at it this way, he'll be home in a minute, and hopefully we can convince him to stay out this time. You don't have a reason to hang your head. I shouldn't be telling you this, but the night your daddy got busted, I begged him to go home, to just leave the shit alone, but he wouldn't listen. After y'all got back from your little trip, he came to the after-hours joint on Lamar. There was money in there that night, and the dice were hitting. Between me and your daddy, we had both lost around three, four thousand dollars. Enough about that old shit. I wanna help you get your shit straight before your father gets home. Baby girl, I'm telling you, you stick with me, and I'll have you out here drippin' in diamonds, Dior, Fendi, whatever you want. New car, new apartment."

Nova's eyes widened. Teddy knew that he had her interest. He smiled and took her hands in his.

"Nova, you're a grown woman now. You're too old to still have a curfew. Don't you want your own spot where you can come and go as you please? I can make that happen. I can take care of you."

"Yeah, Teddy? And what's it going to cost me?"

"Take a walk with me," he said, tossing three crisp $100 bills onto the table. As they passed the waiter, Teddy winked at him. "Look out, playa. I left enough to cover the check and your tip. Be easy."

They walked a short distance, and on a couple of occasions, Nova even allowed Teddy to hold her hand. The park near the diner had a small pond with ducks, and Teddy bought a bag of breadcrumbs from a nearby vendor and took a seat on a nearby bench. Joggers, mothers pushing whining babies on play dates, and rollerbladers all vied for space on the narrow asphalt path.

Teddy put his arm around Nova and whispered in her ear, "Where your daddy at?"

"In prison—" Nova started, but Teddy cut her off.

"Wrong, baby girl. Yo' daddy is sitting right next to you. Yeah, your biological daddy is in prison because that nigga abandoned you for these streets a long time ago. He's selfish for putting money before you, baby, real shit. Tootie's ass is trying to keep your magnificence from the world because her time has passed. They treat you like a child, and I, for one, am appalled. I mean, look at you! Certified, qualified, and fine as the day is long. Say, mane, you got it, you hear me? You got it. You got that mojo! Damn, let me look at you. Walk over there, then walk back," Teddy ordered softly.

Nova stood and adjusted her jeans and made her ass jiggle. She did it on purpose to impress Teddy and flaunt her curvaceous body. She sashayed along the gravel walkway leading to the pond. Her hips swayed and her rotund ass bounced in rhythmic succession as if dancing to a beat that only she could hear. She stopped and turned to Teddy and locked eyes with him. Angelic slivers of wispy white clouds sliced through majestic hues of purples and blues as the sun descended to its resting place. The setting was perfect, just like in the daydreams that Nova had had on so many occasions. Nova fantasized about Teddy standing and grabbing her, kissing her while the sun set in the distance.

The black silk slacks that he wore were bulging in the front, his arousal evident.

She glared at him. "So I'm supposed to sit back and let you talk about my father and my auntie like that? I thought you all were friends."

Teddy stood up and walked to Nova, looking down on her with a saddened look on his face. He kissed her softly and pulled away. He walked to the edge of the pond and felt the soft, wet mud squish beneath his alligator loafers. "Sweetness, I'm not trying to talk bad about your father or your aunt. I'm giving you some cold, hard facts. Mu'fuckas been running in and outta yo' life since you were a kid, but things are about to change. I'm trying to put you on a winning team, beautiful." Teddy let the compliment drip from his split tongue like venomous syrup from a lecherous viper. He turned toward her with a knowing smile on his face.

"Winning team?" she asked with a befuddled look in her eyes.

Teddy chuckled and Nova grinned, giving life to his credo, "If you grin, you're in." He pulled her to him and kissed her hard, allowing his tongue to swirl and explore the deepest recesses of her young, soft, wet mouth. He pressed his stiff erection against the soft flesh of her stomach.

At first Nova wanted to slap him, but his tongue slithered in her mouth expertly as if it had a mind of its own. He sucked her bottom lip softly and bit it gently before once again letting his tongue swirl and twirl. Their tongues wrestled, and Teddy squeezed her ass cheeks as they kissed like lovestruck teenagers. She felt her knees weaken, threatening to reveal her enjoyment. Nova draped her arms around Teddy's neck and kissed him deeply. Teddy hugged her tighter and kissed her deeper, and then he pulled away and looked at her. "I'm gonna

show you how I get down. I'm the only daddy you gon'
ever need, you can believe that."

"If I do this, if we do this, I'm not going to be your little
love thang you keep hidden away. I'm not sitting home
while you run the streets, Teddy, so if you're trying to
run game, let me save you some trouble. I know you have
women out here. I hear things and I'm not stupid. So to
keep the confusion down, I'll play my role, but I have
some rules. You're going to get me the apartment like
you said and pay it up for a year, in my name. I want a
car, same deal, my name. And there will be no pulling up
to my spot and acting crazy because you see somebody
there. As a matter of fact, don't come by unannounced,"
Nova said, watching his face, trying to gauge his reaction.

"Seems like you've been thinking about this, huh? Well,
I got rules too. You can get at any of these youngsters out
here you want to, but don't fall in love. I'm first before
anybody, ya dig? And if you choose to get a boyfriend,
don't even think about moving the nigga into the spot
that I'm paying for. Just so we're clear, this is a business
agreement. I break bread, and you spread them legs. Is
that what you're telling me?" All the slick pimp speech
had left his vernacular, and now his words bordered on
frenzied anticipation. His dick throbbed, and the harder
it got, the more it hurt.

"You don't have to make it sound so dirty. You're my
man when you're with me and vice versa. I need your
help, you're willing to help me, so what we do is our business. Simple. But don't get it twisted. I'm not a whore."

"I know you ain't no ho, baby. I'm just trying to be to
you what your daddy shoulda been to you a long time ago.
You think Tootie is going to be a problem?"

"I'm grown. If you're not around here putting our
business in the streets, my auntie won't know what I
have going on," Nova said with a shrug.

"This is like some forbidden love shit, huh?"

It's whatever you want to think it is, big man, but the ball is in my court, Nova thought, but out loud she said, "Whatever you say . . . daddy."

Chapter Eight

It was so muggy outside when Jarvis stepped out of Mrs. Marie's house that he started sweating instantly. A single heavy bead of sweat ran from behind his ear and along his neck until it disappeared into the puddle building inside his T-shirt. He glanced at his watch. It was 3:47 in the morning, and there was no way that he wouldn't be hearing Angela's and Fred's mouths. Jarvis wasn't worried about it because he had made enough money to buy their silence for another week. And if that didn't work, he would get a room until he could stack enough money to get an apartment. Jarvis crossed the street and saw a few guys he knew from the neighborhood.

"What's good, youngsta? Let me holla atcha right quick," a gravelly voice said from the shadows.

Every bone in Jarvis's body rattled, and his bladder felt heavy. "Sheeeit!" he screamed. He wasn't afraid because he knew who it was before he ever saw his face.

Lizard was a reformed dopefiend who spent his time on the streets with the same people he once got high with, trying to pull them into sobriety with him. "Look out, young blood, I didn't mean to scare you," he said with a sly chuckle. Lizard stepped from the darkness and extended his fist, which Jarvis bumped.

"You didn't scare me, old school. You just always doing that spooky shit hiding in the shadows and shit."

"Better to see than to be seen, fool. Better to hear than to speak, you feel me? But look here, I wanna rap wit' you a taste if you got time."

Jarvis peered down the street to the corner where his friends were. They were entertaining a group of girls in front of the Grand City Grocery. "Yeah, I got a few minutes Lizard, what's good?" Jarvis said. His eyes were still trained on the group on the corner.

"I ain't never been one to get into nobody's business, but I need to pull your coat."

"G'on and speak ya mind, old head. I'm tryin'a get to the crib." Jarvis was growing impatient, and it showed in his tone.

Lizard ran his hand across the white stubble growing on his chin. "You're a smart young'un, Jarvis. You're not like these knuckleheads out here. I knew your parents, and they were good people. They kept you and your sister away from this bullshit for a reason. Why you're going against the grain boggles my mind."

"Is there a point to all this, or are we just taking a stroll down memory lane?"

"Yeah, just like your old man, right to the business. I'ma keep it short. Them boys are jealous of you, mane. They know that you don't have to sell dope. They know that you're smarter than them, and they know that you have what it takes to get out of this hellhole. They're hoping that you follow them down that ghetto-ass rabbit hole. When me and your parents were coming up, we had each other's backs, or at least we tried to. I was a knucklehead like your friends right there," Lizard said, nodding toward Dog Face, Scooter, and a muscular dum-dum named Bumpy. "That's why while your daddy and mama were building a legacy with the shop, I was out here robbing, doing time, and smoking crack. I was hardheaded and didn't wanna listen. All I'm saying is your daddy passed you a real gift. Don't blow it tryin'a run with niggas who will probably be in prison with football numbers in the next couple of years. It's your life, and I know you

probably think ol' Lizard ain't got no right to lace you
with no game, seeing how I squandered my own life. But
experience is the best teacher, right?" Lizard stared off
into a faraway galaxy that was far beyond Jarvis's field
of vision. His eyes were glassy and sad. "Your daddy had
this exact same conversation with me, and I didn't listen
to him. I thought he was crazy with his big dreams of
wanting to open a shop in the hood. I don't think I could
call myself your daddy's friend if I didn't pull his only
son's coattails, ya dig? What kinda OG would I be if I
didn't give you the game?" Lizard had posed a rhetorical
question and didn't wait for a response. He disappeared
back into the shadows he had come from.

Jarvis had never known that Lizard grew up with his
parents and didn't know that they were friends. But he
knew that the old fiend spoke the truth. When he and
Angela were much younger, during happier times before
his parents died, his father's meteoric rise in automotive
care was fabled in the hood. Dexter Lane had single-
handedly changed the landscape with his "for the people"
approach. He offered the same level of care and quality
as the big boys at a fraction of the cost or, as Dexter liked
to put it, "I'm giving our people dealership-warranty
quality at shade-tree mechanic prices." And people loved
him for it. His father not only took the best shade-tree
mechanics and trained them to do it the right way, but he
also trained the wayward teens in the neighborhood.

Jarvis had been raised in the garage. He knew wrench
sizes and tool names before he even started school. He
couldn't remember a time when his father was under the
hood of somebody's car and he wasn't at his father's side,
learning, fully engrossed in the challenge of finding a
vehicle's hidden ailment.

Miriam, Jarvis's mother, had died first. She had been
diagnosed with stage 4 pancreatic cancer. As soon as

they operated on her to remove some tumors, the cancer spread. First it went to her liver and then her lungs. The disease spread aggressively throughout her body, and it ravaged her. Dexter and Miriam had managed to keep her illness away from their children until her failing health made her frailty visible. They could no longer carry on the charade. The night that they sat Jarvis and Angela down for the "talk" haunted him.

"You kids know me and your daddy love you very much, and this is a conversation that we never thought we'd have with you, but here we are."

His father, who was usually a strong, imposing figure with a booming voice, was silent. He looked shrunken and weak. He looked defeated.

"You're probably wondering why I look like this," *Miriam said, removing the silk scarf covering her head. The chemotherapy had taken most of her once-thick mane and left wispy strings of hair. She looked embarrassed, as if the side effects of her impending death were somehow her fault.*

"As you can see, the chemo isn't working, and the doctors have given me three months to live," *Miriam said, her tone soft and flat. She kept her eyes locked on her hands resting in her lap. She was afraid to look up, afraid that meeting their eyes would unleash the waterworks.*

At her words, Dexter broke down. His sobs came in deep, heavy, guttural cries. Miriam put a hand on his knee. The action caused him to quiet some, but only to a whimper.

Three months? *Jarvis thought he had more time. He was only 10 years old, and although he and his father were very close, his mother was his best friend. The feeling of helplessness was gut-wrenching. It didn't take three months, because not even two weeks after having that conversation with his mother, Jarvis, Angela, and Dexter were sitting in a mortuary making funeral arrangements for his mother.*

After her death, Angela had tried to fill their mother's shoes, but it wasn't the same. His father tried to make things as normal as possible, but the void left by Miriam was deafening. Dexter never fully recovered from his wife's death, and a year later he went to sleep in his La-Z-Boy and never woke up. Jarvis remembered the distinct smell of cognac and cigars when he found his father's corpse. The doctors said that his heart just stopped beating, but Jarvis knew better. Miriam was Dexter's best friend just as she was his. That connection, that piece of Miriam she attached to everyone she came in contact with, was gone. His father couldn't live without it, and in the end, Dexter Lane died from a broken heart.

"Dawg, you don't hear me talking to you?" Dog Face said. He had stepped in front of Jarvis, blocking his path.

Jarvis had been so lost in his thoughts that he didn't even realize he was walking. "Damn, my bad, Face. What up, my nigga?"

"I was saying me, Scooter, and Bumpy about to go run a train on this bitch. You down or what?" Dog Face asked.

"Nah, homie, I'm going to catch hell from Angela for being out most of the night anyway. I'll catch you on the next one."

"Yo' loss, nigga. I heard this little bitch a freak," Bumpy chimed in, rubbing his crotch.

Jarvis turned to walk away. There was nothing appealing or enticing to him about being in a room naked with three other men. Not to mention the emotional trauma the girl would suffer whether immediately or later. Jarvis couldn't be a part of that.

He had made it maybe twenty feet from the group when the unmistakable hum of a police cruiser came to a screeching stop. He kept walking, quickening his pace until he heard a Southern-tinged voice yell, "Don't you fucking move!" from behind him. He froze, afraid to move for fear that he might end up like so many of the other African American young men whose faces were ironed on the front of T-shirts with declarations of "Rest in Peace" and "Never Forgotten." Jarvis's legs were quivering, and he felt like he had to pee. If they found the few rocks that he had left in his pocket, they would put a case on him for sure. Maybe he could tell them that he was a crackhead and that the drugs were for personal use, but with a pocketful of money, it was unlikely that they would buy it.

"Damn it!" Jarvis cursed under his breath. His tongue felt wet, and his stomach churned and gurgled. Jarvis turned around slowly. His eyes searched for an escape route as he turned just in case he got the urge to run. He locked eyes with a short, stocky redneck cop. His sleeves were rolled up, exposing his massive biceps. He looked agitated, angry almost as he stared at Jarvis, nostrils flaring. Officer Malnik, as his nametag read, was in definite need of a steroid break.

"What the fuck are you doing? Go where the fuck you're going, or you can get what these assholes are about to get!" he barked.

"I thought you were talking to me, Officer. My bad," Jarvis said.

"Damn right it's your bad," the officer said, but Jarvis was already a block away, turning the corner that led to his house. He stopped walking and took a deep breath of the stale, musty, stifling air. The whole ordeal, from Lizard stopping him to the brush with the police, was weighing on him. He reached into his pocket, grabbed the rocks, and looked at them. He had four $50 slabs left.

"Heyyyyy, Jarvis," a syrupy sweet voice called.

"S'up, Dana?"

"Where you going?"

"I'm going home," Jarvis said. He didn't care for Dana. She was the kind of crackhead who would sell her own child if it meant getting another hit.

"If you going to bed when you get home, you might as well let me suck that dick and drain ya little sack. I'll get you right for a Twinkie," she hissed.

"Nah, I'm good. Appreciate you, though, being concerned with my sack and all," he said, rolling his eyes.

"You got anything left that I can cop? I got fo' dollars, baby."

"Nope, sure don't." Jarvis turned to walk away and stopped again. "Yo, Dana, check this out."

She switched over to him, slender hips swinging from side to side. "What's up, daddy?"

"Here you go. I'm out. You can have this shit." He handed Dana the four slabs that he had left. Jarvis held out the palm of his hand, and Dana's eyes turned to saucers.

"Just remember I took care of you," Jarvis said and walked through the gate and up the sidewalk to his front door. If he was starting fresh, he was leaving all the bullshit outside.

Chapter Nine

Jarvis could have easily slept another two or three hours, but the smell of scrambled eggs pulled him from a sound slumber. He sat up in bed and let his feet touch the cold hardwood floor. As he had hoped, the frigid wood jolted him and forced the grogginess from his brain. He slid on his house shoes, stood, and yawned. Jarvis let his hand glide across his tight stomach. He didn't have a six-pack, but it was hard and flat. He grabbed a T-shirt and headed to the bathroom. Malcolm was coming out of the bathroom when Jarvis reached it.

"What's up, little man?" Jarvis said, throwing a fake punch at Malcolm.

"Don't 'little man' me." Malcolm made to push past Jarvis, but he put a hand on the boy's chest.

"Whooooa, nephew, what's with all the hostility?"

"You lied! You said we would play the game when you got home, but you didn't come home!" Malcolm said. He wasn't yelling, but his voice was naturally loud. Couple that with the fact that the kid had no idea what whispering was and Jarvis was sure Angela had heard him.

He looked down the hallway toward the kitchen and then back to Malcolm. "Chill, G, that's my bad. I got caught up, and by the time I made it home, you were asleep."

Malcolm's anger was palpable, and tears lined the rims of his eyes.

"But look, by the time you get out of school, I'll have a regular job, with regular hours, so I'll be home a lot more. If you forgive me, I will make it up to you. How about if I take you and Martin to Urban Air when I get my first check?" Jarvis said, putting a comforting hand on his nephew's shoulder.

At the mention of Urban Air, the boy's mood changed. "You found a job?" he asked excitedly.

"Not yet, but I'll have one before the day ends," Jarvis said. His confidence was high, and he was going to manifest a job. He didn't care if he had to shovel shit. He wouldn't come back to his sister's house without a job.

"Cool," Malcolm said, then went into his room to get dressed for school.

Jarvis went to the kitchen and saw Angela still in her bathrobe pulling a pan of biscuits from the oven. "Hey, Angel," Jarvis said, kissing her on top of her head.

"Don't 'Angel' me!"

"Jesus Christ, what is with the people in this family?" Jarvis said.

"What?"

"Never mind. Look, before you start fussin', I was dead wrong for being out all night. I should have at least called and let you know that I was safe. That was my bad, and I'm going to do better. Also, I'm jumping on the bus today, and I'm not coming home until I find a job. I'm done with the streets." Jarvis had said he was getting out of the streets on more than one occasion, but Lizard's words had made him call his mind back.

Angela was speechless because he had said exactly what she had intended to say. There was no sense in flaring up because Jarvis had stolen her argument. "Who are you, and what have you done with my baby brother? Do you have bus fare for the day?" she asked.

"I'm straight, sis. I appreciate you though."

"Go take a shower and put some clothes on. By the time you finish, the food will be ready."

Jarvis showered slowly, mapping his job search route in his head. He would go to north Dallas first because it was his farthest point of consideration. He would end at his father's old shop. It was still a garage, but it was owned by a car dealer. Even if they didn't hire him, at least he would be closer to home, because the dealership was only a few blocks from his house. If he did have to face disappointment, it was only a short ride home. There was nothing worse than being in a bad mood and have to deal with the weirdos who frequented the city bus.

Jarvis dressed in a pair of navy blue khakis and a white slim-fit polo. He completed his ensemble with a pair of cognac-colored chukka boots and the belt to match. Jarvis brushed the thick black beehive of waves on his head. He looked in the mirror and gave an approving smile.

"You look nice! I'd hire you," Angela said with a wide smile. She put a plate of scrambled eggs, smothered potatoes, and bacon with a side of biscuits and gravy in front of him. "Sit down and eat. Malcolm, Martin, hurry up before you miss the bus," she said, craning her neck toward the hall.

"This looks good, sis. Thank you."

"You're welcome. Now eat. Early bird gets the worm."

Malcolm and Martin came out, dressed in school uniforms, their book bags hanging below their butts from the weight. Angela handed each of them a butterscotch hard candy. It was a practice that she had started on Malcolm's first day of kindergarten. The candy had been the only thing that had been able to quiet his cries from first-day jitters. Malcolm had gone through extreme separation anxiety, but the sweet treat had calmed him and had become a welcomed routine.

"You are both brilliant, beautiful boys. You have everything to gain and nothing to lose from paying attention and learning. I love you, and I want you both to shine today. What are the golden rules?" Angela asked.

"Listen more than I talk. Pay attention to everything around me. Honor my ancestors by learning and teaching. And know that I am love and I am loved," they said in unison.

"Good job! Have a fantastic day. I love you both. Make good choices," she said, kissing her boys before they left.

"See you later, Uncle Jarvis," Martin said.

"I'll see y'all later," Jarvis said.

Malcolm ran back to him and gave him dap. "Good luck today. If you find a job, I might let you win tonight." The boys scurried from the house, slamming the door behind them.

"I guess I'm going to get going too, Angela," Jarvis said. He stood and took another swig of his orange juice and grabbed the large manila envelope that held his résumés. He went to the door and turned back to Angela. "If you've ever been ashamed of me or have ever been disappointed in me, I'm sorry."

Angela walked to him and placed her hand on his cheek. With her free hand she placed a butterscotch hard candy in her baby brother's palm. She knew that he was searching for himself. Jarvis was trying to find his place in a world that oftentimes prejudged and categorized young men like him. She had done her best without their parents, but his journey to manhood was a challenge that she could not walk him through. She could only encourage him. "You are brilliant and intelligent, and the world needs you, black man. You got this! I'm proud of you, Jarvis, and always remember that you are love and you are loved."

***

By 2:00 p.m., Jarvis had submitted more than twenty applications along with his résumé. He even had copies of his high school diploma and his transcripts from El Centro College. He only needed one elective and a macro-economics course to get his associate's degree. But none of the garages or dealerships he went to were interested in anything that he had to offer. Some would smile and look at him with pity like he was the poor black boy out of his league. Some were blunter: "I'm sure you're good with the cars in the hood, but we're not hiring." Or after looking him up and down: "If we're interested, we'll call. Here at Blah Blah Motors, we blah blah fucking blah." The rejection made his ears hot, and slowly discouragement and self-doubt started to creep into his head like a foggy mist.

He had one more stop before he called it a day. The sign read ROTH MOTORS, written in fancy script. It looked out of place in the semi-drab neighborhood with a liquor store on one corner and an abandoned dry cleaner on the other. The garage and car lot weren't for the people in the neighborhood. It was for the well-to-do whites, Hispanics, and bourgeoisie blacks who were pushing in as gentrification spread.

Jarvis took a deep breath and walked inside. The shop had changed from when Dexter owned it. It looked like they had added a lot of lights, along with more state-of-the-art equipment. The walls had been painted a sterile white and the floors red. He was still admiring the shop when a short white man came and stood next to him. "It's beautiful, isn't it?"

"Yes, it is. It looks more like an operating room than a garage," Jarvis said. Even the car lifts were spotless. The red paint looked fresh and new, and there were no oil spots.

"You must really have a love for cars, kid. I'm Saul, Saul Rothberger. I own this place."

"Nice to meet you. I'm Jarvis Lane. I came in today hoping that I might leave you my résumé."

"Are you a mensch or are you a meshuggener?" Saul asked.

"I'm sorry, sir, I don't know what that means, but I'm hardworking and dependable. I'm a fast learner, and I'm really good with cars," Jarvis said. The nervousness he experienced when interviewing was excruciating. But this wasn't a formal interview. This was the owner. He could feel the moisture collecting in his armpits. His desperation was tangible, and he hoped that it didn't show in his face.

The old man adjusted his yarmulke and grew quiet as if he might be considering Jarvis's pitch. "I like your chutzpah, kid. Unfortunately, I'm closing these doors for good. My beautiful Francine has gone to sing with the angels, and I have no desire for the car business anymore. So the car lot has been sold to a property developer, and they are building a plaza there. They didn't want the garage in the deal, so I'm going to sell it independently," Saul said.

Jarvis had grown quiet at the thought that the shop, a part of him, being lost forever was a real possibility.

"Don't look so glum, kid. I'm sure there are plenty of garages that would love to have you. If I weren't selling it, I'd hire you. Truth is, I only bought this place because a really good friend of mine owned it once. Good kid. I couldn't let his dream turn to dust, you know," Saul said.

"My dad used to own this shop. Probably after your friend, but I grew up here. When my dad died, I was still a kid. I wish I had some money, Mr. Rothberger. I'd buy it from you myself."

"You say you grew up here, huh? You kind of remind me of my friend: young, full of piss and vinegar, full of confidence. He was my student back in the old days when schools had automotive shop. He stayed in that shop, turning wrenches, diagnosing problems." Saul stopped talking, and his mouth dropped open and his head snapped toward Jarvis.

"Hey, kid, what did you say your name was again?" Saul asked.

"It's Lane, sir."

"Would you be any relation to Dexter Lane?"

At the mention of his father's name, Jarvis's heart sank into the pit of his stomach. "That's my dad."

"Your father was a brilliant mechanic, Jarvis. Let me show you something." He led Jarvis into his office. It was the opposite of the actual shop. Where the shop had been clinically clean, Saul's office was an OCD patient's worst nightmare. Files and papers were thrown across his desk in haphazard piles, and file boxes were stacked behind his desk. A row of file cabinets with different-sized snow globes were aligned by scenery. In the corner a water cooler with a five-gallon water jug on top gulped lazily as they walked in. "You see this? He was special," Saul said. He handed Jarvis a picture and took a seat behind his desk.

It was a picture of Mr. Rothberger, Dexter, and a woman Jarvis assumed was his beautiful Francine. Dexter was holding a trophy and a check with a huge smile on his face.

"The day that picture was taken was when I realized that this kid was the real deal. There used to be a magazine, not sure if it's still around, called *Popular Mechanics,* that was having a contest for kids fifteen to eighteen. They supplied the car, and the kids had to diagnose it, go into a massive warehouse, find their parts, and fix whatever the problem was. Your dad was a prodigy, Jarvis. He found the problem, picked the needed parts, and had the engine repaired in record time. That check that you see him holding in that picture was for ten thousand dollars. He went there with the intention to win the seed money to start this place, and he won. That's my Francine, standing with us," Saul said. He beamed with pride as he recounted more old stories about Dexter and his love for cars. "There was only one thing that Dexter loved more than cars and that was—"

"Miriam, my mom," Jarvis said proudly.

"Miriam is your mother? She was a wonderful woman, and Franny and I absolutely adored your mother. I wish there were more I could do to help, kid. I'm sorry," Saul said.

Jasper shook the old man's hand and left the shop. The sun was sneaking off to slumber, and in its wake, it left an array of dark blues and orange hues.

Chapter Ten

The tension in the small apartment was thick as frozen peanut butter. Tootie hadn't really spoken to Nova since she came home with the new black Acura, and now she was coming to her to tell her that Teddy was putting her in an apartment. "Nova, I don't like this shit one bit! Teddy is old enough to be your damn daddy. He done bought you a car, putting you in an apartment and shit. I never figured you as a sugar-daddy type, but you're grown," Tootie sneered.

"It's not even like that."

"What's it like, Nova? Do you know what kind of reputation Teddy has in these streets, girl? He just wants to use you up and throw you away. Just because you lost your job fucking with Chino's grimy ass doesn't mean you need to jump out of the frying pan and into the fire."

"I got this. You're worried for nothing."

"I sure hope so. You can play a lot of ways, but a man's money and his heart are always off-limits. If you're going to play the game, you have to be ready, because ain't no love in these streets and these niggas make the rules as they go along."

Part Two:

Funny How Time Flies

Chapter Eleven

She was the only bright spot in his life, and Jarvis knew he needed money to keep it that way. Not that it was a requirement to have her, but as a man it was his job to provide and protect. She didn't like hustlers, but desperate times called for desperate measures, and Jarvis was at his lowest. He'd jumped from job to job, most of them lasting no more than a few months at best. Some of the jobs he was fired from for tardiness, but being dependent on public transportation didn't exactly advance his cause. Other jobs he just walked away from because of a lack of interest.

Angela held true to her word and had Fred toss him out on his ass. He worked for Mr. Rothberger on the weekends, but that was barely enough to cover the rent for the efficiency apartment he lived in. He looked around the sparsely furnished hovel and sighed. He wanted to move in with his girlfriend, but she wasn't having it. She said she needed to make sure that he wanted her and didn't need her. She'd told him point blank, "Most of these lames out here aren't looking for a relationship. They're looking for help. I'm not taking care of no man, but I will put something with something to make something." She didn't care that his place was small or that every penny he made was dedicated to not starving. She showed him on more than one occasion that she had his back, but he was still a hustler by nature.

The streets had a way of either pushing you toward legal greatness or dragging you into the gutter where you squirm the rest of your life to claw your way out. The average woman would have folded and left, but Nova wasn't average. She swore to him that they would be rich if he believed in her, and he fell headfirst. He was all in. Jarvis felt that familiar stirring in his loins thinking about the things that she could do to his body.

He was lying in bed naked, arms folded behind his head, staring at the ceiling. He climbed from his bed and stood in the full-length mirror. He pulled the shirt that he wore over his head, exposing his slender, muscular frame. The tiny gold chain and cross that he wore glimmered brightly against his dark skin. He stripped out of his pants and boxers and admired his own semi-erect penis. She was in his head bad, and she knew it, teasing him with salacious phone calls and touching him seductively in public.

He smiled, because as sprung as he was on Nova, he knew that she was just as gone with the heavy, veiny muscle hanging between his legs. The thought of her thickness drove him crazy with lust, and he could feel his manhood start to stiffen. He grabbed the lotion from his dresser, sat at the edge of his bed, and stroked himself until he was hard. He pulled his favorite picture of Nova up on his phone and thought about the night he'd taken the shot. That night, Nova had professed her love for him after months of playing cat and mouse. Their conversations were innocent at first, a compliment here, a subtle touch there, until he turned up the heat.

"What do you want from me, Nova? I mean, it's obvious that I'm still not that nigga you referred to when you shot me down the first fucking time."

"I want you to be everything that I believe you can be, baby, trust," she'd said, reaching into his boxers, massaging his manhood. She'd rocked back and posed, instructing him to take the picture. She was lying back on her elbows across his bed in nothing but a bra and panties in front of him with a look on her face that begged him to take her. Nova's legs were parted, and the print of her pussy was pressed firmly against yellow satin. Her dark nipples were visible through the sheer fabric, and her chocolate skin shimmered under the glow of a red bulb.

Jarvis stroked a little more and stopped. The last thing he needed was to start playing with it, bust one, and Nova wanted to fuck later. He would never be able to convince her that he wasn't cheating. "See? She got you so gone you don't even wanna waste your seed, soft ass," he scolded himself.

"It's me, babe. Open the door," Nova said from the other side of the door.

"Shit, girl, I thought you were coming closer to seven thirty!" Jarvis said as he scrambled around the room looking for something to cover up with. He snatched the musty tank top from the back of the office chair beside his dresser, sniffed it, and winced. Jarvis stretched the shirt around his waist and held it with one hand and opened the door with the other.

"Hey, baby, come in. What's up?" Jarvis asked, nearly out of breath.

Nova looked down at the imprint bulging beneath the thin material. "Hmph!" She pushed past Jarvis and swiveled on her heels until she faced him. "What you in here doing, Jarvis?"

She hated when he laughed at her, but he couldn't help it. Her voice was light and airy. It was the type of voice reserved for kindergarten teachers and pediatric doctors. "Oh, you think it's funny? You're going to make me fuck you up!"

Again, he laughed, this time letting the shirt fall from his hands to expose his now fully erect penis.

"You got somebody in here? Keep playing with me, I'ma chop your little pretty dick off."

"Man, ain't nobody in here, and chill out with the dick threats. You tripping," Jarvis said. With the mention of chopping off his Johnson, his sense of humor and his erection both died at the same time.

"Uh-huh." Nova walked to the closet and snatched the door open as if she expected to see some scared thot cowering behind a pile of dirty clothes. With her aha moment dashed, she kneeled and peered beneath the full-size bed, but there was nothing there save a few socks that had gone missing, waiting in darkness, where socks go to die.

"Your little ass is crazy, but I love it." He pulled her close to him.

Nova glared up at Jarvis, her Hennessy-colored eyes burning holes into his smoky retinas. "I'm serious, Jarvis! If you fuck me over, I'ma cut it off. That's my dick!" she hissed, grabbing his tool, stroking it gently. It seemed to fill her entire hand, and she felt the heat and moisture building between her legs. Her clit twitched and throbbed as she thought about the way his dick was arched and hung slightly to the left. Before Jarvis could ever get the chance to use the sliver of pink heaven in his mouth, his perfectly shaped penis had already brought her to at least three orgasms. She didn't know how a man could find her G-spot so easily, and with his dick no less. Nova shook her head, trying to snap herself out of the trance of Jarvis Lane.

"Girl, if you knew how I felt about you, you wouldn't even trip. I don't want nobody but you, baby."

"Prove it then." She pouted.

"How? Just name it."

"Tell me you're ready to hit this lick so we can open this shop and leave these streets alone."

"You already know I'm with it, babe. What's the play?"

"You know my uncle Teddy I'm always telling you about? He's looking for somebody to make collections. I'm gonna get you put on so that you can see how this shit works. Then we're going to hit all the houses at the same time."

"Won't he be suspicious that it was us?" Jarvis asked, not really understanding.

"You let me worry about that. I'm working out the details in my head. The important thing is to get you inside his camp. I will set up everything, and if all goes well, it's on, baby," Nova said, stroking him a little more before backing away toward the bed. "Besides, I know you love me, right?" She lifted her summer dress above her waist and bent over the bed.

Jarvis's eyes were glued to the puffiness beneath the ruby red lingerie she wore. He licked his lips and reached out and caressed her ebony butt cheeks. "You know I do." His voice was husky and dripping with lust and anticipation.

"If we can pull this off, we'll be making love on the beach under the stars in Jamaica somewhere, sipping on Mai Tais and Rum Runners."

Jarvis had gotten lost in her fantasy and subsequently bought it hook, line, and sinker. "I'm going to jump in the shower. You coming with me?" he said from the bathroom doorway.

"No, babe, I'm going to call my uncle and put things in motion."

Nova watched him disappear into the bathroom and waited until she heard the water running before dialing Teddy's number.

"Hello? Hey, remember the guy Jarvis I told you I wanted you to put on? I'm going to bring him by tonight so that you can meet him, is that cool?"

"Yeah, it's cool, but I ain't no rest haven for dumb niggas. If this nigga can't keep up with my paper, we're gonna have a problem."

"The dude is going to be a collector. You act like he's going to be your accountant or something." Nova chuckled nervously.

"And you sound like you're falling in love with this nigga. All giggly and shit," Teddy hissed through the phone.

"I love you and only you, Teddy. Stop playin'. He's just my little friend."

"Don't let your little friend get you dumped in a cold, dark alley somewhere."

"Like Chino?" Nova asked, but Teddy didn't answer.

Chapter Twelve

As the saying goes, "The more things change, the more they stay the same." Teddy had more money than he could count, he had endless women at his beck and call, and he had the streets on lock. What else could a young 44-year-old playa ask for? He wanted something real to call his own.

He had grown bored with Nova. The little bitch was expensive, and she always had her hand out, but she was a freak, and the more money he gave her, the freakier she got. When Teddy wanted to screw, he called Nova, and when she needed or wanted money, she called him. It was the perfect arrangement, but things were different now, and it wasn't lost on Teddy. She wasn't as attentive and nowhere near as sexual as she used to be.

He wondered if this kid Jarvis was the reason for the change in Nova. She had the audacity to bring her boyfriend to him to help get his money right. Nova would be getting paper on both ends, and Teddy wasn't sure she had even figured that out. The way Teddy saw it, it was all his money anyway because he'd be paying Jarvis.

"In that case, I might as well be getting it all. Right now, fuck that bitch," Teddy said. He walked to the window of his apartment and opened the blinds. Below were zombified crackheads on their way to their next deadly fix. Teddy felt most comfortable here among the broken glass and crack vials that littered the streets of south Dallas. His people loved him, and he loved them right back, basking in their special blend of adoration and terror. Of course, he had haters, but who didn't? Anyone who thought that he was a monster had obviously done something to provoke him, right? Like Chino.

Nova had come to him about helping that clown, too. Teddy, trying to play the role and putting one of her friends on, put Chino on house count. All he had to do was go from trap to trap and count money. The fool didn't even have to pick up money, just count it and turn in a tally. He had come short on quite a few counts, and when Teddy confronted him about it, he bucked and tried to put it on the trap workers, saying that they were coming up short. The problem with it was he only did it in houses where he had Nova doing pickups and deliveries. Teddy had cameras installed in all the traps, and just as Teddy had suspected, Nova didn't know shit.

He had her ask Chino to meet her at a remote location on the outskirts of Dallas under the guise of reconciling their relationship. When he got there, he was confronted with Teddy's pistol in his face and video evidence of his thievery. Teddy handed Nova the pistol and told her that since she was the one who introduced him to their world, she had to be the one to do it. She refused, and even though Teddy threatened her, she couldn't pull the trigger. Teddy knew that Chino was a street cat, and if he let him go, he would have to look over his shoulder. Teddy shot Chino and left his body at the base of the rocks by the water. Nova loved helping strays and playing house with niggas who couldn't afford to walk in his shoes, and he was sick of it.

He pulled the cell phone from his pocket and dialed Dog Face and Scooter. They had a Mexican homeboy who could make anybody disappear and stay disappeared. He hadn't given a damn about killing Chino and leaving his body to be found, but Jarvis and Nova had family. If they came up missing, there would certainly be questions. Especially from Tootie. She knew that Nova was fucking both him and Jarvis, and she liked Jarvis more, so if anything happened to Nova or her precious boyfriend, Tootie would send the police to him first. Nah, he would rely on his shooters and cleanup man to take care of this one.

Chapter Thirteen

Nova's black Camry turned into the parking lot and backed into a spot marked RESERVED. Teddy couldn't see inside the car, but he knew that he was in there. A little drizzle had begun to blanket the streets, and Nova's headlights danced from raindrop to raindrop. It was as if she were intentionally sitting in the car, taunting him with her lover. He snatched the blinds closed and walked to the bar. Teddy poured a shot of vodka and downed it quickly. It burned his throat, blazing a fiery trail toward his stomach. He poured another, this time making sure to drop a couple of ice cubes in the glass so that he could sip this one.

Nova eased her way into the apartment with her key and smiled widely. "Heyyyy, Uncle Teddy."

"Hey, baby, what's crackin'?"

"Nothing. This is my friend Jarvis I was telling you about," Nova said, nodding toward her man.

Teddy gave the young, handsome kid the once-over. He could see why Nova was infatuated with him. His features were stern, and he looked strong. His body was lean and powerful, and he looked at Nova like she was the only thing in the world that existed. Yeah, aesthetically Jarvis was her type, but Teddy had an advantage: money.

"Look out, bruh. Nova tells me you're interested in making some real money," Teddy said, extending his hand.

"Yes, sir, I'm ready to make a come-up, you feel me?" Jarvis blurted, cursing himself silently for sounding overly eager.

"Good. I'm going to start you off slow, see how you do. If you play your cards right, you can move up really quick and make a ton of money. You fuck me over, you're a dead man, period."

Jarvis swallowed hard, but the lump in his throat didn't move. Every fiber in his body told him that the handshake was literally with the devil. He wanted to decline the offer because the look in Teddy's eyes terrified him, but he needed the money. "I won't fuck you over. That's not me. I just want to make money so that I can keep your niece happy."

"I believe you!" Teddy said, clamping his shovel-head-sized hand over the boy's shoulder.

Jarvis shook visibly under the weight of Teddy's hand. His knees threatened to buckle beneath the pressure of Teddy's thinly veiled threat. Jarvis Lane was nobody's gangster, not by a long shot, and he had the nagging feeling that he had stepped into something that was deeper than he knew, something that would drown him before it ever let him go.

"Go wait in the car, baby. I'll be out in a minute. I want to talk to Uncle for a minute," Nova said softly, gently brushing Jarvis's cheek with baby-soft hands.

Once Jarvis was outside, she watched him through the blinds until he made it to the car. The sun had all but burned the stormy clouds away and left an air of muggy misery in its wake. She kept her eyes planted on Jarvis as she spoke. "I need the money you owe me, Teddy."

"Sheeeeeeiiiiit, what money? You know what I need? I need for you to stop acting like I'm your personal ATM, like I'm a mu'fuckin' employment agency for these little niggas you be fucking! I need you to put me in that pussy

without rushing my time wit' ya. That's what I need."
Salaciousness dripped from Teddy's perverted tongue
with every word. He slid up behind her to let her feel his
semi-erect penis.

Nova sidestepped and pivoted and put her hand on
Teddy's chest. "Hold up. I already got Jarvis thinking
you're my uncle and shit. I already feel foul as fuck, man.
Just break me off. I'll be back later after I drop him off."

"A'ight, how much you need?" Teddy said, rubbing his
crotch, thinking about what later would be like.

Nova only extended her palm. She'd let him make the
decision. If it was too much, cool, and if it wasn't enough,
she would use it to throw in his face later. Teddy handed
her a wad of $100, $50, and $20 bills. Nova riffled
through the bills. It wasn't a lot, only $1,700, but it would
be a help in saving up for Jarvis's shop. She needed a life
away from Teddy, and that life would be with Jarvis. She
loved Teddy for all that he had taught her over the past
couple of years, but she was in love with Jarvis. They had
talked about moving away on more than one occasion,
but Nova doubted Jarvis would leave his family. She
just wanted to be somewhere people didn't know them,
where they could start fresh.

"Ay, while you're standing in my shit asking me about
my fuckin' money, you could at least not stare out the
window drooling over that nigga and shit. You're so
disrespectful, Nova, I swear, one of these days I'ma—"

"You're gonna what? All the shit I know about you,
Teddy, really? Don't try me. I'm not one of these little
hood rat bitches you've brainwashed out here. Stop
playing with me."

Nova eased out of the front door and shivered. The
more that she was around Teddy, the more her respect
for him dwindled. He was crass, arrogant, and extremely
abrasive, and she couldn't stand his ass, but he was never

stingy with the money. Nova had fallen into that trap like many of her friends. The dope boys and hustlers were flashy and always into shit, but the players? The players were older, treated them like queens, and made the sky the limit. The only problem with the players or sugar daddies was that they wanted complete dominion over their young subjects.

She threw on her best smile as she descended the stairs. Nova was still smiling when she threw her arms around Jarvis's neck and kissed him deeply. "My uncle really likes you, baby. That's the good news. The bad news is we gotta hit this lick like yesterday," she whispered in his ear.

Jarvis looked up toward Teddy's door to see him standing beneath his porch light. Moths flittered between the glowing light bulb and the smoke rings that Teddy blew from his cigarette. Jarvis nodded at Teddy, but there was no reciprocation. Only cold, evil eyes stared back at him, burning holes through his soul.

Chapter Fourteen

While Jarvis worked for Teddy, most of his time was spent in Teddy's bar on Lamar. It was just a hangout spot, a place where they all awaited Teddy's orders. Whether it was collecting rent from his tenants or money owed for drug debts, or picking up money from his whores, they were at his disposal. A lot of the guys were hired muscle to impose his distinct brand of street justice.

Jarvis had learned early not to cross Teddy. A john had refused to pay one of Teddy's girls, so Teddy had him kidnapped from work and brought to the bar. They dragged him through the bar to a storeroom in the back and tied him to a chair. The poor man begged and pleaded for them to let him go before Teddy got there. "I'll pay her and y'all, man. Please, just let me go!" he'd cried. Teddy had come in and immediately started to beat the man savagely across the face, all the while keeping his eyes trained on Jarvis.

Tonight, he would be meeting Scooter and Dog Face on the east side to do a pickup from some Mexicans, and he felt uneasy. His stomach churned as trepidation and hesitation did somersaults in his gut. He'd dealt with the Mexicans on more than one occasion, and they were never a problem, but Dog Face was trigger-happy and Scooter was his flunky, which made him even more dangerous. Maybe it was because it was so close to his house, or maybe it was because he knew that he wasn't built for the aftermath if things went wrong.

He reached beneath his pillow and removed a dull black small-caliber pistol and shoved it in his waistband. Jarvis went to the mirror hanging from his door and stared at himself. He was lean and muscular, but the black velour sweat suit only served to make him look skinnier. He adjusted his beanie. Yeah, he looked mean and tough, standing dressed in black from head to toe, but his gut was quivering, and he felt like he needed to poop. "Breathe, Jarvis, breathe," he scolded himself. Jarvis felt his butt pucker at the force banging on his door. "Who is it?" he screamed. It was screechy, and he cursed himself for sounding like a coward.

"Man, open the damn door. It's time to ride!" Dog Face yelled.

"Yeah, yeah, open the do', fool." Scooter snickered through rat-like teeth.

Jarvis eased the door open as if not trusting that the men were who they said they were. "What's up?"

"Move, nigga!" Dog Face said, pushing his way into Jarvis's apartment.

"I thought that I was supposed to be meeting y'all on the east side. At least, last time I checked, that was the plan," Jarvis said, trying to deepen his voice to sound tough.

"First of all, homeboy, take some of that bass outta yo' voice when you talk to me! Second of all, I don't work for you, playboy. I'm here to put you up on game."

"He tryin'a help you, l'il ign'ant-ass boy!" Scooter concurred.

"Now either you want this free game I'm tryin'a put you down with or you don't. I don't really give a fat rat's ass. If you listen, you'll have enough money to start your little mechanic shop. If you don't, you'll still be flunking for Teddy in these streets while he's fucking your old lady behind your back." Dog Face laughed, giving Scooter dap.

The look on Jarvis's face caused his uninvited guests to double over in laughter. "Y'all niggas trippin'. That's her uncle!"

"Bruh, you can't be that blind! That nigga ain't bit mo' that girl's uncle than I am yours. Nah, Teddy been dumping dick in Nova for years. Tried to turn her out like his other girls, but Nova was different. She didn't give a damn and played the game just like Teddy, and that nigga fell in love." Dog Face pulled a joint from his pocket and lit it. He inhaled deeply and continued his lurid tale.

"Her daddy and Teddy were childhood friends, and they fell out about Nova when he found out, you feel me? Her old man felt like Teddy had groomed his daughter, finessed her through the years, and got inside her head some type of way. Her old man was gon' kill the nigga, but word is Teddy spent some paper to keep that fool behind bars because he didn't want to lose Nova. So he tried to have somebody shank him, but Roland ended up killing the dude in self-defense but still caught a charge. Truth is, dawg, I don't know how else to say it. Nova got power over niggas to make them get all the way out there. Always been that way, even in high school. Like it wasn't even sexual. Niggas just rock with Nova. She treats everybody different but everybody the same type shit."

Dog Face pulled on his stick of rancid skunk weed. He stared past Jarvis into emptiness as if lamenting some long-ago pain. Scooter slinked deeper into the corner, no longer commenting. Nova was a source of contention among many men.

"Wait, wait, Nova is sleeping with Teddy? She said that he was her uncle!" Jarvis repeated. He was hot, his chest heaved, and his neck burned with the heat of his anger.

"Listen, man, I'm just tryin'a put you up on game. I can show you better than I can tell you. When we show you, whatever you decide to do to this nigga, keep me and Scooter out of it."

The truth was that Dog Face and every other hustler in the south wanted Teddy gone, but nobody had the balls or the brains to put the play in motion. When Nova had come about hitting the lick, she made it clear how she wanted things to go down. Jarvis needed to know everything so that they could start fresh. They would split four ways whatever they got off Teddy. She would send him a text message when it was time, and she had left it at that.

"Whatever." Jarvis waved him off. Were they telling the truth? If so, then he was the biggest fool alive. Thinking back on it, there were little hints and signs that Jarvis had noticed but brushed aside. The more he thought about it, the madder he got. "What about the meeting with the Mexicans?"

"We'll cross that bridge when we come to it," Dog Face said with a sly grin. He locked eyes with Scooter and exited Jarvis's apartment.

Chapter Fifteen

"Stop, Teddy, for real. Stop touching me!" Nova screamed, nearly backing over his desk.

"Look out, you need to stop playing with me. You've been acting real brand new lately like you don't know what's going on. This is mine, you understand me? You can play house with ya l'il friend all you want to, but what I want, I get!" Teddy said, grabbing Nova by her shoulders and forcing her to her knees. He pulled his erectness from his sweatpants and tried to force it into her mouth, but her lips were pursed tight.

"You got me fucked up, Teddy. Move!" she screamed, clawing at his manhood.

"The fuck is wrong with you, girl? You must be losing your goddamn mind!"

"I'm tired of this shit, Teddy. You're happy taking money from women and selling dope. What about my happiness though? Doesn't what make me happy count at all? You run from bed to bed, pillow to post, sticking your little skinny dick in any wet snatch that will have you!"

"Watch your mouth!"

"They love you because after a long day of whoring for you, they can go home to their fleabag motels and decide what they want to give you. You will always be second to their real pimps: their children! Some of them your grimy ass made. Nah, you're a piece of shit, and I'm out. This shit is over."

Teddy slapped her violently. "Bitch!" he spat. "This is about that nigga Jarvis. Keep it real. You think I'm stupid? You fell in love, didn't you? As much game as I've given you over the years, you fall for a flunky? He ain't got shit, and what he does have, I made it possible for him to have it."

"It's not about money. It's about being here for me. It's about somebody seeing me as more than a fucking cum receptacle. It's about knowing more about me than what my favorite position is. It's about romance, about love, about living a normal life around normal people."

"I offered to give you that, but that's not what you wanted." Teddy shrugged, sitting on the edge of his desk.

"That's where you're wrong. I do want it. I just don't want it with you. You're my father's age, and we could never have a life together. You isolated me from everybody who loved me. Made empty promises you knew you wouldn't keep. I just want to be happy, free to be me, free to live my life."

"You ungrateful little—" Teddy screamed, but his words were cut short by the menacing look that Nova shot his way. She stared at him with death in her eyes as if daring him to strike her again. He lowered his hand and turned his back to her. "What do you expect me to do? I made you, Nova. Am I supposed to just let the next man come in and reap the benefits of my hard work?"

"You're supposed to love me enough to let me go so that I can chase my own happiness. You're supposed to be a man of your word."

"All because of whassaname, huh?"

"His name is Jarvis, and what does it matter who it's with? If you love me like you say you do, you'll let me go," Nova said, hugging Teddy from the back.

"Little girl, little girl. You take a playa outta his element every time. I just can't tell you no. I'll let you go under one condition."

"What's that?" Nova knew that Teddy would come with some sort of stipulation, probably something having to do with sex.

"I'll let you go be with this nigga and I'll give you what I promised if you put me in that yummy one more time," Teddy said, huskily nodding at two duffle bags in the corner.

"I knew you would come with some bull. Here I am professing my love for someone else, and you want me to continue with the madness," Nova said, but her eyes were on the duffle bags. "Is my money in there?"

"Every fucking dime. But look here, just one more time for old time's sake. You say I'm a minute man anyway, so what's one more minute?"

"Okay, but—"

"Nah, ain't no buts. If you want that bread, you'll make me feel like the king I am, bitch. Pretend I'm your sweet little Jarvis. Earn your freedom, unless of course you'd rather I kill that nigga and keep you on this leash forever."

Nova slunk to her knees and slowly pulled his sweat-pants down to his ankles. She unzipped the matching jacket and rubbed his hairy chest. She closed her eyes and tried to imagine being in this position in front of Jarvis. Nova took his rigid penis in her hand and knew immediately that it wasn't Jarvis. She thought of Jarvis's smile and the way it filled her with happiness. Every word that he spoke was true with an innocent type of ignorance, and she loved it. He was no one's fool, but there were just things that he didn't know. At first, she'd only found him to be amusing and cute, but over time he had shown her what most men could only claim. He was different.

She stroked Teddy's hard dick only seeing Jarvis's chocolate face. If this was what it took to buy the life of her and her lover, then so be it. They would move far away where no one knew who they were. She took him into her mouth . . . for freedom.

Chapter Sixteen

They parked across the street from Teddy's warehouse and killed the lights. "A'ight, from the looks of it, both of them are inside," Dog Face said, pointing to Teddy's and Nova's cars parked out front.

"If we go in there unannounced, that fool might just start shooting!"

"Shut the fuck up, Scooter! Stop trying to think. You're going to hurt yourself. We'll go in from the side. That door ain't never locked, and coming in from there we can see the office and the entire building, plus ain't no cameras on that side. Leave this bitch running, Scooter."

Darkness blanketed the deserted street as the trio made their way up the driveway, shielded by the warehouse on one side and massive hedges on the other. Just as Dog Face had said, the door was unlocked. They made their way inside and took up posts in the darkest corner of the building.

Jarvis stood in the shadows and watched in horror as Teddy knelt in front of Nova, threw her thighs over his shoulders, and buried his head between her legs. She held his head with one hand and fondled her breast with the other. Her head was tilted in the throes of ecstasy, and even from a distance, Jarvis could tell she was enjoying it.

"I told you, nigga! Sheeeeeiiiiiiitt, if that's his niece, Popeye's a big-legged punk. That fool munchin' on that box like he tryin'a turn her out, fool," Dog Face teased.

He knew that if he pushed the right button, Jarvis would snap. Maybe he'd get lucky and Jarvis would actually kill Teddy. He was a brutal killer, but he respected the code of the street. If he killed him and tried to take his place, he'd be looked at as a grimy-ass hater. On the other hand, if he could gas Jarvis up, put that key in his back, and ring that jealous bell, he would probably kill Teddy and go to prison, leaving Dog Face to take his place with Nova. Jarvis didn't strike Dog Face as a fighter, let alone a shooter. "Bruh, you gonna let this nigga dick your girl down, nigga, yo' baby, the one you out here hustlin' fo'? Couldn't be me. Shiiiiiiit, homeboy would hafta see 'bout me!" Dog Face said, trying to provoke Jarvis.

"Y'all gon' get us caught down here with all that bumpin'," Scooter whispered.

Teddy stopped munching briefly and looked out into the darkness, but the light flooding the room bounced back against the tinted glass. Amid the darkened window, Teddy saw his faded reflection. Staring back at him was a shell of the pimp he had once been. He'd been reduced to a trick, paying for sex and in love with a woman who refused to be his woman or his whore.

He stood and took Nova by her throat and forced himself inside of her violently, and she winced. It was nothing major like Teddy would have liked to believe, but more of a fleeting inconvenience. Teddy loved talkative sex, and Nova knew just how to stroke his fragile ego. An "Ooooooh, daddy" here or a "Fuck me harder" there whispered gently in his ear always made him cum fast.

"Whose pussy is this?" he rasped.

"Ooooohhh, yours, daddy. Fuck me harder, daddy, damn!" she screamed.

"Oooh, shit, baby, ooh, here it comes, goddammit!"

She watched the digital clock above the watercooler as Teddy pumped for dear life. She needed something other than the grotesque fuck faces he made during sex. It was only three minutes before she felt Teddy's hot stickiness spew inside of her, and she felt sick. The stench of his sweat mixed with his foul breath made her wretch. Nova turned her head to avoid Teddy's kiss. In the darkness fighting against the light, she thought she saw a slight movement near the back door.

"Teddy, move. I think someone is here," she whispered, scrambling to put on her clothes.

Teddy stood naked in his office window, his once-rigid penis now flaccid from satisfaction. He walked to his desk, grabbed his pistol, cocked it, and walked to the door. He tried to focus his eyes to see in the darkness, but he only saw black.

"I see you out there," he lied. "If you don't wanna die, you better show yourself!" he said, fear clawing at his chest.

Teddy heard a click, and the room was flooded with light. There near the back door stood Dog Face, Scooter, and Jarvis.

"What's all this? Y'all s'posed to be meeting the Mexicans. You niggas is in violation."

"Nah, you in violation. Now drop that pistol before we have a problem, nigga," Dog Face ordered. He leveled his pistol in Teddy's direction and stared at the curvaceous woman behind him.

Nova stood sheepishly, half-dressed behind Teddy, and she locked eyes with Jarvis. She could see the strained pain written on his face. She mouthed the words "I'm sorry" in his direction, but he dropped his head, unable to meet her gaze. His sadness and confusion gave way to anger as he raised his gun.

"Why, Nova? Why would you play with my heart like that?" Jarvis asked, tears staining his cheeks.

"I'm sorry, baby, I—"

"Shut up, bitch!" Teddy screamed, slapping her violently to the ground.

"What the fuck is wrong with you?" Jarvis said as he closed his eyes and pulled the trigger, but the bullet ricocheted from the metal doorjamb above Teddy's head.

He turned toward Jarvis and aimed, but Dog Face fired his pistol, burying a slug in Teddy's leg. "You little bitch-ass nigga! Disloyal-ass bitch!" Teddy screamed. He raised his pistol, but Dog Face shot him again. Teddy fired his pistol, and the bullet missed its intended target, striking Scooter in his neck. The boy dropped to the floor, gurgling, drowning in his own blood.

"Get out of here, Jarvis," Nova said, kneeling to pick up Teddy's gun.

"What about you?" Jarvis asked.

"Don't worry about her, nigga. Just leave," Dog Face barked.

Jarvis stuck his pistol in his waistband and backed out the door, eyes still trained on the melee in front of him. He stepped out into the night, eyes stinging. He was a grown man and wouldn't cry, but the shit hurt. He still couldn't believe what Nova had done to him, playing him like a sucker. She said that she would do anything to make him happy, and he was willing to die for her, yet she had chosen to step on him.

Dog Face's car was still idling, and Jarvis considered taking it, but he didn't need any more problems than he already had. He went through the field behind the warehouse and walked along the railroad tracks until he got to the Trinity River. He tossed the pistol into the water and headed toward his apartment.

It took him almost forty minutes to get home going through the thickets and high bushes that lined the shore of the river. When he jumped Ms. Celestine's fence, he had a clear view of his driveway and froze, fear tugging at his gut, making him feel like he was about to retch. He inched closer to the big pecan tree with its low-hanging branches, and he melted into the darkness.

Dog Face's car was parked in the driveway of his building, running. Nova was sitting on the hood smoking a cigarette, wiping blood from her face with a wet wipe. Jarvis scanned the area. She appeared to be alone, but where was Dog Face? Jarvis walked along the fence slowly, letting the full landscape of the street come into view. She was alone. He crossed the street and stood in front of her. He didn't speak. He just watched her. What would he say? Shit, what could he say?

"I know you're probably mad at me, and to tell the truth, I don't blame you, Jarvis. I want to tell you something, and when I'm done, if you want to walk away from me, I completely understand. If you decide to stay with me, tonight didn't happen, do you understand?" Nova said.

"Yeah, I understand, but—"

"No buts, Jarvis. I love you, and I told you that I'd do anything for you," Nova said, pulling Jarvis close to her. She whispered in his ear, "When you left the warehouse and me, Teddy, and Dog Face were alone, I made him shoot Teddy, and then I shot him with Teddy's gun, the same gun that he used to murder Chino. Teddy's dead, Dog Face is dead, and Scooter is dead. We're the only people who know what happened in that warehouse, and I'm not going to say shit, are you?" Nova asked, kissing him on his neck.

"Hell naw. I love you, Nova, but I just saw you fucking another dude."

"Pull your emotions out of your ass, Jarvis. I could be the type of bitch to cheat on you with your friends. I could be the type of bitch who only thought about myself. I didn't do this for me, baby. I did this for you. I could have kept dealing with Teddy's goofy ass and kept getting money, but I didn't want him. I want you. Let's just go. Let's leave Dallas."

"And go where?"

"Anywhere we want to. All we need is us. Leave everything. Just go."

An hour later they were on the freeway headed east out of Dallas. Two duffle bags of money were shoved down in the floorboard of Nova's car. She reached over and put her hand on top of Jarvis's hand. She wouldn't stop driving until she was sure that the stench of the streets couldn't touch them.